W9-AXC-191

Dara

Dara

A Victorian Novel

by Anonymous

Grove Weidenfeld
New York

Published by Grove Weidenfeld
A division of Grove Press, Inc.
841 Broadway
New York, NY 10003-4793

First published in 1984
by Panther Books
Granada Publishing Ltd.
London, England

Printed in the United States of America

0-394-62110-7

PART ONE

Journey to Chicago

Reflected in the ornate gilt mirror were all the intimate details of my body. Trying to be objective I searched the reflection from top to bottom for blemishes and to see if the passing years had brought about any changes. In my youth, when my breasts were no larger than two halved lemons, there was no concern in my mind for flaws in my developing body. Running wild over the hills and mountains of the Isle of Man I was only conscious of boundless energy and a strange restlessness each time I viewed my growing breasts and the black hairs that were beginning to cover the vent between my legs.

Now that I was approaching my twenty-second birthday I wanted the mirror to assure me that my body was just as desirable to men as it had been during the past seven years. Tonight of all nights I had to be at my best as Bertie and I would be together for the last time. Bertie, known throughout the land as His Royal Highness, the Prince of Wales, who would soon be married to Alexandra, the beautiful princess from Denmark.

Although we had been lovers for nearly two years, the Prince decided our affair must end because, as he put it in his rather husky voice and rolling his R's as he did when he was most serious, 'A married man must be more circumspect than a single man and, besides, if ever our affair became public knowledge, my mother and the British People would be extremely displeased. Considering that I will be a married man with a particularly beautiful young bride they would think that there could be no possible excuse for infidelity.'

He paused for a moment and then with a smile, 'Alex has a mischievous, gentle, childlike innocence about her that I find absolutely fascinating. I have quite lost my heart to her and would despise myself if I betrayed the trust she places in me.' He looked thoughtful for a moment or two and I tactfully kept my silence, waiting for what he might say next.

Coming out of his reverie he looked up and gave me a warm fond smile. He put his hands on my shoulders. 'My darling Dara, I will never forget you. There will always be a corner of my heart especially reserved for you and if ever you need my help and support, don't hesitate to call me. You were my first love; indeed you taught me how to love, naturally and spontaneously. Mainly because of what I learnt from you, I will be an understanding, gentle husband with my beautiful Alexandra.'

Looking into the mirror once more I could see that the passing years had been kind to me. The breasts were, of course, larger than in my youth but not overblown or drooping. No baby had ever suckled at those nipples and they remained fresh pink and tilted slightly upwards. My belly gently curved outwards with its small navel which gave me a sly little wink when I pulled in the muscles. Pleasingly plump but firm thighs framed the small patch of curly black hairs that discreetly hid the vent. The vent, often referred to by one of my lovers as 'the cavity of enchantment'. Though there was nothing enchanting about the grunts and groans he made when he entered its pink interior. Yes, I was well pleased with the survey of my image in the mirror.

Five years ago I had boarded the steamship 'Packet' lying alongside the jetty in Douglas Harbour. Little did I know on that early spring day in 1858 that I would never return to my island home or that I would, after many adventures, become the mistress to the future King of England. I was bound for the port of Liverpool from where I would sail across the mighty ocean seas to America.

Relatives who had emigrated some years previously to settle in Cleveland, Ohio, had written home paying tribute to the boundless opportunities and wonders of America. Their descriptions of the new land fired my imagination and strengthened my determination to face the hazards of the journey to this far off country. With the optimism of youth, sustained by my experience of men of all classes, and my resilience and zest for life, I faced the journeying alone without any qualms. To bolster my confidence still more I had tucked into the stocking of my right leg a ten inch dagger, razor sharp on both edges.

I had my first man shortly after my fifteenth birthday. John Bruce didn't seduce me: I made all the running. He was the farmer I worked for who had an ailing wife who very rarely got out of her bed. I was obsessively in love with him to a degree that bordered on madness. Just under six feet, thirty years of good food and hard work on the land had given him a broad muscular body. His labourers respected him for his upright character and strong religious principles. They knew that if they fell upon hard times they could always turn to him for charity.

In contrast to his clean, well ordered farmhouse, the poor crofter's cottage where I lived was more like a pigsty than a home. It couldn't be otherwise. My widowed mother and her six children ate and slept in this one roomed hovel. During the winter months, with the door firmly shut to keep out the freezing cold wind, the stench was suffocating, for in addition to the children huddled around the peat fire there were hens roosting in the rafters overhead, ducks waddling across the earthen floor, and a young calf tethered to the foot of the bed. It was worse when my father was alive. He was a loud-mouthed braggard and a bully who treated us all, including my mother, most cruelly and spent most of his time at home on our one and only bed in a drunken stupor.

Although I had the constant company of my brothers and sisters I was a lonely child, detached from all that was going on around me, escaping into a world of my own imagination where John Bruce was my hero and my lover.

All my passionate feelings for him, which I had nursed secretly for years, came to a head on the night of the 'Mheillea', a harvest festival supper held in the school house adjoining St Luke's, the lonely little church on the ridge of the Royal Way, a track the Viking Kings had used in ancient times. I had been chosen that night to be the queen of the harvest festival. Crowned with a wreath of corn and roses, I graciously received with some ceremony, the *Babban Ny Mheilla* or Harvest Baby which was the last sheaf of corn of the harvest dressed in a baby's christening gown. As the queen, I was honoured to lead off the dancing and jigging with John Bruce as my partner. I was delirious with delight as he held me firmly in his arms in the dance and excited beyond measure at the closeness of his body to mine. He obviously found me attractive, I could see that by the way he was looking at me.

Later that evening he left the school hall for a breath of fresh air and a quiet smoke of his pipe. I'd seen his departure and left by another door at the rear to run pell-mell into his arms as he leaned against the meadow stone wall. Reaching up I got my arms around his neck and clung to him, drawing my whole body into his and kissed him with all my pent up passion. It took him a moment or two to realize who was kissing him so passionately on his full lips.

'Dara,' he protested, trying to push me off. 'You are too young for this sort of behaviour,' but I hung on to his neck, determined to give my virginity to the man I loved, and no-one else.

Squirming and rubbing up against him, and pushing my belly hard against his crotch, I sensed him yielding to my embrace and when his large, masculine hands came up under my skirt and cupped the bare cheeks of my bottom I knew that he would take what was offered to him so passionately. He was breathing heavily. To give him further encouragement I pressed myself even harder against him and wiggled my hips. He let out a long groan, it was almost like a cry for help.

Lifting me over the wall on to the grassy field he made haste to follow. I flung myself at him smothering him with kisses. He made a feeble attempt to push me away when I began to loosen the cod buttons of his breeches, but all the resistance faded when his cock, pulsing hard with hot blood, sprang out as I undid him. It stood out proudly when I got my soft, long fingers around it. My hands, as if by instinct, gently explored and caressed all his private parts. Getting a firm grip on his cock, I steered its head between my eager lips and into my mouth. In an effort to try to pull away from me he slipped and fell backwards on to the damp grass beneath us but I was not to be denied and quickly got astride him. Breathing very deeply, he raised me up a little and guided the head of his cock into me. When it penetrated right up into my giny and filled it to full capacity I had to suppress a cry of pain that was about to escape from my lips. As the flesh of my giny yielded and gave way to the thrust of the fullness of his cock I shuffled my buttocks and spread my thighs to get into a more comfortable position. Rather like a hen settling on a nest of eggs.

I had just got myself settled, and being without experience in these matters was wondering what I should do next, when he got his strong fingers painfully pressed deep into the soft flesh of the cheeks of my bottom and pulled me hard up against him and then began to see-saw me backwards and forwards. Suddenly he let out a cry of such intense feeling that I feared that I had hurt him in some way.

'Are you all right, Mr Bruce?' I asked anxiously as he lay back panting for air. Getting no reply, I became more concerned, 'Did I hurt you?' I enquired in a whisper and tried to get to my feet but he pulled me hard down on to him and brought his knees up against my back. I sensed then that I had not hurt him and that he had not cried out in pain but because of the intensity of his pleasure.

Spreading his hands around my thighs he moved me gently into a rhythm that opened my knees wider as he strove to push his cock further up me. It made me happy that I had been a satisfactory lover and in a feeling of exhilaration I wiggled and undulated in keeping with the up-ward thrusts of his hips. I felt proud and innocently delighted when, once again burying his strong fingers into my buttocks, he drew my giny tight up against him as a long deep groan shuddered through his body.

After a few minutes his breathing became more even and struggling out from underneath me he got to his feet and leaned against the stone wall. It wasn't long before I joined him to kiss him with all the ardour a young girl has for her first love. His cock was still hanging out of his open breeches so I got my hand around it and pulled gently until it got big and hard. It brought new vigour back into his loins and with almost brute force he turned me to face the wall and pushed my back down so that I had to cling to the protruding stones to stop myself falling.

Lifting up my skirt he forced his cock deep inside me. It filled my giny so suddenly that it squeezed the breath out of me. The soft curves of my bottom fitted snugly into his strong thighs. Leaning over my back he got his hands under my blouse and around my small firm breasts and then humped me with strong powerful strokes until he was finished with me. He lay slumped over me for some time and then suddenly crying out in anguish, he threw me to one side.

Buttoning up his trousers he said in a hoarse, low voice, 'May God forgive me . . . and you, for the terrible sin we have committed.'

I had no understanding of his remorse and protested emotionally, 'We have committed no sin. I love you with all my heart.'

He stood there in silence with his head hanging down from drooped shoulders.

'Please. Oh, please don't turn away from me,' I cried out with passion trembling in my voice, 'I live only for you. Nothing else matters.'

Without a word he scrambled over the wall and strode back to the school hall. Puzzled and confused by this frightening change in his mood I lay on the grass and hammered the ground with a clenched fist in a fit of angry vexation. Many times since then I have been left bewildered at the various reactions men have after a woman has pleasured them.

During the weeks that followed I pursued John Bruce unmercifully and, taking full advantage of the rare moments when we were alone together, clammered for his kisses and the intimacy of being crushed within his strong arms. He gave me no encouragement and looked upon me as a pestering nuisance.

On one occasion when he was supervising the milking in the byres I ran up to him and flung my arms around his neck. His forbearance snapped, and he spat out in irritation, 'Get off me, you rotten daughter of Satan. Keep your mind on your work,' he shouted and took me by the arm and dragged me back to the cow I had been milking.

I reached for the cow's udder and as I pulled hard on the tit, quickly turned it so that a stream of warm milk shot upwards, straight between his eyes.

He got so angry that there and then he threw me off the farm telling me never to return, but his conscience must have pricked him for the next day he used his influence to get me a job as a chamber maid at one of the largest and best hotels in Douglas.

Rejected and scorned by the man I loved, I resolved to get even by making as many men as possible submit to my female charms. Such is the perversity of a young passionate girl scorned by her lover. Within a few days I had seduced the proprietor of the hotel, and, soon after, his bank manager, who dined every lunchtime at the hotel, insisting each time that I sat astride them as they lay on the bed. I wanted to be on top of all men and was determined that I would sit astride them rather than be spread-eagled beneath them. To have them submitting gratefully to the power of my sexual attractions gave me great satisfaction and to see them begging for my favours and snivelling and sulking when I refused them. Sometimes they were like puppy dogs panting for any tit-bits of favours I cared to grant them. I got my gratification out of seeing their red faces beneath me, distorted in an agony of passion, while I, cold-bloodedly, had nothing but contempt for them.

It wasn't long before the wife of the hotel owner got wind of the shenanigans going on between her husband and myself and, giving me a minute's notice, she ordered me off the premises. In all haste I presented myself at the bank and asked a toffee-nosed clerk if I could have a moment with Mr Scott, the manager.

'Only if you have an appointment,' he said, adding, 'which I doubt very much.' He then looked down at his ledger as if I didn't exist.

'You,' I said haughtily as I prodded him with my finger. 'You tell Mr Scott that Miss Tully wishes to speak to him at once and if you don't I will march into his office and tell him myself. Now look sharp, I haven't got all day to wait on the likes of you!'

He sat there aghast that I dared to speak to him in this manner and he gaped at me open-mouthed.

'Well?' I demanded. 'Are you going to get yourself off that stool and tell him, or should I do it myself?'

As if in a daze he stumbled to the manager's office and returned looking very subdued and told me very respectfully that Mr Scott would see me at once.

Scotty, for that was how I often addressed him when I bounced up and down on him as he lay beneath me, patted me on the hand when I related what had happened at the hotel.

'Leave this to me, dear,' he said. 'When they bought the hotel they had to raise a very large loan from this bank. I can demand the return of that money anytime I wish to do so.'

He rose from his chair and putting on his overcoat said, 'I'll go along now and have a quiet talk with them. Make yourself comfortable in my chair and wait here until I get back. In the meantime I will instruct my clerk to bring you a pot of tea and some biscuits.'

It did my heart good to see the clerk bowing and scraping as he placed the tea and biscuits before me.

'I hope the tea will be to your liking. Just ring the bell on the side table if you require more,' he said as he backed out of the door, leaving me alone with my anxious thoughts as to what the outcome was likely to be after the day's events.

I didn't have any need to worry, for within the half hour Scotty was back to tell me that the job at the hotel was mine for as long as I wanted and that there would be no further talk of dismissal. I gave the dear old boy a hearty kiss and cuddle and returned to the hotel where I was given a polite but cold welcome by Madame. She told me that in future I would no longer be required to sleep in the servants' quarters on the top floor, as one of the guest rooms had been set aside for me.

Sizing up my new situation, I took liberties and worked when I felt like it and remained in bed till midday if I had had a strenuous night with one of the gentleman guests.

They were a mixed bunch of all ages and sizes: tall, short, fat and thin; retired service officers, civil and military; business men and dilettantes. They only had one thing in common: an eye for a pretty girl who was willing to be bedded. But it was I who bedded them, not they me. I picked and chose as I pleased and was always on top when they were in my bed. They either submitted to it that way or got nothing.

There was no hint for money or gifts on my part; nevertheless many of them discreetly left a gold sovereign or two under the pillow or returned later that day with a gift of jewellery. There were an equal number who took what I was giving freely without even a 'thank you' and came back a few days later begging for more of the same treatment. The hotel also prospered from my activities, for many of the male guests, single and even those with families, changed their plans when they made my acquaintance, stayed not just for a few days, but for a few weeks. The owners of the hotel eventually came to look upon me as a valuable asset they could ill-afford to lose.

With all this activity I would, undoubtedly, have become pregnant if it hadn't been for the good offices of the cook who, when she heard shortly after my arrival at the hotel of my affair with the proprietor, called me down to the kitchen for an intimate talk. Being a good Christian woman, she first tried to persuade me to give up my wanton ways and be a good girl in the future. Failing in this task, she then warned me of the terrible consequences that would follow the birth of a bastard child which she said was bound to happen if I continued to bed down with men.

After seeing she was getting nowhere on that tack she threw her hands above her exclaiming, 'Mercy, child, if nothing I can say will change your ways then get yourself along to Ma Bustin, the midwife in Fort Street, and for God's sake listen to her and take her advice for she is well versed in the knowledge of how a girl can be bedded without having a baby.'

After giving the matter some thought, common sense prevailed. Upon enquiring in Fort Street of Ma Bustin's abode, I was directed to a basement room in one of the hovels which composed the street at that time. Descending the rickety wooden steps to the basement I knocked repeatedly on the door without receiving any reply. Angry at wasting my time on a fruitless errand, I kicked at the door and, to my astonishment, it flew open. I stepped cautiously inside and, as my eyes became accustomed to the darkened interior, I saw a wizened old woman lying on a makeshift bed holding to her bosom half a bottle of gin. Ma Bustin I presumed. My deliberate coughing had no effect on her slumbers, so I picked up an empty pan and brought it down on the wooden table with a loud bang which immediately brought the old woman to her senses. She set up such a fearful squawking that it was a wonder the neighbours didn't come rushing to her aid.

She calmed down somewhat on seeing that the intruder was a mere girl. Coughing and spluttering between sips of gin from the bottle she rose from the bed.

Focusing her eyes on me in the dim light, she came right up to me and, looking into my face, mumbled, 'I don't know you. Who sent you?'

Before I could answer, there was another question. 'How many months are you with child? It will cost you plenty, you know that.'

Before she could go any further I burst out, 'I'm not wanting to get rid of a baby. The cook at the Crescent Hotel sent me. She said you would tell me how I could bed with a man and not get pregnant.'

'So that's it, is it? Well, sit down on the bed.' She pulled up a wooden stool and sat facing me. 'You scratch my back and I'll scratch yours. You get my meaning?' she queried.

I didn't and had no intention of scratching her filthy back or allowing her to put her dirty hands on mine.

Seeing the puzzled look on my face, she gripped my knee, took another sip of gin, and whispered hoarsely, 'How much are you going to pay for the secret knowledge that all women would like to learn?'

I opened my purse and offered her half a sovereign.

Displaying three brown-stained teeth in what was meant to be a smile, she said, 'Make it a gold sovereign and I'll tell you all you want to know and show you how to do it.'

I put the coin back in my purse and gave her a sovereign. Money was of no importance to me at the time as I had plenty of it. If she had asked for more I would have given it to her without any argument.

She brought forth from a corner cupboard a piece of sponge about the size of a hen's egg, a small bottle of vinegar and a wooden clothes peg. Pouring a small portion of the vinegar into a cup she then filled it nearly to the brim with water. Putting the sponge into the cup she held it down with a finger until it was well soaked with the liquid.

'Alright, my dear, lie down on the bed and put your knees up.'

Before I had time to cry out in protest she had stuffed the wet sponge right up my giny with the wooden clothes peg. Outraged and angry, I jumped off the bed with the diluted vinegar dripping down my legs and glared at her. 'What the hell do you think you are doing, taking liberties with my privates!'

'Don't get yourself all worked up over nothing,' she replied. 'I had to show you how to do it. Now you know.'

Her voice took on a more serious tone. 'Calm yourself, my dear. Sit down on the bed. I have more to tell you and a question I must put to you.'

When I got settled on the bed she asked, 'When did you last have a show of blood?'

'I've just had one,' I answered.

She nodded her head. 'Then you will be alright. If you follow my instructions from now on you'll never have any worry about your month-lies; they will come along as regular as clockwork. But you must do it the way I say.'

'I don't like mucking about with my privates like that,' I protested. 'It's alright a man poking his thing up there, but it doesn't seem right for anything else to be in my giny.'

'Can you feel the sponge?' she asked.

I shook my head.

'That's alright then, you'll never know it's there nor will a man when he gets inside you. Take it with you wherever you go and you will never be caught napping.'

She got on to her feet and brought me another sponge. 'Don't have a sponge in for more than a day. The vinegar loses its sharpness to kill off his seed so change about, day after day; that is why you are going to need two sponges. There you are,' she said, wrapping the sponge, the bottle of vinegar and the peg in a bit of old newspaper and handing it to me. 'That will be ten shillings.'

I looked at the newspaper bundle in my hands. The whole lot couldn't have cost her more than sixpence, but I gave her half a sovereign as I wanted to get out of the place as soon as possible. Giving her the coin, I noticed her black-rimmed finger nails and made up my mind that as soon as I got back to the hotel my private parts would get a good wash.

*　*　*

Looking back on those days, I'm very thankful the hotel cook and Ma Bustin took me in hand just in time. For there can be no doubt that with the way I was behaving, there would have been a baby in my belly before long. I've seen what happens to unmarried girls who have bastard babies. Their lives are not worth living and I was very fortunate to have escaped such a fate.

As it happened I had my men without any dire consequences. One of the happy consequences of my association with these gentlemen was a considerable sum of money hidden in a leather pouch under my skirt and in a similar pouch my jewellery was tucked in safe and secure. With this small fortune under my skirts I was able to travel first class and well able to afford a shared cabin.

After booking a berth in what was referred to as a 'second cabin' on Mr Samuel Cunard's paddle steamer 'Britannia', all of one-thousand-one-hundred-and-fifty tons as the booking clerk kindly informed me, I made my way through Liverpool's docks, passing several masted sailing ships with their long bowsprits reaching out over the quayside.

Leaning wearily against the chandlers' shops were groups of sailors, glassy-eyed and washed out after a night of debauchery in the city's taverns and brothels.

The gangway was crowded with emigrants and their luggage. An officer standing under a huge red funnel which was belching heavy black smoke waved me below to the steerage quarters when I reached the deck but, when he caught sight of my booking ticket, was all smiles and servility and, with a bow, directed me to the poop and instructed a seaman to carry my leather bag to the intermediate cabins. We made our way across the deck which was cluttered with luggage, masts, spars, and rolls of sail cloth.

As I entered the cabin and before the door was shut behind me a loud authoritative voice demanded, 'Who are you, that you presume to enter my cabin before knocking?'

It was my fellow passenger with whom I was to share a cabin. She was a large, bulky woman and, by the look of her, weighed all of twenty stone.

'My name is Dara Tully and I am to share a cabin with you for this voyage,' I answered.

'Tully? Tully?' she repeated. 'I don't recall hearing that name amongst all the county families that I am acquainted with. Who are your family that they allow a girl of your age to travel alone without a chaperon? From your speech you are no gentlewoman and not a member of society.'

She was obviously going to worm the truth out of me before very long so I thought it better to make my position clear right from the start.

'My family are poor crofters and I have recently been in service in a hotel as a chamber maid. And I would be obliged if you will allow me time to unpack my luggage before you ask any more questions.'

She huffed and puffed as the blood rose to her face when she got the unvarnished truth of my background. She was an aggressive, overbearing woman with heavy features, flabby pendulous lips and protruding fish eyes.

'A common chamber maid sharing my cabin. Whatever next? I won't have it,' she shouted. 'I'll see the Captain at once.' And, before she slammed the door behind her, 'You can pack your clothes back into your bag. You are not sharing this cabin with me.'

I unpacked my luggage and was sitting on my bunk contemplating what I could do next when the door burst open and in marched 'Her Ladyship' accompanied by the Captain of the ship, a short, well-built man with a jovial red face and a merry twinkle in his eye.

He started off by saying, 'I understand, Miss, we are having a problem in this cabin.'

Getting to my feet and offering my hand, which he shook gently in an absent-minded way, he took stock of me.

He was about to say something else when I got in first. Speaking with that high-toned voice that I had heard the lady guests use at the hotel, I said, 'Allow me to introduce myself. My name is Miss Dara Tully and I'm very pleased to make your acquaintance, I'm sure.' I gave him a sweet smile as I looked directly into his eyes and, shaking him by the hand once more, said, 'How do you do?'

He was taken aback by the society accent and answered, 'Very well, Miss.' Then searching his mind for something to say, 'I hope you find the cabin comfortable and to your satisfaction.'

The twenty stone of fatty flesh of 'Her Ladyship' was trembling with indignation. Spluttering in her fury, she shrieked that I was 'nothing more than a common serving wench who had no respect for her betters', and then commanded the Captain to throw me out, bag and baggage, or she would report him to Mr Samuel Cunard.

The Captain smiled when he heard her threat. He straightened his shoulders and drew himself up. 'Mrs Ponsonby, please do calm yourself. I am sure you are mistaken. There seems to be no reason for complaint. Indeed, I think you are most fortunate to have as a travelling companion on this voyage a charming young lady with such refined manners.'

Before she had time to answer, he took me by the arm and steered me through the door saying, 'A word with you, Miss, before I get back to the bridge.'

Closing the door of the cabin firmly behind him he continued, 'It doesn't bode well for you having to share a cabin with such a haughty lady. In time she may come off her high horse and condescend to be more considerate of your feelings. This ship is fully booked and there is not another bunk to spare anywhere, otherwise I would have you trans-ferred to another cabin.'

He smiled at me and, putting a fatherly hand on my shoulder, said, 'I know it's going to be very difficult for you, Miss Tully, but try to be patient with her. Take a promenade around the deck and when you get back to the cabin you may find her more agreeable and sociable.' Step-ping back a pace, he gave a brief salute and hurried back to the bridge.

I was met with stony silence when I got back to the cabin so, after a few minutes of being treated as if I didn't exist, I departed to explore the ship.

My cabin was on the starboard side of the vessel and looking to the left I could see great confusion with officers shouting to seamen stepping over a swarm of luggage. Moving warily towards the aft deck I suddenly found myself overtaken by crowds of people rushing towards the steerage quarters below decks. Pushed about by the crowd, I was jockeyed willy-nilly down the steps with people carrying their luggage pressing hard up against me, intent only on getting below to secure the best bunks for the voyage.

It was sheer bedlam in the steerage quarters and I was thankful that I had a cabin on deck even if I had to share it with an ogre. The whole place was in an uproar. Women screaming at their children, babies suck-ling at their mothers' breasts, others bawling their heads off. Men strug-gling with luggage trying to stow it beneath bunks, occasionally losing their tempers with the children and their women and clouting them across the head with a flat open hand.

There were slatternly women already maudlin drunk, passing a half empty gin bottle to their friends who were droning through a song that was popular at that time in taverns and low dives.

They never got past the first stanza:

> 'Your husband gave to you a ring,
> Set around with jewels rare;
> You gave him a better thing—
> A ring set around with hair.
> Tra-la-tra-la-tra-la.'

But they obviously didn't know the rest of the song because as soon as they finished their tra-las they started on the same words again.

Curses and bad language rose harshly above the general noisy swell of the hubbub coming from the emigrants as they pushed hither and thither. There being little or no ventilation, it was suffocatingly hot with a mustiness adding its contribution to the odour from unwashed bodies and babies' puke. One or two men started to ogle me so I strove to regain the level of the higher decks before they could get their hands on me.

I'd had enough of men with their lecherous advances and was sickened by my own shameful behaviour with them at the hotel. One of the main reasons for my decision to go to America was to cast off the past and begin a new life among people who knew nothing of my background.

The 'Britannia' was just leaving the dockside when I got on deck. Within the hour we were in the Irish Sea and heading for the Atlantic Ocean.

Come nightfall, with Mrs Ponsonby and me undressing in stony silence as we prepared to bed down for the night, it seemed my head had hardly touched the pillow and I was off into a deep sleep. Sometime in the middle of the night the ship began to roll very hard and I was awakened by Mrs Ponsonby moaning loudly in her bunk.

Lighting a small oil lamp attached to one of the cabin walls, I was about to ask her if she was in pain when, with a face greyish green with nausea, she leaned over the side of her bunk and disgorged the contents of her stomach. I thought she would never stop.

She spewed continuously for over five minutes until the floor of the cabin was covered in vomit. The stench was unbearable to my nostrils and the sour smell hung about me like a graveyard wraith. It was in my throat and choking me with nausea.

Collecting shoes, clothes, warm overcoat and blanket, I got out of the cabin before I spewed up myself. It took but a few minutes to dress and put on my overcoat. Luckily there was no one about to see me in a state of undress.

Tearing a small piece of material from the bottom of my petticoat, I wiped as much as possible of the vomit from my bare feet and put on my stockings and shoes, for my toes were becoming numb in the cold night air. Groping my way along the deck, I found a place near the rail sheltered from the wind and under a lifeboat hanging from its davit. I settled down on the deck with the blanket around my legs and the thick overcoat close to me to keep me warm.

Despite the hard wooden deck under my back I must have dozed off because the next thing I remember was feeling a rough calloused hand moving up between my thighs. The fingers of the hand squeezed the lips of my giny before I became wide awake to what was happening to me. Seething between fear and anger at this outrage, I slid my hand down the outside of my right leg and got a good grip on the handle of the dagger hidden in my stocking, brought it up quickly and prodded the sharp end at the arm between my thighs. Whoever it was let out an almighty yell which was followed by a stream of filthy language as he rocked back on his heels. I couldn't see his face but only the outline of his form, for there was only a ship's lantern behind him. By its dim light he could see my face but his remained in shadow.

'You will pay dearly for that, you fucking steerage whore,' he threatened with a hoarse voice. I felt his hand groping for one of my feet. Sitting up suddenly I leaned forward with the dagger in my hand. He must have seen the blade for he moved just out of my reach.

'You rotten stinking cunt, my arm is soaked in blood! I'll cut your bloody throat wide open if I get my hands on you.'

My blood curdled; I was in a cold sweat and scared out of my wits. Swallowing down the fear that was beginning to grip my throat, I whispered in a menacingly gruff voice, 'Make one, just one, move towards me and I'll cut your ears off and stuff them into your filthy mouth.'

He moved back a pace and stood up. He was about to walk away when he turned to me, his voice choked with anger.

'I've got to stop this bleeding, otherwise I would deal with you now. But get this straight, I'll have my eye on you night and day from now on. You won't get away with it. A pox on your twat,' he grunted. 'I'll see to it that you and your dirty cunt go to a watery grave over the ship's rail before we reach New York.'

The man was obviously insane with a dangerous quick temper and I feared for the days ahead. Waiting until I could no longer hear his footsteps, I picked up the blanket and made a dash for the steerage quarters and the safety of the company of the emigrants below decks.

Stumbling down the steps, I emerged into the steerage quarters where there were only one or two small oil lamps to relieve the gloomy atmosphere. I peered fearfully into the dark shadows between the rows of bunks. God knows, I thought, who is lurking in there, ready to jump out at me.

It came to me then that I would never know who it was that threatened me with a 'watery grave'. His face was never visible as it was always in the shadow, whereas what little light that came from the ship's lantern shone on my face. He would, throughout the voyage, be able to recognize me. There was no doubt in my mind from the way he uttered his threat that he meant every word of it and in the days to come would be stalking me and waiting for the opportunity to push me over the ship's rail. It could be any one of the seamen or any of the male passengers on the boat. Shuddering at the thought of being suddenly tipped overboard without warning I resolved I would move about with great care, always on the alert, looking for any man taking too much interest in me, or with an injured arm.

Impatiently waiting for the dawn, I spent the rest of the night wide awake sitting under one of the oil lamps with my hand resting on the hand of the dagger in my stocking. Escaping from the fetid air of the steerage and emerging into the bright daylight made me blink my eyes until they became accustomed to the change of light. Leaning against the ship's rail and looking at me with some amusement was a tall open-faced clergyman of middle years.

Because of my fears and the need of a trustworthy man I ran to him exclaiming, 'I'm in great danger. Will you please help me?'

His face immediately became serious and showed concern.

'Of course. What can I do to help you?'

Offering my hand I said, 'My name is Miss Dara Tully.'

'And I am,' he answered, 'the Reverend Robert Blake of the Presbyterian Church. You appear to be in some distress. Now tell me what can I do to relieve your anxiety?'

Leaning against the rail with us both looking out to sea, I told him of the night's events. As I related what had happened his face became more and more serious. He was silent for some time after I had finished speaking, and continued to look out to sea with a very stern expression on his face.

'What can I do?' I asked anxiously.

'You, Miss Dara, you cannot do anything, but I can. From now on, until we get to New York, I will be as close to you as your own shadow, guarding you night and day. When you are in your cabin you will keep the door locked and will open it to no one but me.'

His voice, rich and elegantly pedantic, reassured me that I was now safe under his guardianship.

When we opened my cabin door the stench was overpowering. I looked inside; the oil lamp was still burning and I caught a quick glimpse of Mrs Ponsonby still lying on her bed covered in blankets with her face to the wall.

As I had already given the Reverend Blake my reasons for sleeping on deck, he expressed no surprise and, shutting the door, said, 'Come with me; that cabin will have to be cleaned before you can use it.'

He spoke to a seaman who fetched a mop and two buckets, one with a long piece of rope attached to the handle. Throwing the bucket over the side, he played out the rope until the bucket was full of sea water.

Mrs Ponsonby, on her bed with her face turned away, ignored us while we watched the seaman who mopped and rinsed the floor three times with fresh sea water before we accepted that the floor was now as clean as a new pin. His face lit up when I proffered a few shillings as payment for his service.

'Now, young lady,' said the Reverend, 'into bed and catch up with lost sleep. Lock the door as soon as you get inside and don't open it to anyone but me. I will be back at midday with some food.'

From that day on I was in the constant company of Robert, as I came to call him. As the days went by I almost forgot about the menace of the man intent on murdering me and, much to Robert's concern, became forgetful about always being on my guard.

When he learnt of my desire to improve my education, almost all my daylight hours were taken up with lessons in English literature and grammar, Robert's favourite subjects. He set me essays to write so that I could improve my spelling and use of words, and fired my imagination with his enthusiasm to such an extent that in the years to come I never lost interest in the written word and became an avid reader of English literature whenever books were available to me.

When we were about four days' sailing time from America the ship began to roll very badly shortly after we got to bed and it tossed so heavily that more than once I nearly fell out of my berth. Within the hour the wind began to roar and howl as if determined to destroy everything afloat. Mrs Ponsonby, moaning and groaning, turned over and spewed on to the cabin floor. Making a quick decision to move myself below decks, I collected my clothes and got out of the cabin. The force of the gale winds was so violent and the pitch of the ship so steep that I found it almost impossible to keep on my feet, and I was flung against the ship's rail.

Terrified, clinging with all the strength of my arms and hands to the rail, I viewed with horror and abject fear mountainous forty feet high waves crashing down on the deck. Shivering with cold and drenched to the skin, I heard the planks and woodwork of the lifeboat above my head splintering and cracking as it swung like a mad thing from its davit. The smoke stack was making loud cracking sounds and I feared that it would be blown over and set fire to the cabins on the deck. Seamen came from below, no doubt on Captain's orders, with strong heavy chains and began to lash the stack more firmly to the deck.

Peering through the sea spray and catching sight of the entrance to the steerage quarters, I got to my feet with the intention of making a dash for it. As I was waiting for a lull in the wind the ship suddenly pitched hard over to starboard. Seeing the deck heaving up before me I turned round to hold on to the rail with all my strength and then fell to my knees as the ship lurched further towards the raging sea until it was almost lying on its side. Something hard struck me on the back of the head and before my forehead hit the rail and I passed out, I heard above me a man's voice cry out in fear. When I came to my senses, my hands were still clinging fiercely to the rail. Feeling very dizzy, my head throbbing painfully, I crawled on hands and knees back to the cabin and collapsed on the bed. Oblivious to the storm raging outside, I dropped into a deep sleep.

By morning the raging wind had blown itself out and, although there was a heavy swell, it was calm in comparison to the night's violent gale. Robert awakened me about eight in the morning by which time the seas had gone down very considerably. Briefly, I explained my adventures during the storm, after his startled exclamation at seeing the swelling on my forehead, and asked him to allow me to sleep till noon as my head still ached. When he departed I fell into bed thankful that I could continue my slumbers.

By the time he returned at midday I was up and dressed and, although feeling rather delicate, was much refreshed after sleeping most of the morning. He had given a lot of thought to my account of what had happened during the storm and told me of his suspicions that the man who had threatened me with a watery grave had attempted to do just that when I was standing at the ship's rail the previous night, and no doubt would have succeeded in his evil intent but for the ship rolling so suddenly on to its side. It was his opinion that the man had rushed towards me with outstretched hands as I turned to hold on to the rail but flew over my head when I dropped to my knees, kicking me accidentally with his boot on the back of my head as he passed on to his own watery grave.

Later that day, in conversation with the Captain, Robert was informed that one of the seamen was missing and was thought to have been swept overboard during the storm. It seemed to Robert that the Captain felt no sorrow over the loss of this man as his reputation was of the worst. Constantly getting into fights because of his vile temper, he had become most unpopular with the rest of the crew and it was rumoured that he was responsible for the death of a man during a brawl in one of the back streets of Liverpool. One of the crew had seen him washing the blood from a deep arm wound on their first night out from Liverpool. No doubt the result of another fight in that port, the Captain had concluded. I thanked God for my lucky escape and looked forward to arriving at New York and getting the whole dreadful affair behind me.

Three days later we were piloted into New York's bay and its magnificent harbour. In the distance I could see the 'Great Western' and other ocean-crossing vessels lying off Sandy Hook, waiting for their next voyage across the Atlantic Ocean. The sun was blazing down on hundreds of wooden cottage-type houses which made up the city on the lower part of Manhattan Island as I gazed with rapt attention at all the bustle and preparation for our docking.

Having landed in America, the promised land for many of us, we immigrants had to face the officials at Castle Garden on Battery Park. The interviews and official papers were mere formalities for Robert and me as we were not considered 'undesirables', and we were given a warm welcome.

There was a crowd of people of all nationalities waiting to greet their immigrant relatives. Robert pointed out how easy it was to guess their origin in Europe: the Irish by their breeches, top hats and holding cudgels which they wouldn't hesitate to use in a fight; the Swedes with their vests of different colours; the Germans smoking their meerschaum pipes and wearing distinctive caps and short jackets.

I wasn't impressed by what I saw of New York as we were driven to the steamship 'Drew' that would carry us the one-hundred-and-fifty miles up the Hudson River to Albany. The streets were mired in slush and were without pavements, only an occasional high wooden sidewalk. There was filth lying about everywhere. The alleys running off the streets were knee-deep in mud from the overnight rainfall. I had expected to see a clean new city with impressive buildings, whereas it was mostly dilapidated wooden houses and broken down shacks and, to complete the depressing picture, there were chickens pecking at piles of garbage and pigs rooting in the gutters.

The steamer had comfortable cabins and a dining room where we ate our first American meal. Famished, as I had been without food since landing, I soon supped up the first serving of oyster stew and then tucked inside me chicken and lamb chops served with potatoes, peas and cabbage, and finished this substantial feast with buckwheat pancakes swimming in maple syrup. All around us people were gobbling the food in huge mouthfuls as if they hadn't got a minute to spare.

There was a lot of strong earthy language with exclamations of 'Sodom and Gomorrah' or 'I'll be God-damned' and similar oaths coming from the male passengers, many of them chewing tobacco after their meal and spitting the dark brown juice all over the floor. I was to learn in later months that this filthy habit was prevalent all over America and even carpeted floors were stained with tobacco spittle. Nevertheless, their frank and unconstrained manners appealed to me and were a good deal more honest than those in England.

With that lovely satisfied feeling that comes with a stomach full of good food, Robert and I made our way up on deck where, leaning against the rail, we admired the beautiful scenery on either side as the steamship splashed its passageway up the Hudson River. It was then that Robert told me about his life in Edinburgh as a Presbyterian minister and of his beloved wife who had died of cholera after twenty-six wonderful years of a marriage where there was never a cross word spoken in anger by either of them.

After she had died he became a recluse and neglected his work, much to the dismay of his church members who tried to no avail to rouse him from his torpor. Every article of household furnishing, indeed nearly every feature of the streets of Edinburgh, reminded him of his dear Charlotte. When he received a letter from his brother in America commiserating with him on the loss of his wife and inviting him to come to Montpelier where there was a vacancy to be filled for a minister of the Presbyterian Church, it took but only a day's thinking to accept the invitation and remove himself from all that raised memories of his dearest Charlotte whose love he had cherished since he was but a young man of twenty years.

He informed me that our friendship which had developed from his guardianship on board the steamship 'Britannia' had lifted him from his three months of sorrowing and that he was now taking a new interest in life. I was totally unprepared for what was to come next.

Taking both my hands in his and looking down at our clasped hands he said, 'My dearest, you may be unaware of how fond I have become of you. You are constantly in my thoughts and although there is this difference in our ages I know beyond all doubt that I would be the happiest man in the world if you would become my wife and help me in my work as a minister for God.'

It took me a full minute to recover my senses and realize that this dear man who had gained my respect and admiration was actually making a proposal of marriage.

'Oh, Robert,' I sighed, 'if only I loved you as a girl ought to love her future husband I would accept your proposal with great joy. But the truth is I don't. You are my dear, dear friend and mentor and I am very fond of you.'

I paused for a moment trying to find the words that would put my refusal more tactfully. 'You deserve someone much better than I could ever be. I cannot see myself as a minister's wife and for that matter I have no intention of becoming anyone's wife. Marriage is not for me or ever will be. Please don't be hurt, dear Robert. I am honoured that you have asked me and if I had to get married I would rather be a wife to you than anyone.'

Without another word he kissed me on the forehead and departed for his sleeping quarters.

During our journey to Albany where we would have to part company no further reference was made to marriage and we resumed our friendship as before.

Disembarking at Albany, our first task was to take rooms at an hotel, for the next morning I would board an Erie Canal barge for Buffalo, three-hundred-and-sixty-four miles away, and he to set off for the green mountains of Vermont.

We would be going for hundreds of miles in opposite directions and would probably never see each other again. The thought of our parting made me feel very sad and I wished we could continue our journey together, but I knew no good would come of that.

Nevertheless, desiring to show my appreciation in some way for his kindness and protective friendship that had been constant from the first moment we met, I invited him to dine with me at the best eating place in Albany at my expense, adding that he must order only the very best dishes on the menu whatever the cost.

The dinner was a most excellent meal and we arrived back at the hotel after stumbling and falling about through dimly lit streets, both a little intoxicated from the wine we had drunk throughout the dinner. A gentle kiss on the lips and then he went to his room and I to mine.

I was slipping my nightdress over my shoulders when I thought I heard a light knock. Opening the door, I was surprised to see Robert standing there, bare-footed, dressed only in trousers and shirt, with tears rolling down his cheeks. Concerned at his distress, I brought him inside and shut the door.

He just stood there with bowed head. Going up to him I put my arms around his neck saying, 'There, there, Robert, don't take on so; we may meet again some day.'

He slowly put his arms around me and drew me in close. So close was I pressed up against him that I could feel the prominent bulge at his crotch. Experience of other men told me what that meant. The thought came to me that he had been without a woman for at least three months and if that was what he was in need of I would be only too happy to oblige. I would willingly have done a lot more to make him happy before we parted.

It took but a moment, crouched in a corner, to insert the sponge, slip off my nightdress and return to his arms, naked as the day I was born. He had his eyes closed and was breathing heavily as I unbuttoned his trousers and got him to step out of them.

When his trousers dropped his cock sprang up stiff and erect. I fondled it for a little while, then put it between my soft plump thighs. He groaned like a man being tortured beyond endurance. Pressing hard up against him, my tits flattened against his chest, I milked him by tugging at his cock with my thighs which had a firm grip on it. I could feel it sliding along the moist groove of my giny when I pressed hard on to him.

He suddenly gripped the cheeks of my bottom and pushed the head of his cock right through to my backside. It was pulsing strongly when I felt his arms crush me to him as his emotions climaxed. Then he swayed and his whole body seemed to crumple as he leaned heavily against me. I had to support him with my arms to stop him falling.

The tears were coming down his cheeks again and he was mumbling to himself. I could only catch some of the words: '. . . Oh, God, forgive me . . . Oh, Dara, I am deeply ashamed . . . I'm just a fornicating sinner like the rest of them . . . I'll never forgive myself.'

When I realized what he was saying I got annoyed. 'Don't be silly, Robert. You are not a fornicating sinner. You are a kind, decent man who has been without a woman for too long. We were not fornicating,' I said, 'you didn't even get it inside me. The truth is you haven't committed a sin. You love me and I did what I did because I'm very fond of you. Please don't take on so, it isn't anything to get into a bother about.'

Blinded by tears, he pushed me away from him and groped for his trousers. He needed my assistance to get into them and get through the doorway back to his own room.

Confused and unhappy that we should part this way, I slept uneasily throughout the night.

When I got downstairs in the morning Robert had gone, leaving a note in an envelope which read, 'Dara, please try to forgive me, Robert.'

I frowned and stamped my foot. How could he, I asked myself, deny his own natural feelings because of his religious beliefs and then take on so because they had got the better of him. I had been prepared to give him a whole night of love and kisses and send him on his way a happy and contented man. Instead it had all turned sour because of his damned religious beliefs.

Tearing his note into small pieces, I threw them into the street. I was doubly annoyed because, for the first time since John Bruce, I had wanted to give myself to a man freely, with affection, respect and a warm heart, and once again I had been pushed off.

The long days spent on the barge taking me through the Erie Canal to Buffalo were dull and boring, apart from the beautiful countryside which was like none that I had ever seen before. After boarding another boat I arrived at Cleveland, a town at the mouth of the Ohio River. My relatives had a farm about twenty miles south of Cleveland. A few enquiries in town led me to a carrier who was willing to take me to within a mile of Peel Farm.

They had named the farm after the town in the Isle of Man where they had emigrated from some eighteen years before. Since they had left the island a year or so before I was born, the only knowledge I had of them was gained from reading letters that they had written to other relatives. The Quirks were not close relations, Mrs Quirk being my dead father's cousin, but being Manx, like themselves, I was sure that they would give me a warm welcome. As I had departed within a few days of making up my mind to emigrate, I had not written to inform them of my intentions as I knew I would arrive at the farm before a letter could reach them.

The farmhouse was like two log cabins adjoining each other to form a letter L, giving the impression that originally there had only been one log cabin and the second had been built at a later date when more house rooms had been required. There was a porch door on which I knocked repeatedly without getting any answer, so I wandered around to the back where there was a door held open by a small wood log. It was the door to the main room of the house. A spotlessly clean combined kitchen and living room.

A lovely appetizing smell of baking bread emanated from the room and the first thing I saw was half a dozen newly baked loaves on a very large wooden table. On the other side of the table a blonde haired woman, nearly six feet in height and stout with it, was kneading dough. She looked up for just a brief moment as I entered then stooped over her dough again. As I stood with my leather luggage bag, not knowing what I should do or say next, she asked without looking up from her work with the dough, 'And who might you be?'

'I'm Dara Tully from Baldwin Valley in the Isle of Man,' I answered.

This news was greeted with silence as she continued to knead the dough.

'I suppose you are Mrs Quirk, my father's cousin.'

She quickly filled six baking tins with the dough and put them in the oven, then turned her full attention on me. 'So you are Sam Tully's daughter. How is he keeping these days?' she asked.

'My father is dead,' I replied.

She gave this information some thought for a moment then said, 'I always thought he wouldn't last very long. Too fond of the drink, that one,' and then, 'What are you doing here in America?'

Perplexed at receiving such a cold reception, I was a little nervous about that question. I tried a smile to see if that would soften her, but her face remained expressionless.

'Well,' I said hesitantly, 'I was hoping you could find me work on the farm or in the house.'

She began to roll out some pastry. 'You don't look strong enough for farm work,' she snapped. 'In any case, my husband and son don't need any help on the farm. We cannot afford it, and I don't need any help in the house. You might find some work in Cleveland. I don't know what we are going to do with you.'

'I can milk cows. I used to work in Mr Bruce's dairy,' I said hopefully.

'We haven't got any milch cows, only hogs and they don't need a dairy maid.' Her remarks struck her as being very funny and she guffawed herself into a fit of coughing. She paused in her coughing and shouted as she pointed a finger at me, 'You, milking hogs, that's a good one; I would like to see that!' She was obviously enjoying mocking me.

She was still bent over coughing when two blonde giants entered the kitchen. Although my body is slim without an ounce of fat on it, I am of good height and taller than most women, and yet I felt like a dwarf beside these men. With massive shoulders about a yard wide and legs like tree trunks, they seemed to fill the kitchen with their presence. I presumed they were Mr Quirk and his son and stood waiting for an introduction, but none was forthcoming.

Mrs Quirk got her coughing under control and pointing a finger at me and looking at her husband said, 'This is Sam Tully's daughter, from the Isle of Man. She has come to help us milk our hogs.'

The absurdity of her introduction set her off again. She neighed like a horse and whooped with laughter. The men just stood there looking at me and then at Mrs Quirk and back again to me, not understanding the joke but with big oafish grins spread across their faces.

In an effort to bring this ridiculous situation to an end, I extended a hand to Mr Quirk saying, 'I am pleased to meet you. I hope you are keeping well.'

'Tolerable, I thank ye,' he replied, politely.

My slender hand disappeared from view when he enclosed it in his huge paw. Going to the son I said, 'My name is Dara. What's yours?'

His face was still occupied with a stupid grin and he stared down at me with pale blue eyes for a moment. 'I'm Billy,' he grunted.

In the meantime, Mrs Quirk, recovered from her laughter, was setting the table with cold meat, a pan of boiled potatoes and a great mound of cabbage. When four large china plates were placed on the table it became apparent that I was expected to join them at their evening meal. Filling three of the plates with meat, potatoes and cabbage, she took the fourth and placed less than half the quantity of the provisions of the other plates on it and handed it to me.

Nevertheless, it was ample for my appetite but her deliberate inhospitality didn't escape my attention and I made up my mind that first thing on the morrow I would be on my way back to Cleveland and out of reach of her insulting uncouth manners.

Our meal was eaten in silence. When we were finished, I asked Mrs Quirk if I could help with the washing up. Receiving no reply I declared a need for fresh air and said that if it was alright with them I would take a look around the farm. On hearing this, Billy lifted his huge body off the bench and said, 'I'll show you round.'

His mother immediately interjected, 'Now don't you be long, our Billy. You've got to get to bed early. You've a hard day's work to do tomorrow.'

She obviously didn't trust me with her precious son. She needn't have worried; the hulking great brute was of no attraction to me. I would rather have been left to my own devices but he stood in the doorway waiting for me to come out, determined to accompany me on my walk.

'This way,' he said as soon as I emerged through the doorway and strode off to a barn only a short distance from the house. Coming up alongside him, as he stood in the open doorway, I was about to make some excuse and wander off when his hand came around my back and pushed me with tremendous force into the barn. Stumbling and trying to keep my balance, I fell on top of a heap of hay. For a man of his size he was surprisingly quick in action. He had turned me over onto my back and was on top of me, squashing all the breath out of me before I had time to rise. Pulling my skirt up over my face and forcing my knees apart, he knelt between my legs. I was in darkness and trying to bring my skirt down from over my head when I cried out in pain as he roughly forced two fingers, coarsened with farm work, up my giny.

He was digging away inside with his fingers as if trying to find something at the top of my giny when the barn door was flung open and I heard his mother shout, 'Billy, where are you?'

By this time I had got my skirt off my face and saw her stride over to us. She clouted Billy hard around the head and told him to get back to the house.

'As for you, you trollop, keep your filthy hands off my Billy. He is already spoken for by a decent girl on the next farm to ours.'

I pulled my skirt down over my knees as she made a move to leave and was about to rise to my feet when she turned. 'Out you go first thing tomorrow morning, and make no mistake about it.'

Flabbergasted at the ferocity in her voice, I lay there for a moment or two before getting onto my feet.

I walked about for a while and then reluctantly returned to the house as there was nothing else to do under the circumstances. She glared at me as I entered, muscles tightened with aggressive hostility, husband and son absent, no doubt in bed.

'Follow me,' she ordered, and led me along a passageway to a bedroom. Before she closed the door on me she yelled, 'And remember, first thing tomorrow you are out, bag and baggage.'

I'll say this for her, the room was spotlessly clean and well furnished, the chief articles being a wash stand and a massive double bed. Undressing quickly I was about to put on my nightdress when the thought struck me that Billy might waylay me on my way from the farm. Preparing my sponge took but a moment and, crouching, I inserted it up my slot. Being raped was bad enough but the thought of that great brute fathering a baby into my belly was too dreadful to contemplate. Then I remembered the bedroom door and made sure it was well and truly locked in case he tried to walk in his sleep.

Getting into bed I felt the cuddly softness of the feather mattress under me and was about to dim the small oil lamp on the side table when I heard a noise coming from the window. Getting out of bed to investigate, I had just got to my feet when the window opened and a breeched leg came over the sill followed by the rest of Billy's bulky form. Before I had time to protest one of his big hands pulled my head back by the hair and the other closed hard over my mouth.

'Now you keep quiet. If you make a noise, I'll bash your face in so you'll never be the same again,' he threatened.

Looking around the room and getting a firmer and more painful grip around my mouth, he growled, 'Are you going to keep quiet?' The menace in his voice made me nod my head in agreement.

If I cried out, I thought, his mother would only blame me again and throw me out into the dark night. Girls always get the worst of it in a situation like this and are often accused of encouraging the man and leading him on. It has always been that way and always will be. Society shuns even the maid who gets raped in a most cruel fashion.

He dropped his breeches, stepped out of them and then pulled my nightdress off. Lifting me up as if I weighed no more than a child, he threw me on the bed and forcing my knees wide open knelt between them. Getting his fingers around the base of his cock, he wobbled it about, looking down at me and grinning all over his face. I watched horrified as it swelled and hardened and grew larger and larger. In all my experience I had never seen anything like it. It was frightening just to look at. How he was going to get it in to a young girl of my age I didn't dare to imagine.

Putting his hand under me he raised my buttocks and shoved the head of his cock hard at my giny. Under its pressure the lips of my giny began to stretch and strain to such an extent I thought he would split me. The pain was awful and I made a move to rise and get away from him but it wasn't to be. He brought a heavy hand over my face and pushed my head down on the pillow. At the same time he came hard down on me.

I was gasping painfully for breath and squirming to get away from him. The more I wriggled about in an effort to get out from under him, the more he seemed to like it. After a while I resigned myself to his cruel humping and shoving for I was pinned down and couldn't move. He had the constitution of an ox and wasn't to be denied. Oblivious to my gasps of pain, his eyes were fixed on the wall behind me like a man in a trance.

Coming to a climax with an animal grunt, he collapsed on me covering my face with his chest and knocking all the wind out of me. Suffocating, I struggled and pushed against this mass of flesh and hair as I tried desperately to get some air into my lungs. He rolled off just as I was about to black out and lay on his back with his right hand firmly clasped around my left wrist.

I lay flat out like one crucified, with his muscular right leg lying heavy across my thighs making it impossible for me to escape. With bruised ribs and painfully panting for breath I lay there dreading the thought that as soon as he recovered from his exertions he would probably get on top of me again. To my surprise I heard him snoring.

My legs began to get the cramp under the weight of his heavy leg as I waited for him to get into a deep sleep and, easing them gently up, I got them free from his leg without awaking him. He still had a good grip on my wrist so I turned very slowly and, with great care, lifted his little finger from my wrist. The next finger showed more resistance but eventually straightened. I was sweating with the concentration needed for my task and the fear that I might awaken him from his sleep. The longest finger of his hand proved to be more difficult and wouldn't budge.

Losing patience with it, I pulled it towards me. He awoke with a start, sat up, and looked around the room as if puzzled at finding himself there.

The now familiar grin began to slowly spread across his face when he turned and saw me beside him. From the look in his eyes I could see he was going to give me another battering and that there was no hope of appealing to him for mercy.

He went through the same motions as before: kneeling between my outstretched knees and swinging his enormous cock from side to side until he was good and ready to enter me once more.

Moving at a more leisurely pace this time, he played it out for as long as he could. When he did come, I was prepared for it and had my head turned to one side so that I was able to breathe when his chest came down crushing my ribs and head. Finishing with me, he rolled onto his back, holding my wrist as before, but remaining wide awake this time.

When he recovered he scoured my tits with his coarsened hands until my nipples were fiery pink and sore. Tiring of that game, he got astride me with knees over my arms, wobbling his cock about until it got big and hard. Moving up on me he slapped my face with it and kept on walloping me until my skin was flushed red from the beating it was getting. All this slapping made his cock get bigger and harder and made him so excited that he couldn't get it in me fast enough and, becoming impatient when he missed the hole, scowled and slapped me hard across the head with his hand as he prodded frantically at the wrong place. When he did get it in, he went at me like a rutting beast and came in no time at all. I expected him to roll onto his back as before, but he got out of the bed when he finished with me, pulled on his breeches and disappeared through the window.

Too tired and weary to get up and close the window after him, I fell into an uneasy sleep and slumbered fitfully until the first light of day when I was awakened by Mrs Quirk hammering on the door and yelling at the top of her voice, 'Get out of bed, you slut. I'm having you out of here. Unlock this door.'

Dragging myself out of bed I walked painfully bowlegged to the door and turned the key. In she strode and stood glaring at me with arms akimbo. I stood looking at her sleepy-eyed trying to gather my senses together.

'Well?' she said. 'Don't just stand there. Get your things packed.' And, raising her voice, bawled, 'GET OUT!'

Feeling bruised and battered and particularly sore and tender around my privates, I picked up what few articles I had unpacked and put them in my bag.

At the kitchen door I was about to ask her where someone might be found to take me into Cleveland when she got her hand on my back, heaved me out and slammed the door.

Stumbling with my heavy bag which seemed to weigh a ton, I made my way slowly towards Cleveland. By midday, hot and sweaty, I stopped for the tenth time to rest, wearied beyond endurance, my thighs tender and sore, my private parts burning painfully. Easing myself on to the grass, I sat down and burst into tears.

After a good cry my will to overcome my problems strengthened and, staggering to my feet, I was about to take up my bag when I heard the shrill laughter of children ahead of me around the bend in the road. Hurrying along as best as I could, my spirits rose when I saw a tethered horse and wagon and, sitting in the shade of a tree, a man with a woman and three small girls having a picnic around a cloth well laid out with pies and cakes. As I hobbled towards them the woman got to her feet and, coming up to me, took my leather bag and led me to the rest of the party.

Beckoning me to be seated she handed me a cool glass of cider saying, 'You look exhausted, my dear. Have a long drink; it will help to revive you,' adding, 'it is uncommonly hot today.' And then with a kindly smile, 'Too hot for a young girl to be walking with a heavy bag.'

I thanked her and attempted to give her some explanation of my situation by telling her that I had been informed that I would meet up with a carrier on this road and had set off early for this purpose but had met no one up until now.

Spying the water of a stream nearby as I was talking to her, I bent forward and whispered in her ear that I would have to make a call of nature and would she keep her family where they were while I hid behind the bushes near the stream.

She nodded her head and said out loud for the benefit of the others, 'Yes, my dear. Go down to the stream and splash some of the cool water on your forehead; it will freshen you up I'm sure.'

Hidden by the bushes, I removed my skirt, petticoat, stockings and shoes and quickly got into the stream gurgling in the shade of a tree. The cold clear water was like balm to the burning skin of my under parts. Sitting on the pebbly bottom of the stream I sighed with relief, thankful that in my haste to get into the water my legs had not been encumbered with lace-edged pantalets, a fashion recently taken up by the better bred ladies of society. Females of a lower class never wore such hindrances as they were most inconvenient for women who had to work. My mind was made up when working at the hotel that I would never ensnare my thighs in such garments as I liked to feel cool air between my legs.

Hastily splashing some water on my face, I reluctantly climbed the embankment before the good lady on the road came looking for me. Quickly drying myself with my petticoat, I dressed and rejoined the picnic party feeling much better and more at ease below the waist.

After formally introducing myself, I learnt that they were Mr and Mrs Garnet and that their children, whose ages ranged from five years to nine, were named Bella, Emily and Alice. Bella, the eldest, was a very pretty child with long curly chestnut hair. She took it upon herself to wait on me, supplying my plate with portions of meat pie, pickles and fruit cake. I was very hungry having partaken of no food since the previous evening and made short work of disposing of the delicious food placed in front of me.

During the course of our conversation, I learnt that Mr James Garnet was practising as a lawyer in Cleveland, and that they would be very happy to make a place for me on the wagon for the return journey to town. Mrs Sarah Garnet's plump, good-natured face showed much concern when she learnt that I intended to travel alone all the way to Chicago and she wasn't reassured on learning that I journeyed alone all the way from Liverpool in England.

On enquiring about hotels, she became very agitated saying, 'Such places are not for young ladies travelling alone. You will lodge with us while in Cleveland.'

When she turned to her husband for his agreement, he nodded, saying, 'You will be most welcome,' and added that there was no need to board the boat for Toledo on the morrow as they would be pleased to have me stay with them for as long as I wished. They were indeed a kindly couple, with three charming daughters, and I thanked providence that these good samaritans had come to my assistance at a time when I was in great distress.

Tucked in a corner of the wagon with a blanket wrapped around me, I was sound asleep when the vehicle came to a halt outside their home in the centre of Cleveland, and, with Bella's arm to help me, I stumbled indoors.

Mrs Garnet was much concerned at my condition and felt my forehead which was covered with sweat, exclaiming in alarm, 'My dear girl, you have got a fever. You must go straight to bed at once.'

When we got to the bedroom she wanted to assist me to undress, but I insisted on doing this myself despite my weakness, thinking she might see the bruises or some other ill-effects from the previous night's ordeal.

'Very well,' she said. 'Get into bed as soon as you are undressed and I will bring you a mixture to suppress the fever.'

I had only just got into bed when she was back again bearing a glass of her home-made medicine. When I enquired what it was, for I'm not the sort of person who drinks anything that is offered me, she smiled. 'My dear, it will do you no harm. It's for your fever; all my family swear by it. It's a mixture of orange, lemon, tamarind, nitre and cream of tartar. Drink it up you'll find the taste quite pleasant.'

As my throat had become very dry the liquid quenched my thirst and after a little while reduced the heat of my body. I was restless throughout the night, awaking frequently with a dry throat. Luckily, dear Mrs Garnet had left a glass and a jug full of her mixture beside my bed. By morning my fever was much reduced, but on Mrs Garnet's insistence I remained in bed and was allowed to join the family for two hours only in the evening.

The next day the fever had gone and my health was as normal, much to the relief of Mrs Garnet and her family. The girls were delighted to see me out and about and, as the weather was warm and sunny, I spent much of my time during the next three days playing games with them in the garden. In this happy atmosphere my resolution to resume my journey to Chicago wavered somewhat but, on the other hand, I felt that it was not good manners to continue to take advantage of their kindly hospitality any longer and regretfully announced that I must board the boat to Toledo on the morrow.

Despite their pleading for me to stay longer, I was packed and ready the next morning for Mr Garnet to escort me to the docks. On the way he pointed out various places of interest and informed me that Cleveland got its name from Moses Cleaveland, a surveyor for a Connecticut land company which bought the land. At a later date the early settlers dropped an 'A' from the spelling of his name.

On arrival at the boat, he told me to seek out in Toledo a Mr Arthur Selwyn, a carrier of good repute, who would take me on his wagon overland from Toledo to Chicago.

Now, fully restored to good health, my aches and pains gone, I made myself comfortable and prepared to enjoy my voyage on the waters of Lake Erie.

We had just cast off when a furious uproar started up from the dockside. Going to the rail to see what it was all about, I beheld two men struggling at the dock's edge restraining, it seemed, an old man from jumping into the water. The man they held had a wizened, wrinkled face, weathered and tanned a dark brown from a lifetime of working out of doors. His language was appalling and got worse when he saw the ship's Captain standing alongside me with an amused expression on his face.

'Stop the boat, you goddamned, pot-bellied son-of-a-bitch,' he yelled as he strained against the men holding him, cussing and swearing something awful.

The Captain, who indeed had a great swaggering belly spilling over his trouser belt, shouted, 'Now then, Tom Cuff, behave yourself and mind your language; we have a young lady here.'

As the ship got further from the dock he explained Cuff's peculiar behaviour. 'He is not a bad old codger. Unfortunately he has got a noisome sewer for a mouth,' he said almost apologetically. 'Some ten years or so ago his wife got sick when visiting relatives in Toledo and died before he could reach her. Every now and then when he has had too much to drink he re-lives those days and tries to board a boat to see his sick wife, long since dead. On the occasions that he does get aboard he sails to Toledo, then returns to Cleveland on the next boat with a haunted grim expression, dejected and drooping with the heaviness of his misery.'

I looked at the men still scuffling on the quayside and felt a deep sympathy for an old man who still carried an endearing love for the wife he lost over ten years ago.

Captain Houseman and I became very good friends on that voyage. He was a mine of information about Lake Erie and its neighbourhood. Inviting me to dine with him, he held me fascinated with tales of the early settlers. Learning that I was hoping to find in Chicago some people named Cubbin, from my island home, he told me that Chicago was named after an Indian called 'Checaqua' and that some of the best soap came from that town, manufactured by James Kirk who built his factory on the site of the first house ever built in Chicago. He went on to relate how early settlers floated inland on flatboards or barges down the Ohio River scrambling ashore when they came to unoccupied land and hacked a clearing in the forest to set up their first home in America. I listened to him for hours, learning a great deal about the Northern States and the people who lived there.

Disembarking at Toledo, I made haste to find Mr Arthur Selwyn who I hoped would be able to take me overland to Chicago. After making a number of enquiries, I met up with his wife who informed me that he was not at home but would be back shortly. She was an agreeable, plump woman with a chubby rosy-apple face and, without asking, placed before me a plate of sliced beef and buttered bread. I was to discover that this kindly hospitality was customary in most American homes.

Having finished my meal, I was sipping at a glass of root beer when the clatter of a wagon was heard outside. It was Mr Selwyn, a bluff and hearty man with a snuff-stained bulbous nose; he gave a fat smile of welcome to me and to a Mr and Mrs Smith who were also to join us on our journey to Chicago. Mr Selwyn had been out and about collecting a variety of goods that people in the neighbourhood were dispatching to our destination and other places on route. The wagon was piled high with parcels large and small and I wondered how we were to be seated. But Mr Selwyn, who knew the nature of the freight he was carrying, soon arranged it so that we could sit amongst it in comfort.

With a 'gid-ap' to his horse, Mr Selwyn had just got started on our journey when a neatly dressed young man with a peaked cap carelessly pushed to the back of his head hailed us to stop and asked Mr Selwyn if he could take him to Chicago. The freight was rearranged alongside me for our fourth passenger on the wagon.

Before climbing aboard, he swept off his cap and bowed to the company, introducing himself as Elmer Varley. He shook my hand, learnt my name, and then did the same with Mr and Mrs Smith, a timid, mousey couple who had little to say to each other or anyone else.

After making several unsuccessful attempts to open up a conversation with them, Elmer Varley turned his attention to me. He had the shameless charm of a born salesman, a bright and breezy manner with a merry look in his eyes and a sly humour which, to begin with, I was slow to take up, not being familiar with his style of wit.

In no time at all, in low tones so that the others couldn't hear, we were exchanging risque jokes, some of which would have scandalized our fellow passengers if they had heard our banter. He was slightly above average height, lean and muscular and had a pleasant open face with clear confident honest blue eyes which you felt you could trust under all circumstances. With a checkered brown and beige jacket and trousers, he wore a coarse striped waistcoat fastened with brown cloth-covered buttons.

Amused and stimulated by his witty conversation, I found him disturbingly attractive and my senses quickened to his captivating gaiety. Before very long we were sitting thigh by thigh, holding between us a book of humorous verse from which he was reading for my ears alone various amusing passages. Bewitched and bemused by his warm personality, time passed quickly.

The day was clear and sunny, a light breeze wafting over the fields on either side of us, but Elmer and I had no eyes for the scenery, only for each other. When daylight gave way to twilight, I looked up in surprise as Mr Selwyn drew up the wagon for our first overnight stop. The day had gone over so swiftly that I hadn't noticed the passage of time or the sun setting low in the west.

Two small tents were soon erected, one for the ladies and another for the men. Mr Selwyn, I was informed, would sleep in his wagon guarding his freight. We gathered a stock of wood and twigs and soon had a blazing fire to sit around while we ate the sliced beef, bread and hard-boiled eggs provided as part of the carrier fare.

After our supper I sat in the blushing glow of the firelight and gazed into the flames as I sipped at my mug of coffee. Mr and Mrs Smith soon retired for the night to the tents and so it was with Mr Selwyn, who settled down amongst the freight on the wagon.

Bewitched by the eerie light that comes on a warm summer evening just after the sun has set, I watched them without interest go to their beds. I was in a quiet mood and sat as if suspended in time and space.

After some time Elmer, on the pretext that the fire was getting low, invited me to join him in search for more wood. His voice came to me as if far off. I could see through his manoeuvre to get me away from the light of the fire, but wasn't averse to a kiss and a cuddle in the dark.

Completely bedazzled by his charm and warm personality, I let him take me by the hand and lead me behind a large clump of brushwood. When he sat down on the lush, thick grass I lay on my back beside him, looking up at the stars shining diamond bright in the canopy of the night sky.

Laid back, I felt his hand on my blouse, but made no attempt to stop him when he gently squeezed my breast beneath the silk. Overcome by the magic of the silent night I felt detached and, as far as I was concerned, was in a mind to allow him to do what he liked with me providing it didn't hurt.

Slowly undoing my blouse buttons, he played freely with my bared breasts and bending over me kissed them repeatedly with eager lips. His kisses made them glow with a warm sensuous feeling and for the first time in my life I felt the nipples swell and stand up firm. When his two hands clasped one of my breasts and he sucked at it like a babe I pushed the swollen nipple up further into his mouth, eager for more caresses from his lips. He nibbled it for a little while and then, abandoning my breasts, he kissed me very gently on my mouth. It was like a breath of heaven on my tender lips.

As the tip of his tongue explored my mouth, his right hand came up slowly under my skirt and softly caressed its way up over my thighs until it came to my giny. One of his fingers delicately stroked its way through the moist groove between the tender lips and up to the little nub above. Gently circling this centre of delight with the tip of his finger, he continued to manipulate it until my inflamed senses were burning with a desire to feel the fullness of his cock inside me.

The fervent sensuality of his tongue licking the lower lip of my mouth added more fuel to my ardour. In a fever of impatience to get him between my thighs I brought my hand up to his crotch and caressed the masculine bulge stored there.

My storming emotions subsided a little as he fumbled with his buttons to remove his trousers. Once he was free of them no time was wasted in getting between my pliant legs and easing his hard thickening cock between the moist lips waiting to welcome its entry.

My passions were stimulated to a white heat as the warm fleshy luxury of his cock filled my belly. The rapture that suffused my body and limbs was like nothing I had experienced before. Rising in me was a tenseness bursting to be released and I pressed my belly and the baby belly above my giny into him and rubbed them hard against his muscular flesh.

My feelings rose to an almost unbearable intensity as I frantically wriggled my hips under him. The passion that shook my innermost self took wing and soared up to a peak of exultation, spiralling up and ever upwards to explode into a thousand fragments of passion spent. Trembling in anguished joy, I floated down swirling around in dreamlike clouds of sensual ecstasy. Bathed in a golden glow of bliss and joy, I heard myself murmuring words of love to the man who had lit a flame in my heart that would never be extinguished.

PART TWO

Goodbye, My Love

Mr Spinks was my last call before I returned to Chicago. He was a little man wearing, as always, a grey coat with black calico sleeves. His sharp eyes, looking out of pinched-up wrinkled features, peered at me suspiciously and with deep distrust. It was far from a warm welcome, considering that he had been buying soap from my firm for years.

I waited impatiently while he fiddle-farted around his store, picking up articles then putting them down again and occasionally looking doubtfully at the few bars of soap he had left from his last order.

The first words he uttered immediately irritated me. 'To tell you the truth, Mr Varley . . .' (I cannot stand people who preface what they are going to say with the words 'to tell you the truth'. The implication is that they usually tell lies, but on this occasion they are going to tell the truth.) He continued, 'My customers don't care much for the James Kirk products, but if you will give me a special discount I will consider giving you an order. The *Shandon Bells* and the *Juvenile* brands of your toilet soap are asked for sometimes. I could give you a small order for them, providing you give a good discount. You see, your prices are too high for the folks of Toledo.'

Anxious to catch the next carrier to Chicago, I was in no mood to spend the next couple of hours bargaining for a piddling little order. 'I'll have a word or two with my employer about your discounts, Mr Spinks, and let you know his answer next time I'm in Toledo,' I said. Before he had time to answer I was out of the door and making my way as fast as I could to Arthur Selwyn's wagon and laughing at the thought that the mean bugger would be without soap for his customers for the next two months.

Mr Selwyn's wagon, with its three passengers, was just moving off when I came alongside his house and I had to hail him to stop. Removing my cap and making an exaggerated bow to my fellow travellers, a middle-aged married couple and a young girl, I climbed aboard and seated myself by the girl.

When I meet people for the first time I'm always a little apprehensive, talk fast and try to get a laugh to start with. A salesman has to appear confident otherwise his customers will be dubious of the goods that he is selling. You have to get on top right from the beginning and keep it like that from then on.

There was no response from the married couple to my overtures, so I concentrated my attentions on Miss Dara Tully, the young lady sitting beside me. She was a stunner, about seventeen years I guessed, and, unlike a lot of English people, not distant and reserved. With a captivating gaiety and a sharp sense of humour, she giggled and laughed at all my jokes.

Wavy chestnut hair, held back by a twist of broad pink ribbon, framed a face glowing with youthful vitality. Her hazel eyes twinkled in teasing merriment when she revealed teeth as creamy white as fresh milk in a smile which brought forth seductive dimples to her cheeks. There was a shapely pair of ankles beneath the cloak wrapped around her legs and an open-sleeved silk blouse with pearl mosaic buttons outlined firm little breasts which had a pert, upward tilt.

As we sat side by side chattering and laughing like old friends, I discovered that not only were my jokes being appreciated as they got more saucy, but her flesh was also responding to the intimate pressure of my leg against her thigh. It is my experience that when it comes to intimacies between the sexes the flesh never lies. The tongue can speak falsehood in abundance, but the flesh can only reveal the truth of the senses under the skin.

Come the evening, when my hands held her firmly around the waist as I helped her down from the wagon for our first overnight stop and she fell against me with her arms around my neck, the signs were clear—she was ripe and ready for 'it'. By the time we got ourselves disentangled 'it' was getting embarrassingly hard inside my trousers. With encounters like this one there was, after all, something to be said for the life of a travelling salesman. Although a twenty-five-year-old married man, who could blame me for falling for the temptation of a pretty young girl with beckoning eyes.

In the darkening twilight after our supper I invited her to help me to search for more wood for the fire. She rose to her feet without a word and like someone in a trance allowed me to lead her by the hand to a patch of grass surrounded by thick leafy shrubs.

As she lay on her back looking up at the stars above us I made my first tentative move. Unbuttoning her blouse I made free play with her firm young tits with the nipples pressing into the palm of my enfolding hand; they became firmer and larger when my lips nibbled at them. It wasn't long before my tongue was between the luscious lips of her mouth and my hand was travelling lightly over the soft full flesh of her thighs which opened out as soon as I touched them. As I said, she was ripe and ready for 'it'.

The slight swell above her cunt with its fine curly hair felt as warm and smooth as a dove's breast and when I cuddled it in my hand it arched upwards like a cat's back when stroked. Gently fingering the nub under this 'Mount of Venus', I brought her passions to a head. She was gasping for breath as the intensity of her pleasure increased. In no time at all, my trousers were off and I was between her pliant legs with a lusty cock throbbing hard to get inside her. The warm, moist vent clasped him firmly when I thrust him forcefully up her as far as he could go.

Pushing hard up against me, she wiggled frantically and getting her hands on my back pulled me to and fro until I was having a hell of a time just trying to keep my cock inside her. For the first time in my life a girl was screwing me—I didn't like it. By the time she reached a climax my cock was beginning to droop and was losing interest in the proceedings. This was something right outside my expectations, although I must admit that, up to then, my only experience had been with my wife, Maude, who always lay like a placid cow when I got on top of her.

Up till the time I met Maude my life had been confined to the farm, working from early morn until nightfall. We had the land, but not the means to work it properly or to stock it with cattle. Barely scraping a living, we struggled on year by year making slow progress in enlarging our herd of cattle. There were very few opportunities for me to meet girls, or for social activities. I was nineteen when I attended my first barn dance and then it was only by accident that I did so.

After delivering a load of hay to a farmer about twenty miles from my home, a wheel shaft cracked just as I had started on the return journey. Getting the shaft repaired took three days and on the third night I was invited across to a nearby farm to a barn dance where I met Maude. She was patient with my ignorance of dance steps. I was clumsy to begin with but soon got the hang of it as I have a natural rhythm in my limbs. Drinking a lot of cider before the dance got under way loosened my legs and helped me to overcome my shyness in strange company. To get to the point quickly, Maude suggested a breath of fresh air would cool us down as we were both sweating after three or four dances. Being unaccustomed to alcohol, the cider had dulled my brain and I have only a vague memory of Maude loosening the buttons of my breeches and her guiding my cock into her. It was my first fuck and to this day I cannot recall anything about it.

Waking up with a splitting head the next morning, I set off home, giving no thought to Maude and what had happened the previous night. Apart from the fact that she was a big, plump eighteen-year-old girl, I couldn't bring to mind any features of her face and wouldn't have recognized her if we had met again the following day. The good God says, 'Take what you will—but pay for it.' And believe me, I have been paying dearly for that drunken fuck ever since.

Three months later, two very angry parents turned up at our farm with Maude to announce that I had fathered a baby onto their daughter. My upright parents, after recovering from the shock of this news and learning further details of how it happened, made it plain to Maude's folks that I would do what was right and marry their daughter.

Confused and embarrassed by the outcome of some event that was but a blur in my memory, I stood dumbfounded, unable to grasp what they were saying. This big, clumsy lump of a girl was a total stranger to me and yet both her parents and mine were discussing dates and places for a wedding when Maude was to become my wife. Someone who was to share the intimacy of a bed with me for the rest of my life. It was like a nightmare from which I longed to awaken, relieved that it was only a dream after all.

Turning to Uncle Andrew, my mother's brother, in the faint hope that out of his great wisdom some other solution could be found to solve this problem, achieved nothing. He sat with head bowed, taking no part in the discussion about arrangements for the wedding, gazing into the fire as if the sparks from the burning logs were of more interest than the talk going on around him. I had more respect and confidence in my Uncle Andrew than any other man alive. He was the source of my education and knowledge of the world and had taught me to appreciate good books and the wisdom that was to be found within their covers. Although physically broken by a chest complaint that brought on frequent fits of coughing, he hadn't spared himself in giving me an education that was to stand me in good stead for the rest of my life. My faith in him was limitless and that was why I devoured every book he gave me and studied hard under his tuition, yet in my hour of greatest need he remained silent and withdrawn.

I didn't know what to think. Was this man who loved me as if I was his own son leaving me to a fate too horrible to contemplate? It was only after the wedding when cold reason took over that I saw clearly that there was nothing he could do to stop this marriage which was to be ill-starred right from the beginning. As he explained to me many weeks later, we each of us must be responsible for our own actions, and it is not excusable to claim that we were drunk at the time. I now realize that it was my undoing, drunk or sober, to take what was offered to me.

Before the wedding I was taken to meet the minister who was to perform the ceremony. To my surprise he berated me, giving me no opportunity to defend myself; calling me a fornicating sinner was one of the milder accusations he threw at me. Working himself up into a fury, he informed me that I was an immoral, unprincipled, depraved, degenerate sinner whom God would never forgive. He demanded that, for the sake of the well-being of my soul in the future, I get down on my knees there and then to pray with him for my escape from the fate of Hell's flames when I died.

Deeply disturbed by the force and power of his oratory, I approached my uncle to seek his more enlightened views on my so-called heinous sins. When he heard what the minister had said to me he laughed himself into such a fit of coughing that I began to fear for his health and reason. It took him nearly half an hour to recover his breath and get some colour into his face which had gone deadly pale after his bout of coughing.

'You look like a whipped cur,' he commented when he got himself composed. 'I'm disappointed in you, Elmer. After all the teaching and philosophical talk I have given you over the years that you should let a ranting minister of religion disturb you and fill you with concern for the destiny of your own soul.'

Seeing the misery in my face, he changed his tune. 'Alright, I'll give it to you straight. God gave you a cock so that you could fuck, in the same way as he gave you a mouth so you can eat your food. Everything has a place and a function in this life of ours.'

He stood pondering on what he was going to say next then, speaking very slowly, 'Running through all living matter is a life-force which has to be used for everything we do. Don't make the mistake of calling it pure or impure because it's neither; it dissipates its power in a great diversity of forms and in none is it entirely good or bad, for there are no absolutes in this world of ours. It is up to each and every one of us as to how much of this life-force we use for whatever we have got in mind and, believe me, we have very little control over what goes on in our mind. The mind is just as mysterious as the rest of the universe and that goes for your ministers of religion as well as everyone else. God only knows what goes on in their minds when they are not telling the rest of us what we must and must not do. I'll bet they have just as many shameful thoughts as you and me.'

He turned toward the house. 'When you get into your head, Elmer, that you are no better or worse than most everyone you will have just about got it right. Look on the bright side; everything is changing all the time; bad times don't last for ever, nor do good times. Every day there is something to laugh about—if you look for it—and every day brings a new challenge. If you face up to each challenge you will become stronger in mind and body. Don't let life get you down, remain undefeated by its trials and tribulations; laugh in adversity, for life is only testing the strength of your will and character.'

Marriage to Maude wasn't as bad as I feared. She was as strong as a horse and a willing worker in the house and on the land. Being a farmer's daughter, she knew what was needed and got on with it without complaint. She hardly ever spoke to anyone. It was the same when we got to bed. With her knees wide open she would wait in silence for me to enter her. She would make no movement as I panted and pushed on top of her. Impassive and patient she would wait for me to finish then turn on her side and go off to sleep.

I longed for her to show some interest in what we were doing and consulted with an older and more experienced man as to what I could do to rouse her. He told me to try caressing her private parts before mounting her. I tried it dozens of times but it had no effect on her. She was devoid of any sensitivity and sensual feelings.

I know all women are not like her because once when I was away from home the opportunity came for me to try my caresses on a girl. Although she got all hot and worked up, she wouldn't let me put it in because she was determined to remain a virgin until she got married but, from the way she sighed and went all slack in the legs, I knew my fingering had made her come. To make up for not letting me have it, she milked me with her hands like you do with a cow, pulling away at my cock until the spunk shot out of it. It's alright that way, but it is better when you can get it between a woman's legs.

To get back to Dara. Her ardent, passionate wiggling under me took me by surprise. I had often day-dreamed of meeting a girl like this, but was totally unprepared for it when it happened. A new experience, however pleasant and flattering, takes a little time to assimilate, but my cock soon became stiff and hard at the view of her private parts as I lifted her ankles and placed them on my shoulders. Leaning over her brought the cool, soft cheeks of her bottom up against my thighs. The burning lust came back into my body and I thrust my cock deep into the warm, moist cunt with powerful strokes. There were sweet overtones of joy and satisfaction in her sighs as she submitted willingly to my masterful possession of her limbs. Balancing myself on stiffened arms, she took my whole weight on her buttocks when I came hard down on her with an excited aggressive cock that savaged and ravished her tender parts. It was like an explosion when the spunk, bursting to be released, spurted with force from my cock. I cried out in the gripping intensity of my feelings as my hips rocked to and fro on the backs of her thighs.

When my emotions subsided and she was once more flat on her back with her legs between mine, I felt empty and lonely and yet exulted because I had risen to heights of passion that I had never thought possible. The back-lash of my storming emotions hit me and I shuddered repeatedly. Dara, cuddling my head in her arms as if I was a baby, showered my face with warm gentle kisses, bringing me to a sleepy stillness as I lay across her listening without thought to the murmur of her loving words.

During the days that followed I was to learn a great deal about Dara. She could be self-assured and assertive and, at other times, meditative and withdrawn. In our loving embraces she would be either exciting and stimulating or dewy-eyed and submissive, encouraging me to ravish her with all my masculine strength. There was never a dull moment in her companionship as I fell in with her varying moods of teasing vivacity and dreamy meditation. In those quiet moments she was ready to discuss any subject providing I took it seriously.

Money was of no importance to her and she spent it freely. I had none to spare and had been living most frugally as I had promised myself and my father that I would save enough to stock our farm with all the beef cattle we needed. This was the sole purpose of my coming to Chicago and taking up the work of a travelling salesman. The harder I worked the more commission I earned. The more commission that came my way, the more cattle we bought. During the last three years sufficient money had gone into the farm to turn the tide and bring new hope of prosperity for my family in the near future. I estimated that within two years I would be able to return home and work the land myself.

Once a month the opportunity came to visit my family and my two children, Daniel and Mary, when I would hand over to my father the money saved since my last visit.

The world with all its troubles and problems rarely penetrates the thoughts of lovers but I couldn't escape from the obligations to my family and the financial responsibilities that were mine, and mine alone, nor had I any wish to do so.

When I informed Dara of the situation I was pleased that she took it in her stride. Nothing daunted that girl and it seemed that nothing was going to stop her loving me. Within hours of our arrival in Chicago she had installed us in a furnished room on Lakeside as Mr and Mrs Varley. She handled all arrangements herself and paid for them while I was in consultation with my employers about the orders placed with me.

'We have now got a home,' she announced when I arrived at the eating house where we had agreed to meet each other before parting at midday.

'Where?' I asked.

'On Lakeside. It's only a furnished room, but cosy with a large, comfortable bed.' She grinned mischievously then whispered, 'Tonight you will get the best loving you ever had. Oh, Elmer, I'm so happy and it's all due to you. It's hard to believe that we have just met. I feel as if I've known you for years. Do you think everyone is as happy as this when they fall in love?' she sighed. 'I hope so, it's wonderful.' Then, with a penetrating, questioning look, 'Do you feel the same way, Elmer? Oh, please say yes. I'll kill you stone dead just where you stand if you dare to say no!' Then with a giggle, 'And, what's more, I will never forgive you or speak to you ever again.'

When I attempted to answer her she put a finger across my mouth saying, 'No, tell me tonight when I have got my arms and legs around you in that big soft bed.'

'What about the rent?' I asked anxiously.

The waiter interrupted to place before us our meal of beef steak, German fried potatoes and cabbage which Dara had ordered and asked him to serve as soon as he saw me arrive.

When he had gone back to the kitchen she leaned forward over the table. 'Don't worry about the rent, Elmer. Please don't spoil it for me. I've got enough money for the rent and food. Don't ask any more questions like that, not today anyway. Now eat your food and let's not get too serious about anything. There will be lots of time to talk seriously, if you want, during the next few months.'

I needed no further bidding as I was ravenous, having had little to eat all day.

After we had finished eating our buckwheat pancakes I suggested collecting my personal effects from my present lodgings on the way to our new abode.

Dara would have none of it. 'No, Elmer, let's not waste time. I want to get back to our Lakeside nest and get into that bed.'

The room was on the second floor of an old house facing the lake. It was twilight when we arrived and it was only when Dara applied light to the two candles on the mantelpiece above the fireplace that the details came into view. It was indeed a well-furnished cosy room and in complete contrast to the drab lodgings I had occupied for the past three years. The rich pink cover on the bed matched the curtains of the latticed window, giving the red carpet a lovely warm glow to everything else in the room. There was a wash stand with a large china bowl with a jug of water in it and, underneath, a slop bucket; two comfortable leather armchairs and two high wood stools, a corner cupboard and an oak dressing table with mirror near the window. But it was the table in the middle of the room that caught my attention first. It was littered with packages of food, bags of fruit, pots, pans, china and cutlery.

'I rushed out after paying three months' rent in advance to buy what we might need,' Dara said, all breathless with excitement and added almost apologetically, 'and I didn't have time to clear it away. If you'll set a light to the logs in the fireplace I'll get these things stored into cupboards, then make you a mug of coffee and cut you a slice of fruit cake to go with it.'

Seeing me looking at the window, she took me by the hand, and pulling me towards her, said, 'Come and look; there's a lovely view of Lake Erie and the ships.'

While I was admiring and making suitable comments she clung on to my arm. 'Say you like it, Elmer, say you like our home. It is a cosy room, isn't it?'

Putting my arms around her and kissing her warmly on the lips, I reassured her that she had done wonders in such a little time and that we would both be happy together in such a cosy room. Then, eyeing the bed, I said, 'Reckon that bed is just about the right size for you and me.'

For my pains, I was rewarded with a kiss and another on the neck and an exclamation, 'Oh, I do love you, Elmer!'

Later, after we had drunk our coffee with only the light of the log fire flickering in our faces, we shared one of the large armchairs, kissing and cuddling. We didn't really need the fire for the night was warm despite a cool breeze coming off the lake. Dara got off my knees after a little while and, announcing that it was time for bed, began to undress. When she was stripped she came and stood before me, searching my eyes in the hope of reading my thoughts. For the first time since we met she was a little shy and slightly unsure of herself and looking for my approval. All our loving up till then had been on the grass with her skirt up around her waist. This was the first time I had seen her completely naked. Her smooth finely textured skin was without a blemish from top to toe. She had no need to be concerned; the beauty of her form and features, the tender curvature of the cheeks of her bottom and the fleshy luxury of her rounded thighs were breathtaking. I just sat there fascinated and enslaved.

When she saw the effect she had on me her confidence and high spirits came back to her with a rush and she began to dance sinuously, wooing me with squirming hips and thighs. She raised her slender arms and reached up as if she was delicately caressing something above her head with her finger tips.

I gasped with mixed emotions of lust and admiration when her firm, creamy breasts with their erect rosy nipples tilted upwards as she leaned over backwards.

As I hurriedly started to divest myself of all my clothing, she came over to me and sank to her knees as I sat on the edge of the armchair, with the intention of helping me remove my stockings, but her eyes were distracted at the sight of something else.

'What a lovely soft cock,' she exclaimed as she swooped on it with eager fingers, cuddling and caressing it and showering it with kisses. When it started to rise and stiffen she curled a finger around its base, and with her other hand, gently held its head with the tips of her fingers.

Bedazzled by its sudden growth, she whispered, 'Isn't it a whopper!' It seemed as if she was asking me to join her in her admiration of my swelling cock.

Removing the yellow ribbon from her hair, she tied it in a bow around the base of my cock and, when it jerked upwards at her touch, she frowned in mock admonition. 'Don't be impatient, you naughty boy.' Then, giving it a light kiss on its tip, 'You won't have long to wait before you will get all you want; but do that again; I like to see you jerk so strongly.'

Squatting on her heels she waited expectantly. Joining in the fun, I jerked it again. Giggling and clapping her hands, she cried out for more. 'Again. Go on. Again and again.'

I kept it up, jerking it until I tired of the game. I made a move towards the bed but she held me back, grabbing my cock with one hand and pushing me back in the chair with the other. With the fingers of both her hands firmly curled around it she pushed the head between her luscious lips and rolled it in the hollow of her tongue.

Removing it from her mouth she adjusted the bow of yellow ribbon so that the ends hung on each side of my balls and, with a parody of solemnity announced, 'As your Royal Sovereign Queen, I appoint you Honourable Knight of the Yellow Ribbon. Arise Sir Elmer Cock.' And then sternly, 'Don't ever dare to fly my ribbon at half-mast.'

It was as if my cock had ears for, on this imperious command, it stood up straighter and stiffer than ever.

After gracefully rising from the floor, she climbed onto the bed and lay full length on the pink overspread. Lying on her side she looked at me with challenging, mischievous eyes. The auburn hair disarrayed around her smooth creamy shoulders had a coppery sheen which reflected the blushing glow from the log fire. The hips curving up voluptuously from her slender waist framed the dark triangle of hair that screened the delicious vent I was about to enter.

As I approached her with stiffened cock I reflected how neat a girl is in her private parts in comparison to what normally hangs dangling between a man's thighs. Seeing the ribbon tied around my cock as I got between her open legs I was about to remove it when she pleaded, 'Please, leave it where it is, darling. It will tickle my fancy when you get on top of me.' And, adding plaintively when she saw the look of doubt on my face, a long drawn out 'Please . . .'

I couldn't deny her anything at that moment and, when her soft full thighs opened wide to reveal the spongy pink mouth of her cunt, my loins surged with brutal lust and I plunged my thick, sturdy cock deep into her. There is no pleasure in the whole wide world to equal the feel of the clasping moist inner flesh of a cunt as it yields to accommodate your swollen, hard cock in a warm clinging embrace.

All the dilly-dallying with yellow ribbon had built up within me a passionate urgency that came to a head with a few powerful thrusts. I groaned out loud in relief as the spunk gushed from my cock. Dara's seductive movements underneath me soon brought me back to a rampant heat. Urgency now gave way to pleasure and, remembering her joy at seeing my cock twitching, I jerked it once or twice inside her. The effect was instantaneous; she laced her fingers around my neck and brought her lips to mine in a passionate kiss. Between kisses she pleaded for more.

When I began to tire I asked her to try to do something similar to me by using the muscles around her cunt, promising her a loving kiss for every time she did it to me. There was only a slight twitch to begin with but, as the movements became stronger, I felt my cock being gripped and made it quiver inside her cunt. It was a titillating, provocative and stimulating sensation and I was only too happy to show my appreciation with a loving tongue kiss each time it happened.

When she weakened in her movements, I took over this gentle sensuous stimulation with my jerking cock and so we dillied and dallied with each other for over an hour. Feeling the quickening of my senses, I got my hands underneath her buttocks and, clasping the soft cheeks of her bottom, I fucked her in an unhurried manner. She rose up to meet me and got into rhythm with my movements. The pace increased and caught us up in an excitement which made us cling to each other with a rapturous intensity.

With eyes closed and teeth clenched, her head thrashing from side to side, her hands gripping my shoulders frantically, she rose to a climax of emotion just as the seed from my loins spurted into her. The spasms of tremors that shook us gradually lessened and we lay entwined seeking comfort and gentle caresses. I heard myself saying over and over, 'I love you, I love you, Dara. I love you.'

Getting no answer, I raised myself up to look into her face. Her lips were pale and slightly open and the long silky eyelashes were glistening with tears.

'Are you alright, my darling?' I asked anxiously.

She opened her eyes, giving me a tender, loving look through the tears. She sighed. 'I cannot move. I want time to stand still so that I can go on feeling like this for ever and ever,' she murmured more to herself than to me.

I kissed her gently on the lips then rolled over onto my back to stretch my legs out as far as they could go. I loved Dara, the cosy room and our bed; I loved the whole world and all its people. It was a state of bliss where there were no yesterdays or tomorrows.

The light from the morning sun was filtering its way through the fabric of the curtains when I awakened slowly from a deep sleep. With a feeling of utter contentment I stretched out my legs then turned to look at Dara. She was facing me, hair tumbling all over the pillow, her lips parted like a baby in slumber. My movements must have disturbed her for she looked at me with guileless wide eyes for a while, then came a sunny dimpled smile.

As she nestled in my arms I couldn't help asking myself which was the real Dara: was it the seductive enchantress who bewitched me in the glow of the firelight or the artless childlike creature now seeking the warmth and loving embrace of my arms?

Although I knew she was no virgin from the way she welcomed my cock that first time we got stuck into each other on the grass, any curiosity about her past got lost in the storming emotions she aroused in me. Enamoured with her winning ways, I never gave it a thought, but now I was asking myself had she loved someone else with the same abandonment that she was loving me? Was I the exception or did she often bare her fleshy delights to any man who took her fancy?

Thinking back, I remembered that she had been an easy conquest— too easy—indeed she was more than willing and in the first intimate union of our flesh she had screwed me. The more I thought about it the more the suspicion grew that the truth of the matter was that she belonged to any man who could satisfy her hot itchy cunt.

My breath was coming in uneasy gasps as I stared at the ceiling and my finger nails were digging into the palms of my hands. A storming rage thundered through my head cutting out all thought and reason. In my frenzied imagination I could see Dara in the most intimate positions with another man.

Suddenly my flesh couldn't stand having her near me any longer and I savagely pushed her from me. Startled, she looked at me, hurt and bewildered.

'What is it, Elmer?' she asked in a small voice. 'Why are you glaring at me like that? What have I done?'

'Who were you with before you took up with me?' I growled threateningly.

Impatient at the tense silence that followed my outburst I shouted, 'Well, out with it. Come on, tell me,' then added, 'I know I am not the first man to get between your legs.'

The blood was pounding in my head and I cursed her with all the filthy words that I had ever heard. I knew she couldn't hear what I was saying for she lay all curled up with her knees nearly touching her chin and her hands pressed to her ears. That only made me more angry and I shouted louder and my swearing and cursing went from bad to worse as I grabbed her hands and pulled them away from her ears.

Kneeling over her I yelled, 'Tell me, you dirty rotten slut, who's been fucking you?'

Turning her face away from me I saw her lower lip trembling and she gulped before answering me in a low, dispirited voice. 'I am sorry, Elmer. I would have liked to have kept myself for you, but how was I to know that we would meet some day?'

She gulped again. 'Please don't stop loving me. I cannot live without you.'

'Who was it?' I yelled. 'How often did he fuck you?'

'It was a farmer who employed me as a dairymaid when I was but fifteen.'

'Did he rape you?' I demanded to know. 'Or did you lift your skirts up for him?'

'I lifted my skirts up for him twice,' she answered in a weary voice as she rose to a sitting position.

'You are nothing but a randy cunt, aren't you?' I insisted as I shook her backwards and forwards by the shoulders. When I had finished shaking her, she faced me with unseeing eyes and whispered, 'Yes, if that's what you want me to be.'

'Is there anything else?' I asked and, when she shook her head, I got out of bed, pulled on my trousers and said in a cold voice, 'I don't believe you. You're a bloody liar. I'll bet there is a lot more to it than what you are saying. It is obvious that you learnt a great deal about men somewhere.'

I got the rest of my clothing on and, before I slammed the door behind me, said, 'Go back to your farmer, you randy bitch.'

Calling at my lodgings to collect my soap samples, I went on to one or two local calls, my mind dead and my voice answering mechanically any queries directed at me by the dealers when they were giving me their orders. The next morning, after a restless night, I set off for Milwaukee area where I was due to call on a number of customers.

It was as if I had closed off most of my mind, leaving a small part to deal with the business of selling soap to the few stores in that area, for I had little feeling and observed nothing of my surroundings. My speech, actions, responses, were automatic and without thought. The mind of a healthy normal individual cannot remain inactive for very long and after my last call in mid-afternoon, the thoughts and emotions came flooding back into my mind.

To begin with it was nearly all emotion with very little clear thinking. Torn apart by jealousy I was like a raving lunatic as I walked along a lonely track across meadow land. Luckily there were only trees and brushwood to see my contorted face and to hear my groans and loud outbursts of anger. Bedevilled in turn by uncontrollable fits of blinding jealousy and raging fury, then slowly descending into depths of maudlin self-pity and sickened by shame as my memory recalled the vile, obscene words I had shouted at Dara. Reason, God's greatest gift to mankind, overcame my storming emotions, bringing tolerance and common sense to my tortured mind.

What right had I, a married man with two children, who was more than eager to bed a beautiful seventeen-year-old girl, to condemn the same girl for an indiscretion that occurred at least two years before we met and fell in love with each other? The only excuse for my despicable jealousy was that, having fallen in love for the first time in my life, I wanted complete, unsoiled possession of my beloved; past, present and future. Jealousy, that dark destructive side to love, had exploded into a thousand poisoned thoughts to shatter all my tender feelings for the girl I loved. Even her fervent desire to please me had been suspected as the actions of a predatory lustful female.

Driven by guilt, regret and shame, I journeyed on to Chicago in a fever of anxiety and impatience to reach Dara and make amends for my cruel behaviour. The sun was setting when I arrived in Chicago and in the still twilight of the evening I ran to the house where Dara had rented the room. Our home, she had said, but now I was on the threshold I hesitated, wondering if I had forfeited the right to free access to Dara and the cosy room. Surely after subjecting Dara to the foulest obscenities, slandering her with filthy accusations and then leaving her alone in her misery for two days and nights, it would be the height of arrogance to presume that I would be welcome. Drawn by my great need for a reconciliation, I crept up the stairs quietly and timidly knocked on the door. Receiving no answer after my second knock, I ventured to open the door and enter.

The dead silence of the darkened room was intimidating and I was about to leave, thinking Dara was out, when I heard a slight movement from one of the armchairs. Peering through the dim light I could just discern a shadowy figure curled up in the chair.

Putting a light to one of the candles on the mantelpiece, the glimmer illuminated a most pitiful figure. A picture of Dara that was to torment my conscience for many a day. Her doleful face was tear-lined. Eyes heavy with despair looked at me blankly and then closed with uncaring weariness. Looking around the room I could see that the rumpled bed-clothes and everything else in the room was just as I had left it. I was to learn later that she had moved from the bed to the chair and had sat there, curtains drawn, for the whole of the time that I was absent.

The bile from my stomach rose in self-disgust at the realization that I had been the cause of all this misery. But this was no time for me to wallow in shame and mortification, and I applied my mind to bring things to rights. First the fire, which I relit to warm the room in the hope of bringing some life back into the still, quiet figure in the armchair. Next some hot food.

Searching the cupboard I could find nothing suitable but three eggs which I put in a pan of water and set to boil on the fire. The thought came to me that she would need more than food to revive her and I dashed out to 'The Dog's Head', a nearby tavern, returning with a bottle of brandy. I removed the hard-boiled eggs from the fire. Getting a spoon from a drawer, I attempted to spoon some of the brandy between Dara's lips. Only half of it went down her throat, the rest dribbled down her chin and onto her blouse. What little she swallowed began to take effect. The colour came back into her cheeks and after a little while she opened her eyes. Her fingers explored my face as if to confirm what she was seeing.

'Elmer, darling,' she whispered. 'Is it really you?'

Overcome with emotion, I was on the verge of tears and could only nod my head in affirmation. When I turned away with the intention of collecting the boiled eggs, she cried out and clutched my jacket. 'Don't leave me. Please don't leave me, Elmer!'

'No, I won't leave you,' I reassured her. 'No, never again.' And then added in a soothing tone, 'I'm just preparing some eggs for you to eat.'

When the eggs were shelled I lifted her onto my lap as I sat in the chair, then coaxed her to swallow small portions of the warm egg. After she had eaten the eggs we just sat there, she occasionally weeping and cuddling up to me with eyes closed, and me with my arms around her in a close, loving embrace.

Sometime later the weeping ceased and she slept fitfully for about an hour. Awakening, she put a hand on my face saying, 'Kiss me, Elmer,' and before I had time to kiss her, 'I'm hungry, Elmer, very hungry. Is there anything to eat?'

Knowing there was nothing to eat, I got her onto her feet.

'Can you walk around the room, Dara?'

She was fairly steady on her feet so, after we had walked twice around the room, I proposed that we go to the tavern and have a pint of ale with a large meat pie. She put her arm through mine, looked up at me and smiled. 'Oh, Elmer, you're back, aren't you? I'll do anything you say, only don't leave me alone. Stay with me. Promise.'

Giving her a gentle hug, I promised never to leave her again and, opening the door, said, 'Now, come on, let's get a hot meat pie down us and then we will both feel better.'

Outside the tavern we nearly fell over a horse trough built specifically on the landlord's instructions so that he could take unruly drunks by the scruff of the neck and hold their heads under the water until they sobered up or passed out.

Inside the tavern it was warm and alive with bustling activity and chattering groups of people. We had only got half way through our pies when a grey-whiskered, broad-shouldered giant of a man approached us in a friendly manner and in a voice rich and fruity with good humour boomed, 'You're new to the neighbourhood, aren't you? Welcome. I'm Vladimir Aksakov. What your name?'

'Elmer Varley,' I replied, shaking him by the hand as I rose to my feet. 'And this is my woman, Dara.'

The warm tavern, the food and the brandy had revived her spirits to the extent that she gave him one of her dazzling smiles. Vladimir obviously had an eye for a pretty girl. He couldn't take his eyes off Dara and, in the hope of getting more such smiles, spread himself across the other side of the table.

'Pies good?' he asked.

We nodded.

'They would be better with some of my vegetables in them, but the landlord won't listen to me. "Meat pies are meat pies" he says. "If they want vegetables they can have them separate, but not in my pies." '

He shook his head sadly and sighed. 'He is a stubborn man, is Harry. Won't listen to me.'

Bringing his tankard up to his mouth, he swilled half his drink down his throat with one swallow, leaving a row of beer beads hanging from the hairs of his moustache. He went on about his fruit and vegetable stall that he manned every day further along Lakeside and expressed the hope that Dara would patronize his stall. Talkative and entertaining, he tried a number of times to draw Dara into the conversation, but without success. She was too busy eating her pie.

I could see the look of disappointment on his face because he wasn't having any effect on her and, laughingly, I said in a friendly voice, 'It's no good, Vladimir, she only has eyes for me. She is a one man girl and I'm the lucky man.'

He gave me a searching, quizzical look then, seeing the grin on my face, threw back his head and roared with laughter. The thunderous guffaws that followed had everyone looking in our direction seeking the cause of the uproar. My remarks were not that funny, but I was pleased that he had taken the rebuff in the right spirit.

I found myself weighing him up. It was his eyes that caught my attention first. Pale grey, tolerant and calm, and in complete contradiction to the thunderous laughter and loud talk. I sensed that behind all that boisterous behaviour there was a thoughtful, patient man. When we became acquainted I was to discover that he was indeed a very patient man especially when pursuing a woman with the purpose of seducing her, which probably accounted for his many successes with even the most virtuous of women.

I always remember my uncle saying, 'Never push a patient man too far, for when he does lose his temper all hell is let loose and there is murder in his eyes,' and I made a mental note to steer clear of Vladimir if he should ever lose his temper.

For the rest of him, he had a mass of wolfish grey hair, a bulbous nose protruding from a large expressive face that was constantly changing from clowning pathos to exhilarating humour; a big, cuddly, amiable Russian bear with bulging arms, strong enough to crack your ribs in a mighty hug.

During the ensuing months Vladimir and I became firm friends and, although he still hankered after Dara, I sensed she would come to no harm from his attentions. She complained to me more than once about him buzzing her rear with his great big hand while she was buying vegetables from his stall. I told her to stand well clear of him when she was at the stall and to treat it all as a game of 'catch me if you can'. She must have taken my advice as I heard no further complaints about Vladimir fondling her bum. Indeed, when the three of us were in 'The Dog's Head' together, she began to take his flattery and lecherous looks with a certain amount of indulgence and good humour and often retaliated with teasing remarks about the women she met at the stall who simpered and giggled every time he spoke to them.

Vladimir would shrug his shoulders and deny that there was anything improper going on; they were, according to him, 'just good customers'.

'Oh, yes,' Dara would reply with a laugh. 'They're good customers because they know where to go when they're randy for their *greens.*'

Vladimir, with a good show of indignation, then pretended to be shocked at her reference to *greens,* and changed the subject rapidly.

On an evening shortly after Christmas, he opened up to tell us why he had emigrated to America. But, as he was about to satisfy our curiosity on this matter, his words were drowned in an outburst of deafening raucous laughter coming from a group of men near us.

As the uproar increased we all stood up to see what was going on. A villainous looking brute with a battle-scarred face had his foot on a man's belly as he lay prone on the floor and was pouring ale into the victim's open mouth. When the ale began to dribble from the man's mouth the foot would come hard down into his guts to make it come spewing up again like a small fountain. No doubt very funny to the onlookers, but painful to the man on the floor who was pretending to enjoy taking the part of the victim in this horse-play, but I could see the pain and anxiety in his eyes every time the foot dug deep into his guts.

'Who is the man with the heavy foot?' I asked.

Vladimir scowled. 'That animal arrived here from Buffalo about two years ago and is now feared and hated by nearly everybody because he has bashed into a bloody pulp every man he has fought so far. A ruthless, dirty fighter who will stop at nothing in a brawl. After knocking a man out cold he will kick him viciously until someone pulls him away.'

He took a swig of his ale, wiped his moustache with the back of his hand. 'A boozy, loud-mouthed ruffian of the worst type. That's what he is. Boasting when he has had a few drinks that, drunk or sober, there isn't a man in Chicago who can stand up to him for more than five minutes.

'You asked who he is?' he said. Turning to me, 'His real name is Bruce Brecon, BB to the toadies who are his constant companions, but to the folk around here he is better known as the "Buffalo Bruiser". It is whispered that he is a secret member of the "Know Nothings", an anti-immigrant political party. In other words he is against people like you and me, Dara. So look out. As for myself, I'm a member of the "Free Soilers", a party pledged to campaign for free soil, free labour, free speech and free men.'

I looked at the 'Bruiser' and then at Vladimir, comparing the two. 'But surely, Vladimir, with your strength and weight you would be more than a match for him?'

'I try to avoid brawling and trouble,' he answered slowly. 'A long time ago I killed two men in Russia and had to flee to America. That must not happen again. I've got a wife, nine children and my own vegetable and fruit business. I've got a lot to lose if I kill an American and, believe me, that's just what would happen if I fought with the "Buffalo Bruiser". As it is I've got the measure of the man. He only picks on those who are afraid of him. I've outstared him many a time—there's no likelihood of him ever challenging me to a fight.'

Leaning forward so no one near could hear me I asked, 'How did you come to kill two men in Russia?'

'There's no need to whisper,' he thundered back at me. 'It's no secret. I've told a number of people. It stops them wanting to fight me and that's fine by me. My family lived in a village about one-hundred-and-fifty versts north of the port of Vernoleninsk on the Black Sea coast.' He broke off to explain that one-hundred-and-fifty versts is about a hundred American miles.

'The village was part of a very large estate owned by a nobleman, a former captain of the Imperial Guard. His Excellency, Count Ivanovich Gorchakov, was looked up to by his peasants as a father with a mystic authority. He was an autocrat who had the absolute power of life and death over his serfs, for they were his property to do with as he wished. Everyone on his estate had to pay him a "soul-tax" just for being alive and having the privilege of being his *moujiks,* or, as you would say in America, serfs. Choose any word you like, they all mean the same thing: human beings who are considered by their owner as no more important than beasts in a field.'

Vladimir gave me a long, hard look. 'It is the same in this country with the black slaves in the south. Don't you agree?'

I could only nod my head and tell him that I was an abolitionist.

'I am glad to hear that you have the same views as myself. Last year I had the privilege of attending a meeting where I heard two candidates for the Senate, Stephen Douglas and Abraham Lincoln, debate the question of black slavery. I much preferred the Republican, Lincoln's attack on the institution of slavery to the mild opinions expressed by Douglas.

'But to get back to my life in Russia. My father, although a serf, was an educated man, the leader and spokesman for the *gromada,* the village council. He was a wealthy man in comparison to other serfs, with his own *droshky,* a carriage he had inherited from his father. My sister and I were the only two children of my parent's marriage. At the time that I am talking about she was fourteen and I was eighteen. She was a quiet, shy girl and very beautiful with the blushing purity of a young maiden just beginning to blossom into womanhood. His Excellency cast a lustful eye on her soon after his wife died in childbirth and sent his guards to collect my sister and two other maidens to form the beginning of what was to become a harem of a dozen village girls.

'I shall never forget the look of terror on my sister's face as she was dragged by the arms from our home. My father and I tried to stop the guards as they were pulling her through the door. As we struggled outside the house we were felled to the ground by their cudgels. The shock of losing her daughter affected my mother so deeply that she just faded away until she looked like a bag of old bones. She was dead within two months.'

Some tears began to well up in Vladimir's eyes. Dara leaned forward and offered him her handkerchief. He sighed, overcome by the memories of the past and, after wiping his eyes, continued with his story.

'A month after my mother's death, my sister was brought before His Excellency for the "sin" of allowing herself to become pregnant. She was obliged to crawl towards the man who had ruined her, kiss the hem of his coat and ask for His Excellency's forgiveness for her crime and then banished to the snowy wastes of Siberia for ten years. Transport was too much of a luxury for serfs and, along with hundreds of other serfs who had offended their masters, she had to walk the whole way to Siberia.

'As more and more girls were taken to replace those that our nobleman had tired of, or who had become pregnant, there was much grumbling among the peasants and one or two foolish fathers went to the big house to protest forcibly about the loss of their daughters. For their impertinence, their naked backs were whipped into a bloody pulp and then salted. Feelings rose so high in the village that my father feared there would be an uprising and bloodshed. He had no faith in money and, over the years, had bought a considerable amount of gold and silver jewellery whenever he could afford to do so. Digging up his cache of jewellery hidden under the floorboards, he placed it all in a small wine cask and sent me off in the *droshky* to a trustworthy friend who lived in a small town forty miles south of our village. I was instructed to leave the cask with this friend and to lodge with him for at least five days before returning to the village.

'He obviously wanted me to escape the punishment that would be dealt out most harshly to all who were involved in any way with an uprising. My father had read the signs of a revolt with the instinct of a leader who is as one with his people. At dusk, two days after my departure, all the men of the village, armed with scythes and cudgels and other weapons, half of them drunk with *Qvass*, assembled outside my father's house and demanded that he lead them up to the big house for a talk with His Excellency. They stood in sullen silence unmoved by my father's

appeal for them to wait until he had had a private word with our nobleman, but they would have none of it, insisting that the Count be told that
night that he could ravish no more girls from the village for from now on
none would be allowed to go to the big house.

'They hustled my father before them saying, "You are our *hetman,* you
will speak for us." He had no option but to lead them to the big house. In
grim silence they followed, holding their smoking torches above their
heads. The Count had seen their approach and, with the confident arrogance of the true aristocrat, stood at the top of the marble steps that led
up to the entrance to the house. When all the serfs were assembled in
front of the house, my father came forward and, with one knee resting on
the bottom step, addressed the Count. *"Batiushka,* we ask your forgiveness for disturbing you at this hour." "What do you want, you filthy
scum? Down on your knees, every one of you," the Count screamed.
Without a moment's hesitation they sank to the ground like dumb beasts
of the field at nightfall. With a sneer on his face, he looked at them and
then at my father. "Well! You stupid oaf, what have you got to say for
yourself?"

' "Begging your pardon, Your Excellency, I speak not for myself but
for the *gromada.* These unworthy serfs who kneel before you would have
me inform you that they will allow no more of their daughters to be
taken for your pleasure."

'On hearing these words, the Count's features twisted into a snarl and
he launched into a great tirade of abuse against his ungrateful *moujiks* as
they bowed their heads lower as if to escape from the heat of his rage.
Rushing down the steps, he cracked his whip across my father's back and
then, plunging into the crowd of bowed serfs, he scattered them like
frightened sheep in all directions with his flaring whip.

'I learned all this from my father on my return. The silent, brooding
log huts of the village warned me that something dreadful had happened.
No one stood at the doors of their *isbas* to welcome me.'

Dara interrupted Vladimir to ask what an *isbas* was.

'An *isbas,*' he snapped back at her impatiently, 'is a one roomed, filthy
hovel that the serfs call a home.'

'And what's a *batiushka?*' asked Dara.

Batiushka means father, and in the case of the Count it means a father
figure with absolute authority. Now let me continue. But before I do, I
need some more ale,' he said, looking at me meaningfully.

I soon replenished his tankard and, after taking a swig at it, he continued with his story.

'My father told me of how, after leading the serfs back to their homes,
about ten or more of them, disappointed that nothing had been achieved

that evening, returned to the big house and set it alight with their torches. No lives were lost, but the house was burned to the ground. The Count called on the Military for help and, the day after I arrived back from my journey south, the soldiers came and rounded up all the men and imprisoned them under armed guard in a large barn. The Count was now living in the outbuildings while men worked frantically to rebuild his house.

'I was the first to be called out of the barn and brought before His Excellency. Abasing myself, I crawled to him, kissed his boots, and proclaimed my innocence as I had been absent from the village at the time of the uprising.'

Vladimir broke off to explain. 'I am not ashamed to admit that I abased myself to save my skin, for I knew that retribution with a vengeance was about to fall on all the heads of those who had taken part in the uprising. As it turned out, it was a retribution that was appalling even by Russian standards.

'All that morning men were led out of the barn to be tortured and beaten until they confessed their guilt or informed on their neighbours and friends. I could hear their screams and shrieks of pain and I sent up a silent prayer of thanks that my father, in his great wisdom, had arranged for me to be absent at the right time. Before midday the guards had the names of the twelve men who had fired the house with their torches and wasted no time in bringing every living soul from the village to the walled courtyard of the big house. Mothers with babes in their arms, the old and the infirm, were all huddled together in family groups cowed and fearful.

'There was a large tree in the centre of the courtyard and its spreading branches were used to string up by their wrists the men who had set fire to the house. They had been stripped of their clothes and, with their toes just touching the ground, they hung from the branches writhing and trembling with fear. Their mystic father, the all powerful *Batiushka,* approached them holding a half empty bottle in one hand and a glass full of wine in the other. Behind him were the guards with their whips. He filled his mouth with wine, with a disdainful gesture, signalled the guards to choose a victim for their whips. The air was rent with shrieks as the naked men twisted and turned against the knotted leather whips which cut deep into their flesh. After a time some of them passed out, unable to bear the cruel treatment any longer, but their bodies, criss-crossed with deep, bleeding cuts, continued to jerk and swing around as the whips lashed around them. They were bleeding profusely and pools of blood began to form beneath them. The Count ordered that buckets of water be thrown over their heads to revive them. Satisfied that he had got them sufficiently alive to feel pain again, he set the guards at them with their cudgels. The blows were not hard to begin with, just sufficient to raise bruises where the flesh was not already torn by the whipping. The men hung from the tree branches limp and exhausted by the cruel punishment they had undergone. Feeble little moans escaped from their lips from time to time.

'Once more, buckets of water were splashed over their heads as the Count strolled amongst them sipping his wine. He kicked at the hanging, bleeding bodies and then looked into their glazed eyes to see if there was still some life left in them and then had a quiet word with the guards, who took up their cudgels to commence their grim task again. They had obviously been told to break as many bones as they could with their heavy cudgels. As they swung the cudgels with all the strength of their arms, they sweated in their efforts to crack as many bones as possible.

'The women and children and the rest of the men who had been brought out of the barn to witness this brutal, savage massacre, stood in shocked silence as they looked at the dead, broken bodies hanging from the tree. I heard some of the women scream when they heard the bones crack under the blows of the cudgels but now there was only dumbfounded shock as they faced the bloodied, crumpled, broken bodies with gaping mouths.

'His Excellency, well satisfied with the punishment he had meted out so far, called the rest of the men to come forward and kneel before him. "Your guilt was not as great as those who fired my house but you all took part in the uprising and must be punished. My sentence is ten lashes of the whip on all of you, except your *hetman*. I have something special for Aksakov as he was the leader of the uprising. Proceed with the whippings," he commanded the guards.

'All this happened many years ago and yet there are times when I awaken in the middle of the night to the terrible sound of lashing whips and piercing shrieks of men hanging from a tree.

'When all the men had received their ten lashes, they were all assembled in the centre of the courtyard. My father was then stripped completely naked and placed with his back up against the massive trunk of the tree. We all stood waiting in hushed silence for the Count, who, during the latter whippings, had retired to the house for refreshments. After a few minutes he appeared, dressed in the full uniform of the Imperial Guard. He drew his sword with its razor-sharp curved blade, strolled over to my father and slashed him across the lower part of the belly with the point of his sabre. The bloody gash across his skin opened into a wide, obscene mouth and a pinkish grey tongue of gut slithered out and hung between his thighs.'

As Vladimir took a swig of ale I glanced at Dara. Her eyes were screwed up tight with horror and her hands were clasped over her ears. Nevertheless, Vladimir went on talking as if he was in a trance.

'The Chief Guard, a bull-necked brute in a grey tunic, stepped out, grabbed the gut and nailed it to the tree trunk. Picking up his whip, he lashed my father across his shoulders. Up till that moment I don't think he felt any pain, but the cut of the whip made him cry out loud and spin round and he stumbled and fell on his back. There was now about seven feet of the intestine stretched out between his belly and the tree. They raised him to his feet and whipped him again, making him move further from the nailed end of the gut. There was stark fear in his eyes as he looked at the fifteen feet of intestine extending out from him and he groaned when he tried, with spread out fingers, to close his split belly. The cutting whip lashed out again, flicking his legs to make him stumble further from the tree to release what was left of his innards. Over twenty feet of his entrails lay glistening before him like a straightened snake. His knees buckled under him and his degutted body collapsed backwards onto the cobbles of the courtyard. There was no more life left in him; his spirit had fled from his tortured body and he lay with his mouth gaping open like his disembowelled abdomen, his unseeing eyes reflecting the green-hued light from the leafy branches above him.

'I stood there stunned, an unfeeling detachment freezing my reason and emotions and one part of my mind recording all that the eyes could see and storing it in my memory. I must have blacked out after that, for I have only a blurred recollection of how I got home. When I came to, the contents of my stomach were vomiting out of my mouth as I lay on the floor near my bed. I have no memory of doing so, but I must have climbed onto the bed fully clothed and fallen into a deep sleep. Awakening at noon the next day, I had only one thought in my mind—my father's death must be avenged. Although during the following weeks I appeared normal on the surface, my thoughts were occupied with scheming and planning on how I was going to kill not only the Count but also his Chief Guard, the one who had whipped my father. It needed careful planning for I intended to survive their deaths so that for many years after I would have the satisfaction of having struck back at the absolute ruthless authority above me—unscathed. It would be no victory for me if I was caught after their deaths and then tortured until I, too, had died. The plan to kill them and escape from Russia gradually formed after three months of careful observation of the daily movements of my enemies.

'Awakening one morning at dawn with the conviction that this was the day for the killing, I sharpened my knife on a smooth, wet stone and taking great care that I wasn't seen by anyone I crept into a wood where, for the previous two days, the Count with his Chief Guard walking behind him, had spent the mornings shooting birds that flew up before him. I had to wait four long hours before I heard them entering the wood.

'Penetrating further into the copse, I quickly climbed a tree whose branches covered the now familiar track they had taken on previous shootings. The Count passed and then pressed his way through some brushwood. Twenty paces behind him trudged the Chief Guard, carrying provisions and two extra guns. When he came alongside the tree I dropped onto his shoulders and had a hand over his mouth and my knife in his throat before his head hit the ground. Sweeping the sharp edge of my knife two or three times across his throat, I made sure that he was dead before crawling on my belly through the brushwood. Making as little noise as possible, I crept up to the Count, just as he was raising his gun to take aim at a bird. The gun went off with a bang as I slid the knife from ear to ear across his upward-stretched throat. I don't know what got into me but, with a maniacal grin on my face, I savagely sawed into his neck until his head was connected to his body only by the spinal bones and the skin at the back.

'It took me but an hour to drag both bodies to a swamp, push them under the thick mud and cover the bloodied tracks where they had been with fallen leaves. At home I stripped off my bloodstained clothes, tied them into a bundle, washed myself thoroughly and donned my best smock and coat. Holding my horse by its bridle, I walked through the village, stopping occasionally to gossip and inform those who were interested that I would be away for a few days as I had business to attend to in the south.

'Once the village was behind me and out of sight, I whipped my horse into a gallop and arrived at the house of my father's friend in the early afternoon. Collecting the small cask of jewellery, I explained that there was no time for me to dine with him as I had to be at the port of Vernoleninsk that day to ship the jewellery abroad. He very kindly offered to exchange one of his fastest horses for mine, an offer I could do no other than accept as my own horse was in no state to ride the rest of the journey. At a river crossing further along the road I stuffed the jewellery into copious pockets inside my coat, dropped the empty cask and bloodstained clothing into deep water and rode on.

'Arriving at Vernoleninsk late in the evening, I took a room at an inn and stabled the horse. Wolfing down a quick meal of meat and vegetables, I then sought the harbour taverns for sailors whose ships were about to leave the port. I was lucky, for the second man I approached told me that his ship, with a mixed cargo, was bound for France and was due to sail on the tide at dawn. In answer to my question as to the possibility of his captain taking a passenger with no questions asked, he winked and put his finger to his nose. He then put out his hand, palm upwards. I took the hint and for ten roubles learned that the captain did take aboard, frequently, unknown passengers and charged them two hundred roubles whatever the length of the journey. The sailor gave me to understand that the information was in confidence as the captain arranged these transactions with great secrecy but was unaware that certain members of the crew knew what he was up to. Secrecy was very necessary as there were police spies everywhere. Other enquiries led me to a jeweller who was just about to retire to his bed when I called on him. We bargained a little before I got two hundred roubles in exchange for some jewellery. Going back to the inn, I wrote a letter to my father's friend telling him where he could collect his horse, paid the innkeeper what I owed him for board and stabling, and informed him that the horse would be collected within the week.

'With police spies everywhere you couldn't trust anyone so I waited on the quayside all night and, at dawn, just as the ship was about to cast off, I boarded it and handed over the two hundred roubles to the captain who placed me in a bunk in the cabin of the first mate with whom, no doubt, he had an arrangement to share the two hundred roubles. From Marseilles I was able to board a boat to London where I stayed for over a year before sailing for America. I didn't waste my time in London, for I lodged with a former professor of Moscow University who taught me English as the English speak it and who also introduced me to the best of English literature.'

Vladimir stood up and looked around as if surprised to find himself in the tavern, then looked back at me. 'Russia lies heavy on my heart to-night. That terrible barbarous country will haunt me all my life,' he said and, without another word, left us sitting there.

Shortly after his departure we retired to our room for the night. Neither of us spoke as we undressed and when we got to bed we lay side by side in silence. I guessed that Dara, like me, had been profoundly shaken by the account of the barbarous cruelty that went on in Russia.

After tossing and turning for an hour or two, I got out of bed, stirred up the fire and put more logs on it. I was sitting in one of the armchairs gazing into the fire, meditating on man's inhumanity to man, when Dara slid out from under the bedclothes and came and sat on my lap.

Neither of us had any clothes on as we always slept in the nude. Although the room was warm from the fire, we cuddled up close to each other and soon the pressure of her luscious soft bottom began to stiffen my cock. Dara, feeling it getting hard underneath her, got astride me. Sitting on my knees she played with it until it swelled so large I thought it would burst. Raising herself she moved onto it, guiding it skilfully into the hole between her thighs and then see-sawed her hips backwards and forwards until the cloudy lust-fluid gushed from me. I lay there thinking what a lovely relaxed way this was of being screwed by a girl.

Her wriggling hips aroused me for a second time and I lifted her up in my arms, grabbed a cushion and lurched over to the bed. Placing the cushion under her belly I mounted her raised buttocks doggy fashion and, bringing my hand around her front, steered my cock into her. The sensual feeling of the tender female flesh tucked well into my loins was all I wanted for a while. Seeking more rounded soft flesh I brought my left hand across her shoulders and down onto her right breast. Getting a firm hold on it, my other hand came up under her and fastened onto her other one. Raw animal lust gripped my body as the erect nipples pressed into the palms of my hands. I wanted to dominate this body beneath me until it was in complete submission to my unbridled savage lust. With an animal strength that wouldn't be denied, I haunched her hips higher and strove to get up her as far as my throbbing cock could penetrate. Then, like a man possessed, I rode her hard with deep, brutal thrusts, heedless of how much I might be hurting her. The pace of my stabbing cock increased. Suddenly every muscle in my body was transfixed in a rigid grip of passion that had me crouched over her with teeth clenched in the pain of the intensity of my feelings. When the last drop of my raging lust spluttered out of me, I collapsed over her back panting like a wounded animal that could go no further. I lay there drained of all aggression with a mind empty of thoughts of Russian atrocities and bullies like the 'Buffalo Bruiser'. Dara, generous to a fault in her loving, I hoped would intuitively understand and forgive me for handling her so roughly. I had returned from the tavern in agonized anger over the terrible cruelties going on every day in this world of ours and with these emotions bursting to be released had blown them off in unbridled lust.

The days went by as days and weeks do. Our evenings with Vladimir were intermittent as I was often away travelling. There is some truth in the saying that 'absence makes the heart grow fonder' for always on my return I got a most ardent welcome from Dara. As soon as I got through the door she would rush into my arms and shower me with kisses. Girls can be very generous with their kisses when they are in love. Pressing her little belly hard into me brought the usual response. Flinging our clothes off, we would leap onto the bed to lie well stuck into each other for an hour or two. After a little sleep we would rise, dress and go off to 'The Dog's Head' to listen to Vladimir's outrageous stories while we drank our ale and ate our meat pies. As far as I was concerned, and I'm sure it was the same for Dara, it was the happiest period of my life.

The evening before Good Friday at 'The Dog's Head' was a night I was to remember for the rest of my life. Everything seemed to be as usual when we arrived—with one exception. Vladimir wasn't there to welcome us and, to make matters worse, the 'Buffalo Bruiser' and his friends were there kicking up a hell of a din with their foul obscenities and raucous laughter.

From what I could gather, they were on a spree and had been drinking in two or three taverns gathering up more hangers-on at each ale house before coming on to 'The Dog's Head'. The 'Bruiser' was insisting on everybody buying him a drink because it was his birthday. Even total strangers were being pressed to buy him a drink. If anybody hesitated he stuck his chin out and gave them a mean look until they got him a drink. Then as they were about to take a swig of their own drink he would slap them as hard as he could on the back with the result that they had ale all over their faces as they struggled to keep on their feet. When this happened the noise of shouting and laughter was deafening.

After a while I became aware that Dara and I were receiving a lot of attention from the 'Bruiser' and his cronies. Without Vladimir's bulk to protect us I became a little apprehensive and whispered in Dara's ear that we should go before trouble came our way. Swallowing what was left of my ale I was about to rise when the 'Bruiser' suddenly appeared at our table and grabbed Dara by the hand. Dara leaned back and tried to pull away from the firm grip he had on her and cast a despairing glance in my direction.

Taken by surprise and totally unprepared for what was happening, I rose slowly to my feet. Getting a firmer grip on Dara's hand he pulled her forward until their noses were nearly touching.

'Yo're a real pretty gal—ain't yo' just,' he said in a thick drunken voice. 'We've 'ad a bet that yo' cain't refuse me a little kiss seeing that it's ma birthday.'

One of his friends chose that moment to shout, 'Come on, BB, get on with it or yor'll lose yo' bet an' yor'll be buying drinks all round.'

It came to me that the 'Bruiser' was taking advantage of Vladimir's absence to play free and easy with Dara. Assuming, I suppose that I would be too afraid to object to him taking liberties with my girl. As he made a move to plant a kiss on her lips and she quickly averted her face, my hackles rose and, without giving the matter any further thought, I pushed him in a sudden outburst of blinding red hot anger. The talk and noise died away when he fell over backwards and there was a deathly hush all over the tavern. With murder in his eyes, he got up slowly from the floor and his coarse, unshaven face suddenly loomed up before me. He reached out and grabbed me by the front of my jacket. As we stood, eye to eye, it came to me that he was taller and broader than me and certainly a lot tougher than I ever could be.

Amazed and alarmed at this sudden turn of events, I felt my stomach tense with fear. His bloodshot eyes glared straight into mine. He has had too much to drink, I thought; maybe if it comes to a fight his inebriation will slow him down.

Suddenly he threw back his head and roared with laughter. 'So yo' wanna fight, hey? Yo' must be crazy, hey?'

I didn't answer. The last thing I wanted was a fight, especially with a murderous brute who would stop at nothing once he got started. And then there were my employers. If it ever got back to them that I had been involved in a tavern brawl then I would be out of work. I sent up a despairing prayer: God have pity on me and get me out of this mess.

The 'Bruiser', confident of his superiority and strength, gazed at me with contempt and then blew out a derisive farting sound between wet lips, spraying my face with spittle. Flustered and outraged, I aimed a blow at his head with a clenched fist. He blocked it with his elbow and pushed me to the floor. I would undoubtedly have been kicked in the head as I lay there but for the intervention of the landlord who came between us and took the full impact of the 'Bruiser's' vicious kick on his legs. With raging fury, the landlord, a big tough man, well able to look after himself, brought his elbow hard back into the 'Bruiser's' belly making him crouch over gasping for breath. 'Out back, both un yo'. No brawling in my tavern.'

The next thing I knew I was being pushed and pulled through the door and onto the cobbled back yard. Everybody in the tavern followed, pushing and making bets as to whether I would still be on my feet after a minute with the 'Bruiser'. Surrounded by a crowd eager to see blood and yelling 'Ring! Ring!' I fronted the scowling face of my opponent. While men pushed against each other to form a ring, with slow deliberation he proceeded to take off his coat, neckerchief and shirt, displaying a battle-scarred chest and bulging muscles on his arms. When I followed suit, he watched me with a smirk on his lips, confident that he would soon have me once more on my back and could this time kick my head in without any interference from the landlord.

'He's got a skin like a woman,' he scoffed when he saw me stripped to the waist and, without any warning, came at me with flying fists. I was quicker in the eye and lighter on my feet than he and had no difficulty in hopping out of the way as he stumbled past me. Turning round he growled, 'Stand up and fight like a man, yo' white livered skunk.'

With a snarling curse he rushed at me again. This time his flailing fists struck me about the head with thudding blows that nearly knocked me senseless. I was deafened on one side when his fist struck hard on my ear. Mouth cut and blood flowing from my nose, I was reeling about in all directions. All around me there was a roaring sea of faces, yelling at me like demons out of hell.

Someone stuck out a foot and I tripped and fell to my knees. Determined to avoid a kick to the head by the 'Bruiser', I twice struggled quickly to my feet but was knocked down each time by sledgehammer blows to my face. When he beat me down a third time I made my way on my hands and knees towards the crowd of spectators who ringed us, hoping to find some way of getting away from this merciless battering.

Words were spluttering from my mouth; I didn't know if I was begging for mercy, cursing or praying as I was lifted to my feet by some on-looker who had no intention of allowing me to escape between his legs. Through misty eyes I saw the 'Bruiser' with swinging fists rushing towards me once more. Ducking just a split second before those fists could reach my face, I had the satisfaction of seeing the 'Bruiser' unable to pull up in time, go over the top of me and into the crowd. Striking out left and right with his clenched knuckles, he brought yells and cries of anguish from three or four men who fell struggling in a heap. The man who had lifted me to my feet got the worst of it and lay under the other men, knocked out senseless. I took the opportunity to wipe the sweat and blood from my face and retire to the other side of the ring of faces to await the 'Bruiser' while he struggled to his feet.

He had his back to me while he harangued the crowd with abuse and curses. Gathering up what little strength I had left in my limbs, I ran across and struck him in the back of the neck with tremendous force. He fell into the crowd once more. This time a number of them got their boots into him before he could get to his feet and quickly disappeared behind the backs of other men.

There must have been some vicious kicks inflicted on him because he was in obvious pain when he got to his feet, tenderly holding his hands over his ribs in a crouching position. I rushed him once more but he saw me coming and butted his head hard into my stomach knocking all the breath out of me. A strong blow to the side of my head finished me off and I fell painfully onto the ground. He was on me in a trice pinning my arms against the cobble stones as he sat astride me. He started to butt my face with his forehead, but ceased almost immediately when someone pulled his head back by the hair. His bucking up and down like a horse trying to unseat its rider brought forth roars of laughter from the crowd.

I didn't know what was happening but the 'Bruiser' seemed to know what was going on because there was a big grin on his face.

I could see a way out of my predicament as my mind began to clear. The next time he bucked I brought my knees up sharply under him and had squirmed out from underneath him and onto my feet before he realized what was happening. I could now see why the 'Bruiser' was bucking up and down. Dara had come to my rescue by jumping onto him and pulling his hair. Her skirt had ridden up onto her back and, each time the 'Bruiser' bucked, her round pink buttocks rose, bringing into view the dark hairs between the top of her thighs. A girl upended is not showing herself at her best but the view can send men mad with desire.

With her bare haunches getting an airing it was pandemonium as the men scuffled with each other to get a better view. It was a disturbing and enticing sight to many of the men. One of them was slapping her bare rump and another, with raw lust in his eyes, was pulling one of her legs and I had to lean over and punch him in the face before he would release his hold. As soon as he did so, I pulled Dara off her perch and onto her feet. I didn't know what to do next as all round us were men just aching to get their hands on her. It was at that very moment that the 'Bruiser' was rising from the cobble stones that I spied Vladimir forcing his way through the crowd. Thankfully, I pushed Dara into his arms.

Turning quickly I was just in time to take some vicious punches from the 'Bruiser' on my arms. Sparring watchfully, I took him by surprise with two lightning blows on his sore ribs. Eluding a swinging right aimed at my head, I ducked under his arm and ran across to the other side of the ring for a breather. There were yells of derision from the spectators for what they thought was my cowardice. What little strength I had in me was draining from me fast. Fearing those boots kicking me senseless, I was desperate to finish the fight and an idea as to how this might be done came into my head. I was banking on him rushing at me as he had done when he fell into the crowd. Sure enough, he did just what I hoped for; shouting, 'Come out and fight like a man,' and letting out a hoarse deep roar he charged across the ring. I went out to face him with my arms hanging by my sides. Ducking down swiftly I grabbed his ankles and, with my head between his legs, tipped him arse over head. He landed with a sickening thud behind me.

The back of his head must have hit the cobbles for he lay like someone dead. I was whacked out and, as I staggered back and forth with exhaustion, I hardly had the strength to wipe the blood from my face. The blows I received on my ears had deafened me, leaving only a muffled roar in my head. My eyelids were closing into thin slits as the bruises around them swelled. I had reached the limit of my endurance and my knees were buckling under me when hands grabbed me and lifted me shoulder high to carry me like a conquering hero around the yard.

Too tired to raise my chin from my chest, I felt like a cloth doll as I was swung around on the men's shoulders and, when they tired of their rejoicing at the defeat of the 'Bruiser' and brought me down again, I collapsed in a crumpled heap onto the cobble stones. I have no memory of what happened next but it seems that Vladimir, with Dara's help had carried me back to our room and washed and anointed salve to my wounds. Dara coaxed spoonfuls of brandy between my swollen lips. Then Vladimir undressed me and put me to bed. And there I stayed for two days, blind, deaf, aching all over and unwilling to move.

On the third day, after a good night's sleep, the bruises ached less and I was able to see and hear Dara a little as, with big anxious eyes, she clucked over me like a worried hen. She nursed me back to my normal healthy self with tender cuts of meat and thick chicken soup. In less than a week I was on my feet and ready for work again.

On our next visit to 'The Dog's Head' some days later, we learnt that my opponent, like me, had also taken about a week to recover from the fight. It was thought that the 'Bruiser' had cracked his skull when he fell onto the cobbles, for he lay in a coma and no one could get a word out of him for nearly five days. He was a shaken man when he did eventually get out of bed and, within a few days, had left for Philadelphia. No doubt he was too shamed to face the scorn of the men of Chicago. What was more important to me was that my employers gave no sign that they had heard anything about the fight with the 'Bruiser'.

Some weeks later Vladimir introduced us to a Dr Lionel Shepherd. A tall, thin man with light grey hair that hung down to his shoulders like a lion's mane. We were having a drink in 'The Dog's Head' at the time and I gathered from the conversation which followed that the doctor was about to open a health institution on Lakeside nearabouts where Vladimir had his fruit and vegetable stall.

He was an impressive figure, wearing a white shirt with a high-winged collar that rose up from a dark blue cravat and a black tail-coat. His deep rich voice, elegant manners and scholarly appearance commanded respect and attention from all who were in his company.

On learning that I was in the soap business, he asked if he could call on me as he had something of importance to discuss that might prove profitable to both parties.

Eager, curious and excited, Dara and I sat in our room the following evening awaiting the doctor's call. That's the effect he had on most everyone. You couldn't help feeling, in his presence, that every time he was about to speak you would hear something of grave importance.

When he did arrive, he got down to business straight away. He had, he said, a formula for a medication soap that was an excellent remedy for many skin complaints. The ingredients were a mixture of common herbs that could be obtained without any difficulty. Would my employers, James S. Kirk & Company, be prepared to manufacture the soap according to his formula under contract, he asked, and confine the supply of this soap to him alone?

I agreed to put the proposition to my employers and added that, provided the order was large enough, I could see no problems which were likely to arise in the execution of such an order under contract. He thanked me most politely, impressing on me the need for secrecy in this matter, then invited Dara and me to join him in a drink at the tavern.

As I had thought, my employers were only too pleased to enter into a contract to supply the doctor with his medication, the first delivery to commence after a month, by which time the doctor estimated he would be ready to open his health institution. I was not to see the opening of the institution because, a week before it was due to open, I received an urgent message from my mother calling me home as my father was seriously ill. Although I dropped everything that I was busy with at the time and set off immediately, my father was dead before my arrival at the farm.

The shock of my father's death so numbed my brain that it was only during the funeral did I appreciate that his passing was going to completely change my life from then onwards. I would have to take over the farm, finish my work as a salesman for James S. Kirk and, what was more important than anything else, say goodbye forever to Dara. And what's more, do all of these things within a few days as it was impossible for my wife to cope with all the work of the farm.

After informing my employers that I couldn't continue my work as a salesman, not even for another day, I made my way to the rooming house at Lakeside to spend my last night with Dara. I shall never forget the look on her face when I told her what had happened to bring about the utter finality of this last time we could be together.

All the colour went out of her face as she put her hand to her mouth. With wide-open eyes she just stared at me as if she was unable to comprehend what I was saying. I tried to look away but that wide-eyed stare of hers brought my words to a stuttering halt and held me spellbound. She swayed and I brought my arms around her and held her close.

It seemed as if eons of time went by before she pulled away from me saying, 'Well, if this is going to be our last night together, let's make it a happy one—something to remember. We won't talk about you going.'

She came back to me and, putting her arms around my neck, looked up at me. 'Elmer, darling, don't say goodbye in the morning. Get out of bed while I'm still asleep and just go.'

Her mood suddenly changed. 'What would you like to eat? We have got chicken and slices of cooked beef. While I'm preparing the meal, go out and get a bottle of wine.'

After our supper we talked for hours about all sorts of things, never once touching on my departure in the morning. There was no passion or joy in our loving when we got to bed. Most of the night we just clung to each other under the bedclothes as if we were trying to shut out the harsh realities that would come with daylight.

. . . The years go by. The farm prospers. I have adapted myself to a different lifestyle, but there is an empty space in my heart that only Dara could occupy. When I get low and depressed I go to the barn where I have secreted away an unsigned letter I received from Dara shortly after we parted. Reading the letter lifts my spirits and when I put it back in the little tin box I seem to hear her voice coming to me through the mists of time and space, whispering the words that ended her letter: 'Goodbye, my love.'

PART THREE

The Egyptian Princess

I knew from the very moment Elmer opened the door to our room that something dreadful had happened. He just stood there with a worried expression on his face.

Going up to him, I took him by the hand. 'Tell me, Elmer. I'll understand.'

He gazed at me for a little while as if trying to imprint on his memory the features of my face, and then exhaled a long sigh. 'The milk sickness got my father and he died last Friday. I'll have to leave Chicago and take his place on the farm. They are all depending on me.'

Looking down and speaking in a voice so low that I could hardly hear him, he continued, 'I'm only here for the night; tomorrow morning I'll have to go back to the farm.'

There was a long pause. 'For good, you understand, Dara. I've got to go. They are all depending on me to look after them. I've got to go back.'

He looked so upset and worried I wanted to reach out and put my arms around him and comfort him, but I couldn't move. I couldn't grasp the meaning of the words. They were all jumbled up and swimming around in my mind.

When I got the words sorted out and I understood that this was to be our last night together and after that I wouldn't ever see him again, the blood drained from my head until I nearly fainted. His heartbeat was pounding in my ear as he held me close. It was the sound of his heart that brought home to me how Elmer was suffering too. Up till that moment I had only been thinking of myself and the futility of trying to live without him.

Looking up into his face, I smiled. 'Why waste precious hours weeping before we part forever,' I asked brightly. 'We still have some time left for us to be happy together—and to love.'

I busied my mind organizing a meal and asked Elmer to get some wine, saying, 'Let's not think about it. And tomorrow, just go—just go quietly, and please, Elmer darling, please don't say goodbye. Just go quickly.'

After we'd had supper we talked and talked. Mainly about the past; about Vladimir in Russia, about Elmer's fight with the 'Bruiser' and all sorts of things we had experienced together. And all the time we were talking I knew there was a question I wanted to ask him. It bothered me, but I couldn't think what it was. And then it came to me quite suddenly and I interrupted him in midsentence. 'Elmer,' I asked, 'what is the milk sickness? I have never heard of it.'

Elmer looked at me somewhat surprised and smiled. 'No, I don't suppose you have. They don't get it in England, but we get a lot of people around here dying of milk sickness. As far as I know, it doesn't occur anywhere else. It is thought that about one in ten people in the Northern States die of this sickness; sometimes whole families are wiped out. Abraham Lincoln's mother died of it.'

'But what is it, Elmer?' I asked, 'and how do they get it?'

'It comes from cow's milk,' he answered, 'and the cows get it when they graze near woodlands and eat white snakeroot. My mother calls it "the trembles" because that's what you do when the poison gets into your system—you tremble all the time. This is followed by convulsions and a quick death.'

He was overcome for a moment or two, then pulled himself together. 'My father must have drunk the milk of a cow he had bought only three days before his death. When he was thirsty he often helped himself to a mouthful of milk from a cow, especially when he was working in a field some distance from the house. Many times I have seen him crouch down near a cow's udder, pull at one of the tits and squirt the milk into his open mouth.'

I said, 'You don't need to talk about it any more, Elmer, if it upsets you.'

'No, I had best tell you. It is good that I can talk about it. Well, it was easy for me to find the infected cow by chasing it across a field. Sure enough the beast started to tremble after its exertions and the vinegary breath coming from it confirmed my suspicions that this was the cow whose milk had poisoned my father.'

We were late getting to bed, but I found it was impossible to sleep. When Elmer rose shortly before dawn, I made a pretence of being sound asleep. I held my emotions in control until I could no longer hear the sound of his footsteps as he descended the stairs; only then did I give way to the anguish that had tortured me throughout the night.

An agonized, hoarse cry, coming up from the very centre of my being, filled the room and echoed back to me like the sound of an animal in extreme pain. I was alone in the depths of my own hell, writhing on the rack and crying out for help. My distress was such that it affected my breathing and I had to sit up and gasp painfully for air. I tried to get out of bed, but fell back on the pillow exhausted. Feeble sobs shook my shoulders and the tears began to flow as I drifted into, and out of, uneasy slumbers.

Three days elapsed before I struggled out of bed. Three days of alternatively sobbing and mindlessly floating through time. Dizzy and confused, I clung to chairs and table as I searched for I do not know what. In passing, I looked in the mirror. An old hag with a lined, shrunken face gazed back at me from the mirror with pale, dead eyes. I knew not who she was, nor did I care, for nothing stirred in my mind. A loud knock on the door brought me to my senses. Startled, I moved quickly to the door and locked it.

It was Vladimir asking if I was alright. 'I've heard that Elmer has gone back to his farm,' he yelled from the other side of the door. Getting no answer he knocked again and shouted, 'Are you alright, Dara? Let me in.'

I tried to shout back at him, but I couldn't manage it as my throat was dry and sore. When he knocked again I said hoarsely, 'I'm ill. Get me some food and leave it outside the door.'

He must have heard me despite my weak voice for he answered, 'If you are ill you had better let me in.'

Taking the key from the door, I put my lips to the keyhole. 'No. I don't trust you. You are a womanizer. No man but Elmer can come into this room. Go away, I don't want you. I want food.'

Getting back into bed, I lay there listening to him appealing for me to let him in. Sometime later I awoke to more knocking on the door. It was Vladimir again.

'Dara. Can you hear me?' he asked. 'I've brought you meat pies, fruit and ale.'

I got to the door and said, 'Thank you. Now go away. I will be alright if you leave me alone.'

'Are you sure?' he asked doubtfully.

'Yes,' I answered wearily as I leaned against the door.

After I had heard him leave the house I collected the food and drink. Feeling better, having eaten, I washed and brushed my hair and put some warm clothes on, for I was beginning to shiver although I didn't feel cold. I had just put some water on to boil to make some coffee when there was another knock at the door. Tense with pent up emotions, ready to explode at the slightest noise, I shouted hysterically, 'For God's sake, Vladimir, stop pestering me.'

'It is not Vladimir,' a voice answered back. 'This is Dr Shepherd. May I have a word with you? If you don't want me to come in, we can talk through the keyhole.'

The situation had become ridiculous. I started to giggle at the very idea of us having a serious conversation through a keyhole. The giggling got worse and I abandoned myself to great whoops of mirth. Blind with tears, I fell and rolled around the floor helpless with maniacal shrieks of laughter.

The hysterics eventually blew themselves out and I got to my feet amidst frantic knocking on the door. 'Stop that knocking,' I shouted. 'I'll be with you in a minute.' I recovered my composure and drank half a glass of water before approaching the door again.

'Dr Shepherd, have you got Vladimir with you out there?' I asked. 'If you tell a lie I'll never believe another word you say in future.'

There was some whispering going on outside, then, 'Yes, but Vladimir says he will go away if that's what you want.'

I didn't answer. Then the doctor said, 'Vladimir has gone. There is only me here now.'

Unlocking the door, I opened it and said calmly, 'Please come in, Doctor. Would you like some coffee? I'm just about to have some my-self.'

If he was taken aback by the sudden change in my demeanour he didn't show it, apart from giving me a searching look as he walked to the table where he pulled up a stool and sat down. Leaning forward, with his elbows on the table, he said, 'Thank you. Yes, I would very much like to have some coffee.'

When we sat facing each other with our mugs of coffee, he said, in the same quiet voice he had used when he thanked me for the coffee, 'Dara, look at me.' Holding my gaze he continued, 'You are suffering from a great emotional shock, my dear. I sympathize with you for I know how you must be feeling, having lost your lover. If you want to tell me about it I'll listen. Not with my intellect, but with my heart. If you don't want to talk about it then we will speak of other matters.'

'What other matters?' I asked.

'Of your future, my dear young lady. Life goes on, whether you like it or not. You cannot lock yourself in your room and mope for the rest of your life. Time alone can heal a broken heart. During the days, and maybe the months to come, you will need to occupy your mind with some work that will capture your interest and attention.'

'Work? What work is there for me?' I said in despair. 'The only work I have ever done is milk cows and make beds. I cannot see much interest in either of those occupations.'

'Nor can I,' he said with a smile. 'That is not what I had in mind.'

He paused for a moment, giving me a long and steady look. 'Would you be interested in helping me with the health institution that I'm about to open on Lakeside? I need an assistant, someone I can trust.'

I was about to question him about the work at the institution when he raised a hand saying, 'No, don't give me your answer now. Meet me at the institution tomorrow at noon. The men have not finished the building yet, but I can show you much that will, I am sure, be of interest to you and tell you what I have in mind regarding yourself.'

Promptly at noon the next day I stood outside the building that was to become a health institution. Painters, carpenters and plasterers were busy in various parts. Planks of wood, pots of paint and all sorts of building materials were strewn all over the place. I hesitated to enter in case something fell on my head.

A man carrying a small wood plank glanced quizzically as he passed, then retraced his steps.

'Looking for somebody?' he asked.

'Yes, Dr Shepherd.'

'Follow me,' he commanded sharply.

I trailed behind him and the plank as he traced a path through piles of bricks and stacks of wood. When we got to a small, wood hut at the rear of the building he knocked on the door, shouting, 'A visitor for you, Dr Shepherd.' Not waiting for an answer he turned around sharply, just missing my head with the end of his plank, and strode away on some purpose.

It was a small hut and, when I got inside, there was only one place to sit; that was on a narrow bed which occupied the length of one of the walls. Opposite me sat the doctor at his desk which was littered with notes, ledger books, bills, estimates and other paraphernalia.

'Well! What do you think of my health institution?'

'I don't know, I've only seen the outside of the building.'

'Come on!' he said, and ushered me out of the door and into the main building.

'Here,' pointing to a corner at the rear, 'will be my lodging room and office; next to it a consulting room and alongside it another consulting room, for I expect to be very busy. There will be no time for me to wait for patients to undress and dress. My time will be most precious. The patients must be ready and waiting for me.'

Turning, he indicated the wall opposite. 'On this side, in the corner, will be the Mixing Room where the herbs and mixtures and medicines will be stored and blended. Next to it will be the Electropathic Machine —it will be used mainly to cure complaints peculiar to the female. Of course, we will have screens to ensure privacy for the ladies. They will be seen only in the afternoons and then only by appointment. You will be in charge of that department of the business.'

'What will I be doing?' I ventured to ask.

'There will be plenty of time for explanations later. Now come along,' he said as he walked towards the front entrance. When we got to the end he looked around and waved a hand imperiously. 'All this space will be a reception and waiting area and will be the responsibility of my Clerk and Barker.'

I wanted to question him further, but he took me by the arm and escorted me outside to the front of the building.

Waving an arm upwards he exclaimed with a certain amount of pride, 'And up there, extending right across the front, will be a large dashboard emblazoned with *Health Institution* supported in small lettering by the words *Dr Shepherd—Medical Consultant*. And here on the left will be a raised platform upon which you will perform your Egyptian dance.'

'My what!' I exclaimed in astonishment.

'There is no need for concern, my dear. What I am going to ask you to do in helping me with this business is well within your capabilities. Indeed, you will enjoy your work here and find it most interesting.'

When we got back to his office hut I told him to dismiss from his mind any ideas he had about me and an Egyptian dance.

All I got from him was, 'Yes, yes, my dear.'

He rose from his desk and began to search for something inside a large trunk, exclaiming after removing various volumes, 'Ah, here it is, the book of Shakespeare.' Turning the pages rapidly he came to what he was looking for, muttering to himself, 'Romeo and Juliet.'

He brought the open book over to me and pointed to a certain passage saying, 'Read that out loud and speak the lines with feeling.'

While I was looking at the passage, he asked, 'Do you know the love story of Romeo and Juliet?'

I told him I had read the play, but had never seen it in a theatre.

'Very well. Just imagine you are Juliet. A Juliet who has become disillusioned with her nurse and answers her with indignation.'

'Ancient damnation!' I exclaimed dramatically.

'No, no,' he interrupted. 'Say it again and this time with a great deal more exasperation in your voice.'

He was right, of course, and this time I tried to feel as Juliet must have felt on that occasion. My emotions took over and found expression in the words:

> ' *"Ancient damnation! O most wicked fiend!*
> *Is it more sin to wish me thus forsworn,*
> *Or to dispraise my Lord with that same tongue*
> *Which she has praised him with above compare*
> *So many thousand times? Go, counsellor!*
> *Thou and my bosom henceforth shall be twain."* '

When I had finished the reading I looked at him, not knowing what to expect.

He smiled. 'Just what I thought; you have a sense of the dramatic. Unlike me, you are a born performer. Because of shyness, most of us hold back—afraid of making fools of ourselves.'

Taking the book of Shakespeare from me and replacing it in the trunk he commented, 'In early childhood we are all natural performers, accepting the laughter and the amusement we create as appreciation. As we grow older we fear the laughter of those observing our antics. It is sad, but the truth is that we have learned the meaning of ridicule.'

He took hold of my hands and brought me to my feet. 'It is time to eat. We will adjourn to "The Dog's Head" where I will explain how you will work with me to make my health institution a success.'

During our time at the tavern and in the days that followed I got more details of how the health institution was to function and what part I was to play as the doctor's assistant.

With the aid of burnt cork and greasepaint I was to appear on the platform as a dusky maiden, dressed up in garments of many colours. An Egyptian princess, so everyone would be informed, who had brought with her remedies that had been passed down through the centuries from the temple priests of ancient Egypt.

The Barker, whom I was yet to meet, would commence the proceedings by beating loudly on a drum and only cease when he considered that we had a large enough crowd of people assembled to see my dance. The doctor informed me that he was leaving the movement of the dance to my imagination and he would be satisfied with whatever I did, providing it was bewitching and in good taste. There was some talk of providing me with some music to accompany the dance. After my performance the Barker would take over, going into a long discourse about the wondrous cures that Dr Lionel Shepherd had for the many complaints and ills that inflicted mankind. After all that preamble it was hoped that patients would line up outside the doctor's consulting rooms.

Two weeks before the health institution was due to open I made the acquaintance of the doctor's other assistant. Bob Derry, who was to be the Clerk and Barker to our establishment. About the same height as myself, he wore a black-tailed coat with a velvet collar. His cloth boots with shiny leather toes didn't seem to be in keeping with the coat and the glossy, black hair, brushed close to his skull and neatly parted down the middle. A quick-witted, smooth-talking, restless young man, always on the move, darting about here and there. I was attracted by his bright and breezy manner, but resented his easy familiarity on such short acquaintance.

Under Dr Shepherd's supervision we spent the two weeks mixing herbs and bottling medicines. We worked long hours and, although my hands got sore and my arms ached, I had an enthusiasm and interest in all the preparations. Among the many things I learned were that field horsetail can be useful as a treatment for ulcers and skin eruptions; a syrup made from onions cures coughs and colds; balm is good for a poor digestion and aids sleeplessness; and salt and onions pounded together cure chilblains. I was particularly interested in a mixture of camomile, elder and fennel for the complexion. According to the doctor there was a remedy with herb mixtures for almost every ailment known to man. As a diversion from my labours, I trained two snow-white doves to fly to my hands for grains of corn when I cried out 'Oy! Oy! Oy!' This was to be the grand finale to my performance out front.

It was during this period that I renewed my friendship with Vladimir Aksakov. Apologizing for the shabby way I had treated him when I was grieving over Elmer's departure, I nevertheless made it clear to him that any amorous advances would not be welcomed. After a short talk on the subject I think he began to understand that my heart still belonged to Elmer and that the very thought of being bedded by another man made me feel sick. I expressed the hope that we could continue our cordiality as I valued his friendship and concern for my welfare. It was good to be in his company again and, as always, his mountainous laughter blew away any unhappy thoughts. He had an avid interest in what was going on at the health institution and was often there in the evenings, helping out in all sorts of ways with the preparations for opening day. When I expressed doubts about masquerading as a dusky princess, Vladimir backed the doctor's persuasive argument, saying, 'It is a sin against nature to be solitary and idle.'

When a thousand handbills had been distributed throughout the town to announce that an Egyptian princess, with magical ancient cures for all ailments, would open the health institution the following Saturday evening, it was impossible for me to withdraw from my commitment.

We were all on tenterhooks on the day. Bob Derry the Barker, a restless personality at any time, was anxiously checking details to make sure everything was in order for the moment when our first patients would enter the institution. I was constantly running to a mirror to comb my hair and pat it into position. My head was crowned with a thin gilt band of metal from which arose a fleur-de-lis of white feathers held at the front by a large, jewelled clasp that twinkled like a star. I wore a high-necked, white silk gown decorated with two, inch-wide rings of sparkling sequins encircling each of my breasts. The gown was slit at the sides from hem to mid-thigh to allow free movement for the dance. The mixture of burnt cork and greasepaint applied freely to my hands, legs and face made me almost unrecognizable, even to my best friends. The gown was a perfect fit; gazing into the mirror, I really did feel like a princess. The doctor had very firm ideas about the design of the gown and had employed the best seamstress in town to make it.

Bob Derry came up to reassure me that I was a 'most beautiful princess' and a 'credit to all concerned'. But it was only an excuse to fondle my bum as he looked over my shoulder into the mirror.

Pushing him off me, I told him in no uncertain terms to keep his hands to himself. I was shaking with nervous agitation and biting my lower lip anxiously as I waited for the moment when I would have to ascend to the platform outside. Bob chided me on my nervousness, telling me that I had nothing to worry about. In an effort to distract me from my fears, he asked, 'Have you heard this limerick?' and then proceeded to recite for my ears only:

> 'There was a young girl all afire
> Who succumbed to her lover's desire.
> She said, "I know it's a sin
> But now that it's in,
> Could you shove it a few inches higher." '

It broke the tension and I started to giggle and couldn't stop. If that was his intention he certainly succeeded for, when the doors opened a moment later, I flew up the steps to the platform as if I hadn't a care in the world and faced the small group of people assembled at the front of the building. I had expected to be the butt of coarse and salacious comments from some of the men but I found that one look of disgust and disapproval wiped the lechery from their faces.

Bob remained at ground level, beating ferociously on a big drum. The noise was deafening, and certainly brought people from far and wide to swell the small crowd who stood gaping at me in my princess attire. They jostled, pushed and scuffled to get a better view of this dusky maiden from the far away land of Egypt. Bob, now satisfied that the audience for our performance was of the right proportions, ceased beating the drum and took from his pocket a little flute and began to play a lively tune that set my feet a-dancing.

The music of the flute had a compelling rhythm and I had no difficulty in keeping step with it. Swaying my hips seductively caused the men in front of me, with lolling tongues and goggling eyes, to gape avidly each time they caught a glimpse of my legs. It was an alluring dance that at times bordered on the indecent as I languorously flaunted my feminine charms.

I had prepared myself for ribald comments from my audience, but there were none. They were hushed into silence from the moment I began to dance. Among the gawping onlookers were men who worked at Chicago's main industrial plants such as James S. Kirk & Company, the soap manufacturers who supplied the health institution with its own medicinal soap. Also, there were industrial workers from the McCormick Harvesting Machine Company, the Booth Packing Company, which was the largest supplier of cans in the world, and a few doleful drunks from Henry H. Shudelt's distillery. There were seamen from the ships docked nearby and several country men from the backwoods who were in Chicago to sample the delights and attractions of the town.

With a tender smile on my lips I turned and swirled as if in a trance, occasionally glancing invitingly out of the corner of my eyes at some section of the onlookers. My eyes promised heaven knows what so that every man might think that I was dancing for him alone. For the first time in my life I was on show, performing to an appreciative audience and I was enjoying every moment of it. To finish the dance I spun around like a top. I was spinning so madly that my gown swirled out to reveal my legs almost to the fullness of my thighs. Coming to a sudden halt, I sank to the boards only to arise just as quickly to my full height with arms outstretched, shouting, 'Oy! Oy! Oy!' Right on cue, the white doves fluttered through the doorway to alight gracefully on my hands for the grains of corn I held for them. As I stood there with hands holding the doves high above my head, there were loud calls and enthusiastic handclapping for this grand finale to my performance. But I wasted no time in getting down the steps and into the institution for it was Bob's turn now to entertain and cajole the crowd.

The doctor was proud of my performance and told me so as soon as I entered the building. We stood together, hiding behind the door, full of curiosity and eager to see how Bob, in his role as the Barker, would make out in his efforts to turn idle spectators into patients.

I missed the first few words of his speech but caught up with his praises of the doctor. 'We are indeed fortunate that Dr Lionel Shepherd, a physician who is respected and honoured by all the medical profession, should choose to establish his health institution in Chicago when people of quality and wealth in New York, Boston, Washington and many other cities are crying out for the benefits of his great knowledge and wisdom on all medical matters.

'Dr Shepherd has travelled far and wide in his search for remedies for the ailments that plague mankind and has visited many countries to consult with other famous doctors. In Egypt he met Princess Fatima who has just performed before your very eyes one of the sacred temple dances that, until today, had been witnessed only by the priests at their secret religious ceremonies. He persuaded her to accompany him back to America for she holds in her memory efficacious magical cures written on ancient scrolls stored in the temple vaults.

'Dr Shepherd is a graduate of Columbia College where he took the Literate and Scientific Course.'

'Can he cure madness?' a man shouted out loud from the crowd.

'Why? Are you mad, sir?' asked Bob.

'No, but I have a young son of five years who is undoubtedly mad.'

'In what form does he show his madness?' asked Bob who obviously enjoyed swapping badinage and welcomed the interruption as further entertainment for his audience.

In all earnestness the man in the crowd answered, 'He throws stones at neighbours and at poultry. He rides on the backs of hogs and suffers much bodily harm when he falls off.'

'Is that all?' asked Bob.

'No, there is something else. He is forever pissing in the milk pails.'

The crowd roared with laughter. I couldn't help admiring the way our Barker, nothing daunted, recaptured the interest of the people listening to him.

'Sir, you can do no better than bring your son for a free consultation with Dr Shepherd—but don't bring the milk pails. We only drink pure milk in this establishment.'

Then, pitching his voice so that everyone could hear him, 'That is something you will get from no other doctor in Chicago. Free consultations. Everyone is welcome; there is no charge for consultations, only for the remedies.'

Hardly stopping for breath and never at a loss for words, he went on, 'If you are having spasms of the bowel, and who doesn't from time to time, we have an antispasmodic pill made of extract of camomile, yarrow, oil of nutmegs, castor and saffron that will cure you of that painful complaint.'

He paused for a moment. 'There is a gentleman over there taking notes. A lot of good that will do for him, for only Dr Shepherd knows how much of each ingredient is needed to make up the pill. Don't delay —this is the day for your free consultation with the good Dr Shepherd. We have remedies for baldness, gentlemen—by the way, it is gentlemen only this evening. The afternoons are reserved for the ladies who will have the benefit of our wondrous Electropathic Machine. Now line up for our free consultations.'

While the men were lining up he continued, 'Under Dr Shepherd's treatment, thousands have changed from weakly, sickly, suffering creatures to strong, healthy and happy men and women. Our "Princess" soap cures all kinds of sores, cuts, boils, erysipelas, sties, sore lips and many other skin complaints, at a special low price of one dollar until stocks run out. Now, come on, line up for your free, yes free, consultations.'

The doctor was kept busy moving through a connecting door from one consulting room to the other for the next three hours. After he had questioned and examined each patient he would hand them a note on which was written their name, the ailment that the doctor had diagnosed and the remedy recommended. When the patient was dressed he would take this note to Bob Derry who, now in his official role as Clerk and Medical Assistant, stood behind a long table loaded with boxes of pills, tins of salve, powders and bottles of medicine.

To keep the interest of those waiting to be served and the men in line for the consulting rooms, the walls of the institution were covered in colourful pictures depicting in most gruesome details diseases and afflictions that the body was subjected to. The most horrific were the venereal pictures. These were entitled *The Dreadful Retribution of a Social Vice*. Another picture showed a young man with spotted face, hollowed cheeks, eyes red and filled with tears to the point of blindness. The picture was entitled *The Retribution of the Solitary Vice and the Evil Hand*.

While Bob filled with dollars the cloth bag hanging from his waist, and handed out the remedies recommended on the patients' notes, I stood by in my regalia as the Egyptian princess ready to fetch from the mixing room something not already on the table.

I was ready to sink to the floor with weariness as the last patient departed from the building. The doctor stumbled from one of the consulting rooms haggard with exhaustion.

Bob, busy counting the dollars he had extracted from his bag, seemed to be unaffected by the hectic hours we had all been through. Making a notation on a pad of paper, he looked at the doctor then at me. 'I am not the doctor at this establishment,' he announced, 'but may I take the liberty of prescribing a large glass of brandy for each of us?'

Doctor Shepherd took the hint. Walking, with drooping shoulders, to his private office he returned with glasses and a bottle of brandy. As we sat sipping the brandy Bob Derry continued his counting. When he had finished there was a broad smile on his face. 'This should put new life into you,' he announced loudly. 'We've taken one-hundred-and-seventy-three dollars on our first day.'

I don't know if it was the brandy or the taking of one-hundred-and-seventy-three dollars, but there was now a lot more colour in the doctor's face and the haggard look had been replaced by a smiling, cheerful expression. 'The omens are good. It looks as if we are going to be a success,' he said. Taking his handkerchief from his pocket, he wiped the sweat from his brow. 'I say "we" deliberately, because I couldn't have done it without your most valuable assistance.' He stood up and looked at his watch. 'There's still time to celebrate with food and drink at "The Dog's Head". Clean that greasepaint from your face, Dara, and change your dress for something more respectable. And you, Bob, clear away that table while I put the dollars in a safe place.'

During the weeks that followed we fell into an easy routine of work. Whilst the pace was never as hectic as on our opening day, the health institution continued to draw enough patients to make it extremely profitable. Early in our acquaintance the doctor had told me that he had not only sunk every dollar he had into setting up the institution, but had also borrowed heavily to meet the cost of the building. He had risked everything on this venture and was immensely relieved that he would be free of the debt within a few months of opening the health institution.

Only two women turned up for treatment on the first afternoon we opened the institution for the ladies of Chicago. Another distribution of handbills especially printed to catch the attention of the ladies brought many more female patients seeking consultation with the doctor.

The big attraction was the Electropathic Machine. The patients viewed it with awe on first entering the building. Always punctiliously courteous with ladies, the doctor would take them gently by the arm to the machine, explaining that electricity was a vital force that brought energy and life to the body. Taking up a simple ebony rod that he had placed by the machine, he would rub it with his silk handkerchief and demonstrate the magnetic power of electricity by picking up pieces of paper or material on the smooth end of the ebony rod.

The doctor was revered by nearly all his women patients. There was a pleasant, old-fashioned manner and confidence in his speech that won them over as he explained that the magnetic qualities of electricity not only drew out the harmful poisons from the blood, but also invigorated the entire bodily system.

As they gazed up at him with simple trust in their eyes, he would announce in solemn tones, 'We have, with this machine, an important invention that will do much to relieve the miseries that only the female is subjected to. The Electropathic Machine, through these small coppered pads, puts life and force into everything it touches. When the pads are placed on the afflicted parts it instantly brings relief to such complaints as rheumatism, backache, kidney, liver and bladder troubles. The machine will also cure female functional irregularities, hysteria and loss of appetite.'

I never did understand fully how the electropathic treatment worked. According to the doctor, a high electrostatic shock was transmitted from a friction machine, through wire, to the coppered pads placed on the patient's body. After the doctor had located the seat of the trouble, it was my responsibility to take the patient behind a screen where she bared that part of her flesh that would receive the electric shock. When she had laid herself down on the couch I would place the coppered pads on that part of the body that was causing the trouble and the doctor would then cause the machine to transmit the electricity.

The ladies were most impressed, declaring how much better they felt after the electric shocks. I could do no other than believe them as they came back frequently for more of the same treatment. Word soon spread among the womenfolk of the town of how efficacious this magical machine was at curing ailments peculiar to women that soon we were taking as much money in the afternoons as we were with the men in the evenings.

In the mornings the three of us were kept busy mixing herbs and preparing the powders, salves and medicines. When I was alone with Bob Derry he was usually talkative, self-opinionated and bossy. With the doctor he was always very deferential. Any knowledge Bob Derry had about medical matters was shallow and superficial and he knew it. He was a young man anxious to go ahead no matter how, and never missed an opportunity to ingratiate himself with the doctor in the hope of learning more about the health business. I thought that was all there was to it until I observed him skimming a percentage of the takings. With the sales money he was always perfectly accurate and remarkably quick at giving change and, as he twisted and turned, you needed sharp eyes to see how some of the dollars found their way into his own pockets instead of the bag hanging at his waist. Keeping a very careful watch on him, I calculated that he was stealing about twenty dollars a night.

Much to my surprise the doctor just nodded his head and walked away when I told him what I had seen. Following him into the office, I asked, 'Aren't you going to do something about Bob skimming the takings?'

Seated at his desk, he said wearily in a voice so low that I could hardly hear him, 'No, I am not going to do anything about it.'

Seeing the puzzled, anxious look on my face he said by way of an explanation, 'Bob Derry is excellent as a barker and a clerk. I don't think there is anyone around here who could do it better.'

'But he's stealing!' I interjected.

'He thinks he's stealing and you think he is deceiving me. It's not so and I will tell you why. The institution is taking a lot more money than I ever expected it to and that is mainly due to Bob's persuasive talk at the front and the extra sales he makes after the patients leave my consulting rooms. You must admit that is true.'

I nodded my head in agreement.

'If he had been an honest man he would have asked for commission on the sales or for more money, or both, and in view of the undoubted success of the business and my need to retain his services, I would have given him, within reason, whatever he asked for. But he is not an honest man and prefers to steal what I would have given him freely. It has gone too far for me to do anything about it. If I was to accuse him of stealing now I would have no option but to terminate his employment and then try to find someone as equally good as he is as a barker and clerk.'

I had another complaint about Bob Derry but, in view of the doctor's attitude about the stolen money, I decided to remain silent and deal with the matter myself. Bob was the type of man who, whenever he found himself alone with a young woman, couldn't keep his hands to himself. I was never at ease in his company, not knowing from one moment to another when he would attempt to take liberties with me. Impertinent as a monkey and as lecherous as a goat, he constantly took advantage of me, fondling the cheeks of my bottom when my hands were immersed in a bowl of claggy medical mixture. Oh yes, he knew when to make his approach, creeping up on me when I was least expecting him to attack. Twice he got a hand down my blouse and grabbed one of my breasts. It was most painful trying to loosen the grip of his fingers on my tender flesh.

I began to view him with an excess of loathing and, to make matters worse, when I reprimanded him he would just stand looking at me with a sneer on his face. It was as if he was devoid of any feelings of sensitivity and got some sort of perverse pleasure in seeing me in a state of nervous agitation and distress.

One day, exasperated beyond endurance, I screamed, 'For God's sake leave me alone.'

Nothing deterred him. With a lascivious smile on his face he came up to me and began to stroke my back. 'Now, now, Dara, don't take on so, and don't bring God into this. You don't fool me. You and I are two of a kind. Like me, you live under Sod's Law not God's Law.'

I pushed him away and bent down to pick up a mixing bowl on the floor. He was on me in a trice, holding up the back of my skirt he tugged at the hairs around my slot with his fingers. My forbearance snapped. Turning round swiftly, I grabbed him by the ears and, in a boiling rage, pulled him towards me and brought my knee up sharply against the balls between his legs. With an agonized expression he crouched with protective hands covering his privates. I was so angry I kicked his backside so hard that he fell on his face. As he lay on the floor gasping for breath, I bent down and said in a quiet voice, 'You'll get the same again if ever you try to take liberties with me.'

From that day on he remained distant and reserved, but he never gave me any more trouble.

Thinking back over the years to the times of Bob Derry makes me reflect on experiences with other men who also had his attitude to the female sex. Thank goodness all men are not like that. Nevertheless, far too many, with an innate arrogance, think we females exist just for their pleasure. They cannot understand why we don't swoon with submissive desire when they grab at our breasts and roughly finger our private parts. The sight of our soft delicate flesh so often brings to the surface their animal instinct for dominance and cruelty.

My talks with married women have revealed how few of them have been warmed by loving caresses. Night after night they are raped by their husbands. How else can it be described when a man without one word of love roughly pulls up a wife's nightgown and, with grunts and groans, empties his lust into her, only to roll onto his back to snore and snuffle through the rest of the night. This bondaged enslavement to a man is the price women must pay to satisfy their instinctive desire for a home and babies.

Maidens yearn for the day when some man will sweep them off their feet and into a marriage which will be a romantic love story of a kind so different in every way from the lives of the unfortunate drudges who are already married. In their nubile fancies they live only for true love, for to them it is the only reality that gives meaning to life. Every romantic thought that comes into their heads is a silent prayer for love, prepared to sacrifice everything for the one they favour. If only men were less aggressive and domineering and received their wives' gentle affections with tenderness and appreciation, then conjugal bliss would be within the reach of everyone.

With the approach of the fall the daylight hours lessened before the long shadows of night and so it was with the number of patients seeking our services in the evenings. These extra hours of leisure were absorbed by readings from one or other of the many plays written by William Shakespeare.

Luckily there was no falling off in the number of ladies requiring treatment from the Electropathic Machine in the afternoons. Without their money the health institution could not have continued as a viable business. Bob Derry's income from his skimmings must have lessened too. Rather than see him standing bored and idle, the doctor often sent Bob off earlier than usual. I was always delighted to see the front doors locked after Bob's departure for this meant another evening devoted to the works of Shakespeare.

With a warm fire glowing in the office hearth and each of us with a steaming cup of coffee, we would settle down to readings from the lays. The doctor delivered, with magnificent eloquence, the words of the male characters, and I answered for the females. He would stop me occasionally to correct my pronunciation or to suggest that I deliver certain passages with more feeling and therefore give more meaning to the words. I learnt a great deal under his tuition and guidance and there was a marked improvement in my elocution. At his suggestion I committed to memory long passages that I would recite again and again until I was word perfect and able to deliver the lines with dramatic effect.

Shakespeare created some interesting women who had an almost obsessive hold on my imagination. I was particularly intrigued by characters like Juliet, Desdemona, Olivia in *Twelfth Night,* Rosalind and Viola and the two girls, Hermia and Helena, in *A Midsummer Night's Dream* who 'grew together like a double cherry'. My favourite of all these female characters will always be Juliet because she is the very essence of love. A love that burned so fiercely was bound to end in tragedy.

Whilst most of the evenings were spent in this fashion not all of our precious hours together were given over to Shakespeare. Sometimes we whiled away the evenings in desultory conversation. It was on one such evening that I asked him why he had never married.

He remained silent for some minutes and, realizing that my question had uncovered a sore spot in his memories, I was about to change the subject when he raised his bowed head and gave me a searching look. It was as if he was trying to find pity and compassion in my face.

'My dear Dara, I want to answer your question, but I hesitate to do so because you may find the answer distasteful. I hesitate because I don't want to reveal a side to my nature that would diminish the respect and friendship that I believe you have for me.'

I stifled my curiosity about any secrets he had buried in the past to assure him that my loyalty and friendship were not to be doubted and went on to say, 'Whatever troubles you, Doctor, will only bring forth sympathy from me and, I hope, understanding.'

'Your loyalty has never been in doubt, Dara. When alone together like this, please address me as Lionel. Your friendship warrants, at the least, that privilege. As it happens I am not a doctor. Although my father had a medical degree, I have no registrable qualification to claim the title of doctor.'

My astonishment at this confession must have shown itself on my face. 'You may well look surprised, Dara, for, as you know, I am deeply versed in all medical matters. Without going into details, I learnt a great deal from my father and, after his death, I gathered more from other doctors with whom I was privileged to work as an assistant.

'It was always my intention to become a physician by profession and, with that in mind, my father found a place for me at Columbia College where I took the Literate and Scientific Course. Because of my father's death I had to forsake my studies after only one year to return home to provide an income for my mother and me. And this I did by working as an assistant for other doctors in the neighbourhood.

'I was heart-broken when my mother died two years later, for I loved her most dearly. That was when I started my wanderings, setting up a number of establishments similar to this health institution. They never lasted more than a year or two before some member of the medical profession in the locality discovered that I had no qualifications and hounded me out of town.'

He paused for a moment to blow his nose and I used this opportunity to exclaim, 'So all this moving about from one place to another made it impossible for you to take on the responsibilities of marriage.'

'No! No!' he answered impatiently. 'That is not the explanation. I had many opportunities to wed good ladies who made it clear that my advances would be welcomed.'

'I can believe that, Lionel, for you are a handsome man and must have been even more attractive when you were younger. Why didn't you marry any of them?'

'The answer to that will come later,' he said. 'First allow me to tell you about my youth. I felt the first radiant glow of love at sixteen when I became infatuated with the daughter of a farmer who was a new arrival in our neighbourhood. Just to catch a glimpse of her as she walked past our house would transfix me with breathless admiration and yearning. In my eyes she was an angel of purity and beauty that could only be worshipped from afar. I was too shy to approach her to make her acquaintance and I spent many anxious hours at our front window in the hope of seeing her walking into town. She had a springy step that bounced her virginal breasts which quickened my senses and sent the blood rushing to my head.

'I was in desperate straits, unable to concentrate on my studies and off my food. She was constantly in my thoughts throughout the day and tormenting my dreams at night. Writing poems was one way that I could express my feelings for this angelic girl who stirred my imagination to raptures of heavenly love.

'One drowsy, hot summer afternoon I was sitting in woodland seeking inspiration for another poem that would describe the noble qualities of the one I loved when I was disturbed by the sound of someone kicking the fallen leaves that lay under the trees. Peering through the thorn and brushwood that hid me from view, I trembled like an aspen leaf in a gentle breeze, when I saw it was she, the goddess of my dreams. Carrying a towel under her arm, she gave a searching look at her surroundings before she proceeded to undress. She was facing the river and had her back to me as she slowly removed each article of clothing. In the shimmering light of the river and the woodland her pearly pink skin took on a delicate translucent beauty that caught my breath and held me in silent awe. Her form was perfect and without a blemish. Walking warily to the river she brought into view a proud, shapely breast that matched the fleshy symmetry of her buttocks.

'I had to sit back and try to control my senses as she splashed in the water like a wood nymph at play. The next time I looked she was on the river bank drying her shoulders with the towel. Anger and horror gripped my mind as I gazed in disgust at a large triangle of damp, dark matted hair that clung to the apex of her thighs and crawled upwards to her belly like some grotesque crab. It was as if the good God above us, jealous of her perfect beauty, had taken up a handful of foul, slimy, mud and splattered it between her legs. Nauseous vomit began to gather in my throat and mouth and I bent down and hammered the earth with a raging fist. Before very long I was retching in disgust at this vision of black obscenity normally hidden from the eyes of man. It was this vision of the female body that was to lie at the back of my mind like a festering sore for the rest of my life.'

Lionel had lapsed into a gloomy silence and, curious to know more about his boyhood, I urged him to continue.

He sighed as if saddened by the memories of the past. 'Some weeks after this emotional upheaval to my finer susceptibilities, I had to accompany my father when he was called to the bedside of a woman who had been in labour for five days. At the time he had taken to his bed with a feverish head cold. On learning that the strength of the woman in labour was ebbing fast and that her relatives feared she was near to death, he struggled out of bed and nearly fell as he was so unsteady on his feet. My mother protested most fervently that he was in no state of health to travel the four miles to this woman's home. But, on seeing the determination in his face, she gave way on condition that I drove the horse and buggy. Despite the coverings of two or three warm blankets, he shivered and coughed throughout the journey. Helping him as far as the bedroom door, I then retired to the kitchen to partake of a bowl of hot soup.

'Only two or three spoonfuls of soup had passed my lips when my father cried out for my assistance. He was crouched down between the woman's ample thighs, holding on to the wooden forceps that he had inserted into her vagina. "Hold on to the forceps, my boy," he said, "I am just about all in and will have to rest awhile." There were large beads of perspiration dripping from his forehead as he stumbled to the nearest chair. Taking over the responsibility for the forceps I closed my eyes but had to open them again when my father called out in a hoarse voice, "For God's sake keep a firm hold on that baby or it will slip back again." With a firm but gentle grip I pulled on the forceps until the baby's head came into view. "That's better," my father muttered, and then, raising his voice, "Bear down, woman. And, you, Lionel, go on pulling. We're nearly there. Go on, woman, bear down. It won't be long now." As more of the baby's head began to appear the vagina was distended to an extent that, up to that time, I wouldn't have thought possible. Catching a glimpse of a mass of bushy black hairs above the vagina stirred my stomach and filled my head with nausea. The next thing I knew was a sudden movement of the wooden forceps and there lay the baby between its mother's thighs, covered in streaks of blood. Dropping the forceps beside the new born infant, I got outside, rushing through the rooms with my hand over my mouth, to spew the contents of my stomach outside the front door.'

My heart went out to him, but I could think of no words that would express adequately the pity I felt for the young Lionel of those days. To be subjected to what he thought was a desecration of the pure young girl he loved, and then this messy birth, must have been a terrible shock to his fastidious, sensitive nature. Such events in our youth can scar us for life.

It was as if he had read my thoughts for he said haltingly, 'I am not seeking your pity, Dara, but only trying to explain how this emotional disturbance early in life affected my future relations with decent women and forced me into the company of whores.

'Although I was mentally disturbed about certain aspects of women, physically I was in good shape. Indeed, there was a virility in my body so strong that I was often put to shame on awakening in the morning to find the evidence on my nightshirt of the nocturnal emissions that came with my dreams.

'At twenty, a young widow took me to her bed and, although I made repeated attempts to enter her, the sight of the black hairs spread around her private parts wilted my manhood. With scorn her angry words bit deeply into my pride and self esteem. The mystique and allure of the female body, nevertheless, continued to have enormous attraction for me but, try as I might to have union with those ladies that favoured me, it always ended in miserable failure.

'There is a powerful force that drives us men to expel our seed and, because of frustration and the complexity of my disturbed thoughts, I turned to prostitutes to relieve my passions. Their ribald laughter and coarse remarks when I requested nervously only a hand manipulation of my male member made me cringe with shame. Nevertheless, many of these debauched creatures will do almost anything for money and, after seeing the earnest expression of my countenance, would lead me to some dark, fetid alley where, with skilful hands, they would assuage the burning flesh of my loins. I suffer such unspeakable anguish each time I have to resort to whores to relieve my lustful desires and, each time, leave them with a feeling of degradation and loathing for my affliction.'

He sat in brooding melancholy unable to say any more and afraid to look at me for what he might see in the expression on my face. He had no need to worry on that score, for I only felt a great sympathy for him.

There was no resentment in my mind at Lionel's revulsion of certain parts of the female body. I remembered a similar feeling in myself when hair first began to appear above my giny, but it didn't bother me unduly. Stroking the hairs gave me the same pleasant sensation as I got when I ran my hand over the back of a pussy cat. Indeed, when intimately chattering with other girls, they often used the word 'pussy' when referring to their private parts. Many's the time when I couldn't get off to sleep at night I would play with my 'pussy' and get a sensual gratification from a gentle finger caressing between the lips of my giny.

I have a great need to be attached in fond affection to someone and I had become very fond of Lionel during the last few months. Although I didn't fully understand his predicament, I didn't doubt the strength of his desires and the conflicts they created in his mind. Acting on impulse, but with great pity in my heart, I took him by the hand and led him to the small yard at the back of the institution. He followed me like a small boy who was about to be reprimanded for committing some misdemeanour.

Knowing there would be embarrassment for both of us for what I was going to do, I wasted no time in getting my left arm around the back of his waist and undoing the cod buttons of his trousers. It was but a piece of limp flesh when I first got my hand on it. Gentle caresses soon put some life into it and when it got stiff and large I closed my fingers firmly around the hard cock and tugged at it until his seed spurted out. His body slackened and he let out a long sigh of relief. I felt I couldn't leave him there with it hanging out, so I tucked it back into his trousers and buttoned up his cod buttons.

Putting my arms around his neck I gave him three or four kisses on the chin saying between times, 'There, there, Lionel—I want you to be happy —it is but a small service for me to do for you—think nothing of it—and don't ever resort to prostitutes—not while I'm here.' Getting as far as the office door I called back to him, 'And when you get into the light of the office, look me straight in the eye and give me a bright smile—that's all the thanks I want.'

This shared secret intimacy brought us closer together in the weeks that followed. The number of patients, however, continued to fall off as the cold of the winter began to strike more keenly into our bones. Lionel had a worrying cough which got worse when bitterly freezing winds lashed flurries of snow into the institution each time the front door was opened. He had to retire to his bed near Christmas time with a fever and a hacking cough. One morning I found a pail by his bedside with blobs of blood in it. He seemed, to my eyes, to have lost a lot of flesh. The skin of his face was shiny and the cheeks shrunken. Alarmed, I asked him what ailed him.

'It's consumption of the lungs,' he answered in a weak voice. 'It runs in the family. A grandmother and an aunt died of it.'

'Is there a cure?' I asked.

'There is not a lot of hope when you start to cough up blood but the milk from a woman has been known to cure consumption.'

Taken aback by this reply I could only respond with, 'Are you serious, Lionel?'

'Your eyes are sticking out in astonishment, Dara,' he chided. 'Do you think I would speak lightly about a disease that could be the death of me? When you are as sick and weary as I feel this morning you will turn to any means that may bring about a cure. Besides, the "suck a woman" remedy for consumption has been known throughout the medical profession for over a hundred years.'

Pointing to his medical books neatly arranged on a shelf he asked me to look for a book entitled *Primitive Physic or an Easy and Natural Method of Curing most Diseases*. I soon found the book he wanted and brought it to his bed.

'The author of this book,' he said, 'is John Wesley, the founder of Methodism and a man of high intelligence and integrity.' Turning the pages he exclaimed, 'Ah! Here it is; but wait one moment, I see he recommends the application of salt and onions pounded together as a cure for chilblains. Now that is a mixture I have given to many of my patients with excellent results. You can see that John Wesley, apart from being a very religious man, was also very knowledgeable about medical matters.'

'But what does he say about consumption?' I asked anxiously.

'Yes, alright, I am about to tell you. These are his very words: "In the first stages of consumption, suck a healthy woman daily". He then goes on to say that this cured his father.'

'If that's the case, Lionel,' I firmly announced, 'we must get you a wet nurse as soon as we can. Today if possible. But how do we find such a person?'

'Ask Vladimir. He knows nearly all the women around here, and while you're out buy some beef and vegetables. I think a bowl of meat broth would help to build up my strength.'

After buying the beef I made haste to Vladimir's stall and, pushing my way through the women crowding around his stall, sought guidance about finding a wet nurse. He gave me the names of two women and their whereabouts. One of them, a Mrs Ada Bunt, lived nearby but she was out when I called so I left a message that her attendance was required at the health institution. I returned to Lionel's bedside in case he had taken a turn for the worse in my absence.

Ada Bunt arrived at the institution late in the afternoon, smelling strongly of drink. A blunt, blowzy, heavily-built woman with a coarse laugh. I took a dislike to her on first sight but greeted her politely for Lionel's sake. If he was going to be cured by a woman's milk, what did it matter where it came from. She laughed uproariously when I told her that the doctor required her milk.

She remonstrated in a loud voice, 'What! A man at my tits; that's something I hadn't expected. I'm not sure I want that,' she said dubiously, and then a greedy look came into her eyes as she viewed the interior of the institution.

'You will have to pay double. Two dollars a visit and as much milk as he can swallow. What do you say?'

I nodded agreement and took her to the doctor. She didn't reply to Lionel's polite greeting but settled herself down on a chair near his bed, unbuttoned her blouse and exposed two huge breasts, each as big as my head. The nipples were also very large and hung down like two dark brown pox-marked thumbs. She got Lionel into a sitting position with his knees between her fat thighs and then, putting a hand behind his head, pressed his face into one of her breasts. I couldn't tell how Lionel was taking this treatment, but I found the whole business shocking and revolting.

She was obviously enjoying humiliating the doctor and giving him rough treatment. When the time came for him to change over to the

other breast she was deliberately awkward slurping the wet nipple across
his face and then winked at me, assuming I would also share the joke.
That settled it for me. I vowed she wouldn't enter the building again.
Someone would have to be found to supply Lionel with the milk he
needed to cure his consumption.

When he had finished with the other breast I settled him back into his
bed and, escorting the woman to the door, handed her two dollars and
told her that we wouldn't require her services any more. She started to
protest but didn't get very far with that as I pushed her through the door
and locked it.

Shortly after her departure I set out to call on Mrs Minnie Summers,
the other woman that Vladimir had informed me had recently lost her
baby. When I met her, after a number of enquiries as to where she lived,
I made it clear to her, right from the very beginning, that it was a man
with consumption who needed her milk.

She was a young woman of about twenty years with rosy cheeks and a
fresh complexion, completely unprepared and at a loss for words to answer my request for her to wet nurse a grown man.

'I don't know what to say,' she said. 'I'm all confused. You had better
talk to my husband.'

He was at the table finishing his evening meal when I entered. Sitting
down opposite him I immediately launched into an emotional appeal for
his permission to allow his wife to save a good doctor from dying from
consumption. I went on at some length and made such a passionate plea
to their Christian charity that they were both on the point of tears by the
time I had finished talking.

The long and the short of it was that I left them on the understanding
that they would think about it and, if they decided to help the sick doctor, Minnie would be at the health institution the following morning at
nine o'clock. Before I left Minnie at the door I informed her that if she
was willing to help to cure the doctor of his consumption she would be
paid two dollars a visit which would amount to fourteen dollars a week
for her services. An attractive sum of money for people in their circumstances.

On the morrow Minnie knocked on our front door prompt at nine
o'clock. I had arrived early to help Lionel dress and shave. He was looking better but there were pink patches on the cheeks of his face which
gave a false appearance of good health.

Minnie, blushing with confusion, was plainly embarrassed at the prospect of exposing her breasts to Lionel. To save her modesty I draped a
table cloth over her front and tied it at the neck. When she had her
blouse undone I instructed Lionel to tuck his head under the cloth and

take the milk he so desperately needed to make him well again. To begin with he seemed to be having some difficulty in getting the milk to flow and Minnie, with a tender expression on her face, gently placed a hand on the back of his head and squeezed her breast with the other hand. There were no more problems after that and the three of us soon became good friends in the days that followed her first visit.

As far as Lionel's health was concerned, it was never the same two weeks running. There were times when he seemed to be almost his normal self, seemingly in good health and attending to the patients with great care and understanding. And then without any warning there would be a relapse when he was too weak to get out of bed. I was sure the milk he was getting from Minnie was very sustaining and it provided the nourishment he needed but I had serious doubts as to it bringing about a permanent cure of his consumption. Time alone would tell I thought, but feared the worst.

Lionel could be very kind and generous with his services when the mood took him that way. One morning in early February he received an urgent call to attend a man lying on the dockside with a broken leg. I was reluctant to let Lionel go as it was a cold, wet, windy day and he had a persistent cough which usually was the forerunner to a relapse that brought him to his bed. There was no stopping him. Collecting bandages and tinctures I hurried after him as he left the institution in haste.

Some men were assembling a makeshift stretcher when we arrived at the scene of the accident. Lionel made a quick examination and instructed me to cut the cloth of the trouser leg from ankle to knee and then to purchase twenty eggs from a nearby stall. Taking a bottle of whisky from his pocket, he allowed the injured man to drink a generous portion of it before preparing to set the broken bone. After setting the bone, Lionel bandaged the leg with three large strips of linen, coating each strip with the whites of the eggs which he had mixed previously with flour. After a little while the egg-soaked linen became as hard as wood. On learning that the patient had a wife with seven children and that he was as poor as a church mouse, he told the man that there would be no charge for his services. Before the man had time to thank him Lionel was on his way back to the institution. We had walked but a short distance when the heavens opened and a heavy rain storm descended upon us. We were soaked to the skin before we got back to the institution.

Lionel, chilled to the bone and shivering, quickly undressed and got between the bed sheets. I poured out a large glass of brandy and got him to sip it while I prepared some hot soup.

The next day he looked dreadful, as if he was at death's door. From that time on he was very rarely out of bed and coughing up blood almost every day.

One evening early in March he struggled to a sitting position in his bed and said, 'I haven't got long to live, Dara. Will you stay with me until the end?'

'Don't talk like that, Lionel,' I answered. 'Soon we will be getting warmer weather and then you'll feel much better, so let's hear no more talk of death.'

Gazing across, as if he was seeing the very spectre of death awaiting him, he said in a voice little above a whisper, 'Nearly all my life I've been conscious of some dark indefinable menace forever dogging my footsteps, lurking and threatening, awaiting the time to spring upon me. In a way I'm relieved that I now know its name is consumption and my life is drawing to a finish. It is no good you saying otherwise; I know. I'm asking you again. Will you stay with me until the end? I may yet have a few more months to live.'

He turned his face to mine. 'Will you?'

'Yes,' I replied. 'I promise that, come what may, I will remain with you to the very end, but let's not talk about such a doleful subject any more.'

'I'm sorry, Dara, but we have to talk about it. There are some important decisions to be made. When I die I want to be in Newport by the sea with a boyhood friend who married a cousin of mine. If you can get me as far as New York I can be put on a boat which will take me to Newport. Will you do that for me, Dara?'

'Of course I will,' I answered. 'I'll go all the way with you if you want me to.'

He sank down on the pillows and closed his eyes and after a little while, seeing he was asleep, I made my way back to my one room apartment.

The next day he called Bob Derry and me into his office and, without any further ado, began to make preparations for his departure for Newport. Addressing us both, he said, 'I'm leaving Chicago and going to Newport. The building will have to be sold and as I have no strength to attend to this matter myself I want you, Bob, to negotiate that sale on my behalf. Here is a note which states that you are to act as my agent for the sale of the property. Get the best price you can, but make it a quick sale as I want to be on my way as soon as possible.'

At this surprising turn of events, Bob Derry stood there non-plussed.

'On your way, Bob,' snapped Lionel irritably. 'There is no time to waste.'

After Bob had departed, he addressed me. 'Visit all the medical men and pharmacists in town, Dara. Tell them that I'm closing the health institution and selling off all my effects including the Electropathic Machine. I'll leave it to you to get the best price you can.'

During the week that followed we had 'would-be' buyers viewing the property with Bob Derry in tow, and representatives of the medical profession bargaining about prices for the effects. By the end of the week the building was but an empty shell apart from Lionel's bed. I was sitting on the end of the bed discussing with Lionel the details of our journey to New York when a bluff, hearty man in his middle years walked into the institution.

'What are you doing here?' he questioned us in a loud voice. 'This is my property.'

I was pleased to hear that the building had been sold and made known to him who we were and asked him the whereabouts of Bob Derry.

'Mr Derry,' he exclaimed, 'sold me the building two days ago for cash. He would have it no other way. He told me that he was leaving that day for Cincinnati to meet you, Doctor Shepherd, to hand over the money.'

'But Doctor Shepherd is not in Cincinnati,' I protested. 'He is here as you can see for yourself.'

'Whatever arrangement you made with Derry is none of my concern,' he barked. 'I now own this property and here is the bill of sale to prove it.'

I handed on the bill of sale to Lionel for his perusal. After studying it for a moment or two, he got up and, with a look of hopeless resignation, turned saying, 'That crook, Bob Derry, has absconded with the money. There is nothing we can do about it. This gentleman is undoubtedly the new owner of the building.'

When the full effect of what had happened sank in I punched the air and flung myself about shouting, 'I always knew that swine was as crooked as a dog's hind leg but you, Lionel, like a fool, trusted him. God help us; what are we to do now?'

I looked at the new owner of the institution.

'I'm sorry for you folks,' he said, 'but you'll have to leave now. And when I say now, I mean today.'

Taking Lionel by the arm I got him outside then went back to drag out his bed. Stopping a man who was passing I offered him two dollars if he would carry the bed to my room near 'The Dog's Head'. After a little bargaining we settled the arrangement for three dollars.

When I got Lionel installed in my room we considered his finances and found that there was enough money to get him to Newport with a little left over. I was in much about the same position but still had some jewellery to sell if I needed more. Most of my money had gone for rent

and food for Elmer. After Elmer and I had been parted I earned enough
at the health institution to keep myself without dipping into my savings.

Within two days we were on our way to New York. The journey was
tiring and a strain on Lionel. He became steadily worse before we
reached Albany where we rested for a week with Lionel in bed the whole
time we were there.

He was so thin and haggard you could clearly see the shape of his skull
beneath the skin. His graveyard cough shook his weakened frame and
left him breathless and sweating profusely. He was just skin and bones by
the time we got off the boat that had brought us down the Hudson River
to New York. A cab took us to a hotel just off Broadway where I engaged
two rooms as I was unable to get any sleep with Lionel coughing all
night.

After settling him in bed I purchased from nearby shops sufficient
food and drink to keep us going for a few days. When I returned I ran to
his bedside to see how he had fared in my absence. He lay like someone
dead but he was still breathing so I prepared a meal, looking in on him
from time to time to see if he was alright. I was ravenously hungry and
wolfed down my food and then prepared a plate of cooked chicken that
would be ready for Lionel when he should awaken from his sleep.

Going to my bed I lay down for a little rest but sleep must have
overtaken me for it was getting dark when I next opened my eyes. Making my way into Lionel's room I found him sitting up in bed and talking
to someone, but there was no one else in the room. Nodding and smiling
and looking intently first in one direction and then in another, he seemed
to be in conversation with several invisible people standing around his
bed. Bringing a chair alongside his bed I sat down and held his hand
trying to claim his attention.

'Lionel,' I cried, looking around nervously and fearful as he spoke
seemingly to someone behind me. Pulling at his hand I tried once more
to gain his attention. He suddenly exclaimed, 'Mother! How good it is to
see you again.' His voice quivered emotionally in his excitement. The air
in the room seemed to become eerily cold—and frightening. I withdrew
my hand from his and backed towards the door looking fearfully around
the room as Lionel's voice greeted more relatives and friends from the
past.

There was a creepy sensation across my skull as if hundreds of small
spiders were crawling through the roots of my hair. It was as though the
bedroom was filled with phantoms of the dead who had come to welcome
Lionel to their ethereal life. The room was in complete darkness by now
but I could sense the presence of spirits from another world moving
about in animated conversation with Lionel.

Sinking to the floor, I huddled up with my hands about my head. In my childhood when the wind brought pieces of brickwork rattling down the chimney my mother used to utter the words of an old folk prayer to ward off the evil spirits and I found myself begging the intervention of the Deity in the same manner as I shivered in fear. 'From ghoulies and ghosties and long-legged beasties and things that go bump in the night, the Good Lord, deliver us.' The last words of the prayer had just left my lips when something seemed to brush past me. In a choking agony of terror I struggled blindly with the door handle and with blessed relief managed to open it and escape down the stairs into the lamp light of the street.

I didn't know where I was or in which direction I was going. Emotionally stunned and stumbling like someone who has had too much to drink in one of the numerous beer houses on Broadway, I sought only the well-lit areas where there were many people to keep me company. As I walked the streets seeing myself, as you might say, under the all-seeing eye of eternity, I felt desolate and very lonely. In this pitiable condition I could see no future for me in America or for that matter in England.

Pausing for breath before a billboard with the words 'Pfaff's Beer-Cellar' I felt a great desire for a warm, cosy atmosphere and quickly descended the steps to find myself amidst a crowd of people of both sexes, some sitting at tables, others standing talking noisily in groups filling up the space before the bar. There was an under-swell of conversation that confused the ears. Overwrought and ready to tumble to the floor with tiredness, I have only a blurred recollection of pushing past people to an empty chair placed at a small table occupied by a young gentleman. Sitting slumped in the chair, with that awful hopeless exhaustion that comes when you are drained of all emotion, I slowly became aware that the young man sharing the table with me was attempting to claim my attention.

'If you don't mind me saying so, you look like a young lady who is about to swoon. May I suggest a glass of brandy? The recuperative powers of brandy would be just the thing if you are feeling ill.'

His speech had the accent of the well-bred Englishman who had lived at a high social level. As he bent over me with an expression of concern on his face I couldn't help noticing a birthmark on his neck that looked like a spotted red ladybird.

Sipping the brandy, I viewed him with curiosity. Elegantly dressed in a dark blue frock coat, a pleated white shirt topped with a fine white muslin cravat and a pale blue velvet waistcoat, he looked every inch a gentleman of fashion and good taste. Beneath the fair curly hair his sensitive features still showed anxiety for my health.

'Feeling better?' he asked. 'Allow me to introduce myself: James Richard Kennet at your service,' he said with a slight bow.

'Miss Dara Tully,' I replied with a faint smile. 'Like yourself, I am also from England. How do you do?'

PART FOUR

Wedded But Not Bedded

Shortly after my arrival in New York I was sitting in Pfaff's Beer-Cellar pondering idly whether to have another beer or move on to a theatre when a young girl approached my table and flopped into a chair opposite me. She was obviously ill and in a state of extreme distress. Although all types of people frequented Pfaff's, they were mostly representatives of the arts and the theatre. In other words, a motley crew of cultured and well-educated idiots, living under the illusion that they had within them that spark of genius which would make them famous some day.

The girl intrigued me. She was respectably dressed, pretty, obviously without a male escort and afraid. But of what, I asked myself, as she sipped the brandy I had given her. I introduced myself and she in turn informed me that her name was Dara Tully. Although she spoke with a slight American accent, she proclaimed that England was her native land. The brandy loosened her tongue and upon discovering that I was a fellow countryman she unburdened the cause of her distress. Troubled by some experience which had shaken her somewhat, she was almost incoherent on occasions as she gave an account of her journey from Chicago accompanied by a doctor dying from consumption. From what I could gather she had sat in a darkened room listening to this man talking to his dead relatives until something had snapped inside her and she had fled from his bedchamber.

It sounded a very eerie affair to me—not the sort of thing to be inflicted on a delicate, sensitive young lady. I offered to accompany her back to the hotel when she became agitated at the thought that she had deserted this doctor when he most needed her.

When we arrived at the hotel, Dara was very reluctant to enter the building but I insisted on her showing me which room the doctor was occupying. It was in total darkness. Pioneering my way with outstretched hands and following Dara's directions, I managed to locate the gas jet to bring some light to the bedchamber. I must confess it was a bit of a shock for me, seeing the head of the recumbent man slouched down on the pillow, jaws agape, and staring straight at me with unseeing eyes. I am always nervous in the presence of the sick or the dead. Trying to move him onto his back brought forth from him a loud, stinking belch of wind which sent me scuttling back in haste to the door and Dara.

She asked in a hoarse whisper, 'Is he dead?'

'I don't know,' I said doubtfully.

Ashamed of my sudden loss of nerve I straightened my shoulders and walked back to the bed, determined to find out whether the man was dead or alive. The body was still warm but, after putting my hand on his chest and feeling no movement or heartbeat, I decided the good doctor was indeed dead.

I had heard somewhere that in a situation like this one must straighten the limbs while the body is still warm for, once it gets cold, they remain fixed as at the point of death, creating problems for those responsible for getting the corpse into the narrow confines of a coffin. Removing the pillow so that his head was in line with the rest of his body, I then brought his legs together and placed his arms by his sides. Taking the cravat from my neck, I placed its middle under his jaw and closed the gaping mouth by tying the ends at the top of his head. His eyes were still wide open.

I remembered, as a boy, being taken to the home of one of our grooms to pay my respects to his three-month-old daughter who had died the previous day. When the baby had expired they had placed, as was the custom, a penny coin on each of the eyelids but, unfortunately, one of the coins had fallen during the night. The body had got cold and nothing they could do the next morning would close that child's eyelid. It gave me belly wobbles seeing that baby with one eye closed and the other with a fixed stare heavenwards. What made it worse was that I was asked to kiss the little monster on the lips and to say a prayer for its soul.

The picture of that baby's wide-open eye staring eternally upwards remains vivid in my memory to this day and makes me shudder whenever it comes to mind. I, therefore, took care to see that the coins that I placed on the doctor's eyelids were firm and secure. Having performed these necessary tasks for the corpse, I was extremely nervous and trembling when I returned to Dara and desperate for a reviving glass of brandy. We made short time in getting back to Pfaff's where I quickly downed two glasses of the restoring liquor while Dara was still sipping at her first brandy.

A few more drinks brought the colour back into her cheeks and her hazel eyes lit up with interest when I told her of my wish to join a theatrical company that was about to be formed at the National Theatre under the direction of a well-known New York actor-manager, Jonathan Ede. Dara, I discovered, had a warm, expansive sense of humour and was soon giggling as I described the antics of some of the players that I had met on my first interview with Jonathan Ede.

We were both in a merry mood by this time and, to my astonishment, when I informed her that rehearsals had commenced for Shakespeare's

Hamlet, she cried, 'Ah! Ophelia. Do you think as I do that she was "as chaste as ice, as pure as snow", a character of simple unselfish affection, or are you of the opinion that she is not all she seems on the surface, secretly harbouring lewd thoughts and desires behind her madness?'

In truth, I didn't know how to answer the girl and was given no opportunity to do so as she commenced to quote various passages from the play. Although her speech was slurred by the brandy that she had drunk and interrupted occasionally by giggles, I knew she was word perfect as recently my time had been taken up studying the play and learning the lines of the part I hoped would be given to me when next I met Jonathan Ede. As I listened and laughed at her I couldn't help thinking there was a lot more to this girl than what first appeared.

It was midnight when, with arms linked in support of each other for we were not too steady on our feet, we made our way back to her hotel. She balked at the hotel entrance again, refusing to go in, declaring that she would rather walk the streets than sleep next to a room with a corpse in it. My modest two-roomed apartment above a leather shop was but a block further on so without any further discussion I took her along with me. The thought of sleeping on a hard floor while she occupied my bed wasn't a pleasant prospect, but I resigned myself to the inevitable outcome of an evening I was now viewing with mixed feelings.

As it happened the floor was not to be my bed for the night. Dara, on hearing my intentions, would have none of it saying, on seeing the bed, 'Why, it is big enough for three people never mind two,' at the same time looking at me quizzically. Getting no response from me she said, 'I can't let you sleep on the floor. Not after all you have done for me.' Then she got all maudlin, going on and on about how kind I had been to her. Flinging her arms around my neck, she burst into tears and then slumped to the floor saying, 'No, I won't deprive you of your bed, James, I'll sleep out here in the lounge.' Rolling herself into a ball and, with eyes closed, she murmured drowsily, 'Good night, James, and thank you.'

Confused, I asked myself what could one do with such a contradictory girl? With brain somewhat hazed by the brandy fumes, I stumbled around the bedroom, dropping my clothes in a higgledy-piggledy mess all over the floor. Getting into bed, I was about to put out the light when Dara walked into my room stark naked. 'I've changed my mind,' she announced. 'It's cold out there; please let me share your bed.'

She giggled nervously as I stared wide-eyed at her nude body. There was good reason for my gaping at her as this was the first time I had seen the female body completely naked.

Suddenly, going all modest, she bent over and covered her genital

organ with her hands. 'Well?' she questioned impatiently. 'Do I stand
here all night shivering or can I get into your bed?'

Moving over I raised the bed clothes on her side and she slid in beside
me. She patted the pillow two or three times before snuggling down to
sleep with her back to me. It took me sometime to regain my composure
and settle down for the night.

I awoke late in the morning to find Dara languidly resting her head on
her arm, looking at me with a mischievous smile on her lips. 'You are like
a beautiful, innocent cherub when you are asleep, James.'

Her perfectly shaped breasts were but only inches from my face. They
were two pearly globes, tipped by nipples that invited loving kisses.
Reaching out, I hesitantly covered one of the breasts with a hand. It felt
as cool and as smooth as the surface of a piece of alabaster. The firm
nipple tickled my palm as I caressed the proud breast with the tips of my
fingers. Some biblical words from the Song of Songs came to my mind:

> 'Your breasts are as two fawns,
> Twins of a female gazelle,
> That graze among the anemones.'

There was a softness in Dara's eyes and a warm smile around her mouth
as she looked down at my upturned face. She slowly ran her fingers
through my hair as I gently sucked the nipple of her breast. It seemed to
grow and harden in my mouth as I pressed my lips deeper into the soft
flesh and when I withdrew to pay my attentions to the other breast it was
glowing cherry red. After a little while I raised myself to kiss her on the
lips. The warm, moist breath from her mouth was an open invitation to
taste further delights as her tender ruby lips parted to welcome my kiss.
The silky tip of her tongue snaked sensuously into me arousing my
desires with affectionate caresses. Surrendering lips to me, her slender
body gradually followed suit, moulding the feminine curves into an intimate embrace of my flesh to become a perfect union that made us as
one.

I had always thought that a girl's body would never have any appeal to
me but I was now feeling a bliss and a joy that I had never experienced
with a man. There was a warm affection in the yielding breasts and soft
thighs as they pressed against my body and sent the blood rushing
through my veins in a lust of feelings that was new to me.

Dara eased herself from me and, with her lips on mine, brought her
hands to my dicky and smoothed the wrinkles out of it until he proudly
stood up thick and hard. Her fingertips played sweet melodies on his taut
skin until I was ready to cry out in an agony of pleasure.

Sliding under me she brought up her knees and opened her legs wide. Still caressing my stiffened dicky she guided him into her moist vent. Consumed in a fever of passion I thrust him up her as far as he could go. Dara, warm and submitting, clasped me to her uttering little cries as she gasped for breath. Hugging me with her soft, rounded thighs, she wriggled and rubbed hard up against me until her swizzling, rising hips brought forth a delirious sigh of deep satisfaction from her.

To see her overcome by fervent, storming emotions was flattering and gratifying but I had urgent desires of my own that also needed to be satisfied and I set to with a will, humping into the soft feminine flesh beneath me with forceful thrusts. As the tension of my pleasure increased I instinctively held my breath when my passions came to a head and the sap of my loins pulsated through my throbbing dicky into her womb. In excited exultation there came from my lips a sound of triumph, a long drawn out 'Ye-O-O-e'. The exquisite sensation that released me from my passion held me in a trance as I lay heavy on Dara's soft curves.

Within minutes of finishing off a hearty breakfast of bacon and eggs at an eating house opposite my apartment, we were on our way to Pfaff's for I was in a mood to celebrate.

'Be a man, my son,' my father had shouted at me before I left our ancestral home for America and then working himself up into a rage that bordered on a fit of apoplexy, 'and don't come back here until you have proved your manhood, you filthy, bare-arsed, pederast, milk-sop!' The old man could be quite vile when aroused.

On this occasion he had some justification for his choice of words, as the day before he had caught me bare-arsed in the stables with a young lusty groom bending over me.

Well! I had now proved my manhood. For the first time in my life I had been a rampant lover between a beautiful girl's legs and I got the impression from the fond looks Dara was giving me that I had done all that was required of me.

There is a saying: 'Claret for boys, port for men, brandy for heroes'. I felt like a hero and lifted my glass of brandy in Pfaff's to salute Dara, the girl who had opened up a new life for me, something I thought would be impossible in my case—marriage with children. But would she have me? That was the question that bothered me as I plied her with drinks in the hope that I could get her in the right mood to accept a proposal of marriage.

She was excited and happy. The merriment in her eyes sparkled as she looked with great interest at the variety of people thronging into Pfaff's for their first drink of the day. Henry Clapp, journalist, and leader of a group of outrageous bohemian admirers, was there that morning with his actress friend, Ada Clare, who also had her coterie of followers. Dara obviously liked the atmosphere and the buzz of conversation around her, giving the impression that it was something new in her experience.

When I brought up the question of what we were going to do about the doctor's corpse at the hotel she brushed the query aside saying, 'Please, James, don't talk about the dead—not yet. This has been the most wonderful morning I've had for months and months. I feel so alive and happy I don't want anything to spoil it. We will talk about Lionel later. You are right, of course; we will have to do something about it, but not now.'

Intoxicated by her cheerfulness and the brandy I had drunk, the words came out of my mouth before I had time to consider them. 'Dara, I feel that I've known you for years. Will you marry me?'

She looked startled and, with a frown, asked, 'What did you say, James?'

'Will you marry me?' I repeated. 'We have known each other for only a short time, but I've become very fond of you and am convinced beyond any doubt that you are the only one for me.'

She was all eyes as she searched the expression on my face hoping to find the answer there. Leaning forward and holding my hand between hers, she whispered, 'You don't have to marry me just because . . . well! You know . . . what happened this morning.'

'It's not just that,' I replied hotly. 'I need you and want you to share my life and I think we would be very happy together.'

She was still looking at me very doubtfully.

'And I would like to wake up every morning from now on and find you lying beside me.'

Her face took on a very tender expression. 'I would like that, too, James,' she said with a sigh.

'Well then,' I got in quickly before she got doubtful again. 'Say you will marry me and I will be the happiest man in New York. Please.'

'But, James, you don't know anything about me.'

'I know as much as I want to know. Please say yes.'

'I suppose it's time I settled down,' she said pensively. 'Always on the move and often lonely. I would never be lonely if I was with you, would I?'

'No,' I answered softly, quietly happy that her thoughts were going in the right direction.

'It's true I like you, James. Like you a lot and, although I don't love you, I think it's possible I will in time.'

She sat meditating on the problem. I didn't dare speak and breathlessly waited for the outcome of her thoughts. Drawing herself up straight, she gave a long searching look into my eyes, then laughed nervously, 'Alright, James. I will be your wife and hope neither of us will ever regret it.'

I let out a long sigh and just sat looking at her with a fixed grin on my face, like some witless oaf.

'What do we do now?' she asked. 'Make burial arrangements for Lionel or arrange a wedding?'

'Both,' I answered quickly, 'and as soon as possible.'

The clergyman we met at the Grace Church on the corner of Broadway and Eleventh Street soon recovered his composure when I announced we had come to arrange a wedding and a funeral. An appointment for the wedding was made for three days hence and the doctor's burial organized for the day before that.

On emerging from the church, Dara was nearly knocked to the ground by two mangy pigs struggling over some titbit they had pulled out of one of the many piles of garbage that were stacked in the gutters lining the sidewalks. The City Council had no means of collecting the garbage that was thrown out every day and left the job to an incredible number of scavenging pigs that moved freely about the streets. I was hoping to travel downtown in one of the variety of omnibuses which were the pride of the New Yorkers. They carried between twelve and twenty passengers seated facing each other on two parallel benches and were drawn by either two or four horses. Although a half-a-dozen or so passed us in as many minutes, they were all full to capacity and it was impossible to find a footing on any of them.

The noise was deafening as drivers of wagons, heavily loaded with a variety of goods, hurled abuse at the hackney cabs that pressed their way past them. Every type of vehicle was to be seen: Broughams, the speedy Phaetons, the Clarence and the Rockway for large families, and numerous handcarts, all desperate to arrive at their destinations as soon as possible. There was no time to waste for the average New Yorker who was hellbent to go ahead, outsmart everyone else and make a profit on whatever he undertook to do that day.

Passage along the sidewalks was difficult, what with the pigs, men with bulging arm muscles carrying great blocks of ice into shops and bars, and other obstructions; it's a wonder we made any progress whatsoever. To escape for a little while from the bustling activity and noise of the streets, we entered Contoits to partake of one of their delicious ice creams for which they had a reputation second to none. Feeling rested and refreshed we made our way to Tiffany's main shop on Union Square to purchase a ring for our wedding. The large stocks of precious stones and exquisite jewellery held Dara in a trance and I had some trouble getting her to concentrate on a great variety of wedding rings that an assistant had laid out for our selection. Dara said they all looked much about the same to her so I chose a plain gold ring and tucked it safely into one of my pockets for the day when we would be wed.

Dara was alternately fascinated and repelled by the rowdiness and hectic activity of the street traders as we walked towards the Tombs, a prison that the Americans called a House of Correction. Its peculiar Egyptian architecture dominated the Bowery, an area of the city which was almost as dreary as the filthy, wretched district of the Five Points, notorious for its drunkenness, poverty, brutality and vice.

At midday we went to Mill-Colonnes cafe and drank gin slings while we waited for our oysters au gratin. The place was crowded with men in a hassle to waste as little time as possible in the cafe in their anxiety to get back to their business. Busy as bees, they had no time for small courtesies and tackled their food with great gusto. A midday meal to them was just gobble, gulp and go!

Ah! The curse and blessing of memories. I can pick out picture slides of that day in New York with Dara that bring it all back as if it was only yesterday. Some memories that are good, some bad, but all of them exciting and exhilarating like the bustling city itself.

In the afternoon we admired the handsome residences of the rich in Hudson Square which put to shame the rows of indistinguishable and uninspiring brown stone houses of Fifth Avenue where one could see a number of fenced-in yards with a cow at pasture. Most of the streets of the city were bordered either by wooden houses of the cottage-type or by brick or stone houses, three, four or even five storeys high. But it wasn't the architecture of New York that excited my imagination, but the haste and hustle between the buildings and the tremendous energy of people as they set about the business of getting ahead to make a success in some aspect of life.

As we prepared for bed that night I was looking forward to repeating my lusty performance of the morning, but my hopes were dashed to the ground when Dara informed me that, much as she would like to oblige me, it was out of the question as she had started a period of menstruation. The thought of the blood oozing from her vent turned my stomach and I found the prospect of sharing my bed with her extremely distasteful, to say the least, of such a messy business. In my jubilation after penetrating her in the morning I had forgotten about this disability that females suffered monthly. It was one of a number of reasons why intimacy with women had no attraction for me.

Lying on the edge of the bed, making as much distance as possible between Dara and me, I tried unsuccessfully to still my agitation and get to sleep. I have never been one who could drop off into slumberland shortly after getting into bed. Most nights, before sleep can overcome me, an hour or two or more is spent gazing blankly into the darkness, feeling dreadfully lonely, with my mind musing on events of the past or fantasies of the future. If God was to grant me one favour I would ask that every night, on going to bed, blessed sleep should close my eyes as soon as my head touched the pillow.

On this, my second night with Dara by my side, my thoughts went back over the years to my school days at Heaton, a boarding school for the sons of the wealthy and privileged, considered to be the best in England. I arrived at Heaton in my twelfth year weary with grief and saddened beyond measure. My mother whom I revered and adored had died of a painful disease some days previously. A new boy, stuttering with nervous apprehension, is given very rough treatment in his first year at school.

I was miserable and unhappy most of the time. That is, until a sixteen-year-old prefect, Nicholas Dawney, took me under his care and protection. To a boy of my age he had the power and status of a god. A god who could give you six vicious cuts across your bared buttocks with his cane for infringements of the rules of the house, or magnanimously grant you small favours if he was in a good mood. In lower school life, floggings and bullying were accepted by everyone as normal and I went in daily fear of both. Running blindly along a corridor one afternoon, pursued by a group of boys who had been tormenting me, I collided with Nicholas Dawney and knocked him off balance. His fury was frightening to behold. Grabbing me by the ear, he pulled me into his study declaring in a voice icy cold with suppressed anger that he was going to give me six cuts with his cane. Crazed with terror, I fumbled with my buttons when he ordered me to remove my trousers. I turned almost faint and nearly fell on my face as I bent over to expose my bare bum.

'Prepare to take your punishment like a man,' he barked as he raised his cane in readiness for the first cut. I gritted my teeth, hoping I would not cry out in agony when the cane cut into my tender flesh. Nothing happened; the suspense was unbearable and I looked up trembling with abject fear to see Dawney, trouserless, with a lump of butter in his hand, gazing at my buttocks as if transfixed. Pushing the greasy butter into the hole between my cheeks, he fondled the soft flesh of my bum with his other hand.

I had heard vague hints of immoralities going on in the school, but had seen nothing of what the boys might be referring to and, in my innocence, submitted to the butter treatment and the loving caresses only too thankful that my person wasn't being inflicted with the cutting cane.

When he pushed his rod into my bum I gasped and fell to my knees. It wasn't too painful and much more preferable as a punishment than the cane. Getting his fingers around my dicky he jockeyed me with forceful thrusts of his rod. To begin with he rode me at a rather gentle canter, but in a short while the pace increased to a furious gallop that finished with him flopping over me panting for breath.

Being Nicholas Dawney's fag brought about a change in my daily routine. I had to rise at six every morning and, by the light of a tallow candle, prepare him a breakfast consisting of tea or coffee, boiled eggs, buttered toast and grilled chicken, leaving me with little time for my own breakfast of bread and butter. Apart from a small piece of beef or mutton with potatoes at midday, bread and butter for us younger boys was our main source of sustenance. If it had not been for the food parcels sent by my father who had been through the same experience in his youth, I would undoubtedly have starved to death. It was costing my father two-hundred-and-fifty pounds a year in school fees for this deprivation and the privilege of wearing a uniform of a black jacket, waistcoat and a white shirt with a black tie, whilst being bullied by masters and prefects alike.

This miserable existence was only relieved when my fagmaster, Nicholas Dawney, took me on his knee and showered me with loving kisses. He had a predilection for kissing me on the neck near my ladybird birthmark. Sitting on his lap always made him horny and it wasn't long before he was loosening my lower garments to indulge his taste for buggery. I became very fond of Nicholas and in time came to look forward, each day, with joyful anticipation to our sessions of passionate intimacy. Within months I became his adoring slave, living only for his kisses and prepared to do anything to please him.

I cried myself to sleep every night for over a week when he left school to become a freshman at Oxford University. When, in turn, I became an undergraduate at the same university I discovered that he had finished his studies the year previously and had gone on to become a commissioned officer with the Grenadier Guards.

At Oxford I became an enthusiastic member of the University Theatre Club, helping out as a stage hand to begin with and taking small parts in performances staged by the club. Neglecting my studies I became more and more enmeshed in Oxford's theatrical activities and spent a lot of my time at the theatre in London. Obsessed with the stage, I was determined to make the theatre my career. Reading plays and writing reviews of performances I had seen in London occupied my time most evenings. Very little of my work was published but I got an enormous thrill whenever an article of mine appeared in print.

Life went along reasonably smoothly in this fashion until my last year at the university. It was the summer vacation and I was mooching around at home in a very apathetic way when I came across a groom in the stables who had the facial features and build of a Grecian god. Neither of us spoke, but looks sometimes express what volumes of words cannot. I hadn't felt such excitement in my being since last I saw Nicholas Dawney. After Nicholas and I had parted I had kept myself to myself, veering away from close friendship with anyone however tempted I might be to further an acquaintanceship. Trembling before the lust in this young man's eyes, I turned and strode quickly back to the house determined to avoid the vicinity of the stables in the future.

Possibly because of the agitation I felt that day, I brought the discussion at dinner around to my wish for a career in the theatre. It took a great deal of courage to raise this matter because my father considered: 'The theatre is an ancillary to the brothels, and those who tread its boards are on a par with gipsies and fornicating trollops pandering to the worst tastes in society.'

On hearing my theatrical ambitions, his face went purple and swelled with shocked anger. Some food caught in his throat and he coughed and spluttered as he repeatedly smote the table with his clenched fist. Fearing the wrath that was about to fall about my ears I beat a hasty retreat to my bedroom and locked the door.

The next morning I waited until he had left the house before coming down for breakfast. After my meal I strolled outdoors to enjoy the bright sunshine. It was a heavenly morning when nature's creations show themselves in all their glory. There was poetry in the sun's warm rays as I wandered about hither and thither as if in a dream. I swear that I was not conscious of where my steps were leading me until I found myself in the stables alone with the handsome groom.

He held me spellbound with a long steady stare, his eyes never leaving my face. Moving very slowly he came up alongside me; his hands stroked me everywhere as he gently manoeuvred me into one of the stalls. Buttons were undone and, when my trousers slid around my ankles, he pushed me on to a bale of straw and removed his trousers. As he came down on me an almighty roar thundered through my head and I heard the man above me cry out in pain as my father's riding crop whiplashed his rear.

It is too painful to relate the uproar of my father's anger at finding me in such a shameful position with one of his grooms. Suffice to say that I will never be able to erase from my memory the humiliation and mortification I felt pulling up my trousers with my father viewing me with the utmost loathing.

The next morning, after a sleepless night, I stood before my father's desk in the library, dejected and weary, without hope and not caring whether I lived or died. Such was his disgust that he was unable to look at me when speaking.

'You are beyond redemption and have brought shame to a family name that has always been held in high esteem in society,' he said coldly. 'Nevertheless it is my duty, however hopeless the task may be, to do all in my power to make a man of you. I have been living for the time when you would marry and produce an heir to carry on the family name. You are my only child, the last of the line of the Kennets. Much depends on you.'

He raised his voice a little. 'Have you any appreciation of how much I'm depending on you to produce another heir for the Kennets?'

'Yes, Father,' I muttered.

Taking two envelopes from one of the drawers of his desk, he addressed me again. 'Tomorrow you sail from Liverpool for America where a cousin of your mother's farms land near New York. You will reside with him and work on the farm and there you will stay until you have proved your manhood. Get yourself a good wench soon after your arrival and bed down with her. I don't care how many women you have or how many bastards you produce, so long as you keep your proper distance from men.'

He paused to glance briefly at me. 'Do you take my meaning?'

I could only nod, miserable at the prospect of farming in America.

'In this envelope,' he said, handing it to me, 'is a letter for your mother's cousin giving him strict instructions to work you hard from dawn to dusk. The discipline will be good for you and keep you out of mischief. You will have no difficulty finding the farm, the address is on the envelope. And here is the other envelope, addressed to a New York bank, with a bill of credit and instructions to pay you monthly a sum of money that should be more than sufficient for your needs.'

The anger he felt was beginning to show on his face. 'Now get out of this house,' he shouted, 'you filthy, bare-arsed, pederast, milksop. And don't come back until you have proved your manhood!'

Needless to say, I never reported my presence to mother's cousin when I arrived in New York.

It was late in the morning before I awakened, but not too late for my appointment at the National Theatre at midday. Dara had arisen before me and had a cup of tea ready as soon as I opened my eyes. She had already extracted a promise from me that she could accompany me as she was just as keen as I to become a play-actor with some American theatrical company.

Jonathan Ede met us in the foyer and took us through the theatre to the stage. Introducing him to Dara, I haltingly explained her presence by saying, 'A good friend of mine from England whose dearest wish is to appear in an American play.'

Dara had the power to dazzle and stimulate any masculine acquaintance whenever she chose to do so and he visibly began to soften as she set out to charm him. He was of medium build, about forty, with a freckled face and reddish hair, confident and positive in action and speech and mildly bellicose if anyone dared to contradict him. Wearing an alpaca frock coat, silk cravat and a beige waistcoat, he could easily be taken as a man of business rather than as a man of the theatre.

'James,' he said, clapping me on the back. 'You will be pleased to hear that I have decided to find you a place in our company. We need a man with a strong English accent in two of the plays we are performing. I will have copies of the plays for you to read sometime next week.'

I was about to thank him but he turned to Dara. 'Well, young lady, what can you do? James says you are from England yet, if my ears don't deceive me, you sound more American than English.'

Dara smiled as if he had paid her a great compliment. 'I've been over here sometime now. As for what I can do, well, I can recite Shakespeare 'til the cows come home.'

He answered somewhat sharply, 'No doubt, but can you act and can you memorize your lines quickly? If you're going to be a member of my touring company you must be able to learn lines within twenty-four hours, as we will be putting on three or four different plays every week and often at short notice. Do you think you can do that?'

Dara looked doubtful. 'Yes, er, I think so,' she answered hesitantly.

'Do you know Gay's ballad "The Black-Ey'd Susan"?'

'No, but I'm sure I could soon learn the words,' she replied, confident and eager.

'Good! Here's a copy,' he said, handing a hand-written sheet to her. 'I am in need of a meal, but will be back here in less than half an hour. See that you are word perfect when I get back.'

With a gesture of farewell he disappeared through a side door, leaving Dara and me somewhat bewildered as to what to do next.

There was a very determined look on Dara's face as she made for a seat in the auditorium and began to read the sheet Jonathan Ede had given her. She looked up for a moment. 'Go away, James. I'll need to concentrate if I'm to learn these words in time for his return to the theatre.'

Jonathan was back in about twenty minutes and strode straight on to the stage. 'Come up here,' he shouted to Dara, 'and leave that copy of "The Black-Ey'd Susan" on the seat down there.'

When Dara joined him, he stood her in the centre of the stage and came down the steps to seat himself beside me.

'Alright, off you go, young lady. And speak up so they can hear you at the back of the theatre.'

Dara gave a little nervous cough, announced the title of the ballad and commenced the first stanza:

> 'All in the Downs the fleet was moor'd,
> The streamers waving in the wind.
> When black-ey'd Susan came aboard.
> Oh! Where shall I my true love find?
> Tell me, ye jovial sailors, tell me true,
> Does my sweet William sail among your crew?'

Jonathan stood up and shouted, 'Very good so far, but raise your voice a little; I'm sure they wouldn't be able to hear you in the back rows.'

> 'William, who high upon the yard,
> Rock'd with the billows to and fro;
> Soon as her well-known voice he heard,
> He sigh'd and cast his eyes below.
> The cord slides swiftly through his glowing hands,
> And quick as lightning on the deck he stands.'

Jonathan Ede was leaning forward eagerly to listen intently with admiration on his face. Here, I thought, was a girl whose intelligence and fine judgement told her when to pause for dramatic effect and when to raise the emotions by pitching her voice higher. Her delivery and sense of pathos matched her beauty so stunningly that even an old cynic like Jonathan was visibly impressed.

> 'The boatswain gave the dreadful word,
> The sails their swelling bosom spread,
> No longer must she stay on board;
> They kiss'd; she sigh'd; he hung his head;
> Her less'ning boat, unwilling rows to land;
> Adieu! she cries, and wav'd her lily hand.'

Carried away by her emotions, there were tears welling up in Dara's eyes as Jonathan stood up and shouted, 'You're hired.' Making his way towards the door, he said, 'See you both Thursday week, here, at midday,' and then waved his goodbye.

Doctor Shepherd's burial took place the next day. What few possessions he had—gold watch, ring and clothing—had all been sold. The amount we got from these personal effects and the money I found in one of his jacket pockets was just enough to pay for the coffin, funeral expenses and a small headstone for his grave. It was a simple inscription engraved on the headstone as Dara knew so little about his family connections. The words on the stone, *Dr Lionel Shepherd, died 2 April 1860. RIP.*, occupied my attention as the men lowered the coffin into the grave.

A blazing hot sun shining in a wide blue sky on this cemetery near Brooklyn had no effect on Dara's grief and sadness. I think right up to the moment that the grave diggers started shovelling earth onto the coffin to fill in the grave, Dara had held back from facing the realization of the doctor's death. There was something final about the soil covering the coffin that released the tears which began to stream down her face. Peerless Green Cemetery had leafy avenues of trees and green paths, but the warm sunshine and beautiful surroundings couldn't penetrate her grief. Racked with deep shuddering sobs, she clung to me as I led her away from the grave to a seat overlooking the bay to give her time to regain her composure.

Away from the cemetery, we were able to board a passing omnibus so crowded that it was standing room only. It swayed so violently that, although we were hanging on to anything we could clutch with our hands, there was a danger of being flung into the street as the vehicle lurched around bends. The driver, whipping up the horses to increase the speed as we rounded the bends, made matters worse and, when we reached our destination at Mill-Colonnes cafe, I alighted like a drunk who had lost the use of his legs.

After the quiet atmosphere of Peerless Green Cemetery, the noise in the street was deafening. What with the seething traffic, newspaper vendors and street traders vying in shouting each other down, the cafe was, in comparison, a place of peace and calm. The midday rush hadn't commenced and, as we practically had the place to ourselves, we were able to eat and talk in a leisurely fashion. Dara was still in a sombre mood so I suggested a quiet afternoon at the apartment and then, to cheer her up, a trip to a burlesque show in the evening.

Niblo's Theatre where *The Black Crook* had been on for years, was almost full but I managed to obtain two seats near the stage. The front of the stage was lined with chamber vases, in the vernacular of the hoi-polloi, better known as 'piss pots'. Each of these was a base for a beautiful display of flowers. Clipper built girls, wearing barely enough to be decent, performed something that was a crude mixture of ballet and burlesque. The tantalizing glimpses of tits and bums did nothing for me but it got a rousing response from most of the audience. A disappointing evening for me and I think it did little to raise Dara's spirits.

The wedding, like the doctor's burial, was a quiet affair. Some cleaners and two or three ladies decorating the church with displays of flowers were the only people in attendance. Dara, wearing a modest white frock with a simple design of embroidered pink roses on the bodice, created a good impression with the ladies witnessing the ceremony. Her pale, beautiful face framed by the rich chestnut hair bore a subdued expression as we stood, side by side, listening to the Reverend Holloway solemnizing the marriage vows. When she raised her head up for the customary kiss from the bridegroom I considered myself indeed fortunate and a lucky dog to have captured such a pretty young girl for a bride.

In the evening, to celebrate our wedding, we had a dinner of Virginia ham, devilled turkey legs and creamed chicken hash, followed by endless heaps of waffles served with silver jugs full of hot maple syrup and side dishes of strawberry shortcake. After dinner we went on to a ball at the Park Theatre where we danced quadrilles and waltzes until nearly midnight, arriving back at my apartment pleasantly tired and ready for bed.

On Saturday afternoon we visited the harbour, walking along South Street looking with interest at dozens of ships moored there. Their towering masts and rigging rose majestically from the decks whilst their great bowsprits loomed threateningly over our heads. It was not a particularly salubrious neighbourhood, with its tenement workshops occupied by pinched-up women with shrunken cheeks and heavily bearded Jews sewing dresses or mending shoes. Life for some immigrants wasn't all it should be. On our way back we enjoyed the colourful Italian life of Mulberry Street with its variety of street stalls.

I pointed out to Dara some places of interest and remarked that there was some justification for New Yorkers constantly repeating what a great city it was to live in.

'Although not as big as London, I imagine,' Dara replied.

'True,' I answered, 'but did you know that it's really a royal city?'

'Royal?' queried Dara. 'How do you make that out?'

'Simple,' I said. 'It is named after the Duke of York who later became James II, the last of the Stuart kings. If one can believe all that is written about him in the history books, he was a most unpleasant personage. Like many other kings before him he was an insatiable lecher exercising his royal prerogative to bed any of the ladies-in-waiting at court who took his fancy. When his wife died he sought details of all the unmarried royal ladies that might be available to him and chose a fourteen-year-old, Mary Beatrice, an Italian princess who was about to become a nun.'

'Did she want to marry him?' Dara asked me.

'Certainly not. She had no say in the matter. Princesses marry the man their parents choose for them. She burst into tears on hearing of the proposal and begged her parents to allow her to become a nun as she abhorred the thought of marriage. The Princess of Modena was still weeping and protesting a week later when she was dragged from the convent and carried off to England.'

'How awful,' Dara exclaimed. 'Poor girl. How she must have suffered, journeying all that way to a man she had never seen. How old was he?'

'He was forty, old enough to be her father. He was so eager to get his hands on her that he got his feet wet on Dover Sands when he ran into the sea to meet her. Within an hour of landing she was brought before a bishop and married to the King who, with a lascivious smile on his lips, wasted no time in getting his innocent bride into the royal bedchamber.'

Dara had obviously given some thought to my account of the Princess of Modena's marriage to James II for, when we were getting into bed that night, she said, 'That fourteen-year-old princess. Was it all true—just as you said?'

'Every word,' I said sharply. 'Have no doubts about it. I spent most of my time at Oxford reading history and became most interested in the lives of the Stuart kings.'

'But it is so different from these days,' she protested. 'Our royal family are so respectable. There is never a word of scandal about them.'

'Oh, yes; very moral and upright. But did you know that Queen Victoria's father, the Duke of Kent, lived on this side of the Atlantic for many years? He had a house near Halifax Harbour in Nova Scotia where he kept a mistress, a Madame de St Laurent, who bore him five illegitimate children. On receiving a royal command he reluctantly returned to England to marry a German princess who bore him only one child before he died. That child is now Queen Victoria.

'Mind you,' I added as an afterthought, 'I have nothing but admiration for our Queen. I'm sure that if her husband, Albert, were to start behaving like James II he would get the royal boot right up his backside.'

Dara, looking at me with her hand to her mouth, began to giggle. The giggling gave way to peals of laughter as she rolled around the bed. She laughed so much that she had to get out of bed to squat on the china vase. I understood her need as I get the same trouble with my bladder when I shake with laughter.

* * *

Getting into bed, she sidled up close, gave me a kiss and murmured in my ear, 'You can love me if you want to. My period is over.'

The truth of the matter was that, although I had been looking forward to getting between Dara's legs, now that the moment had presented itself a dark cloud of doubt passed over my mind. I was far from confident that I could repeat the success of the coupling we had had before we were wed. It had been like a dream on that occasion, when one mindlessly drifts along in a gentle breeze of warm affection.

In an effort to recapture that feeling again I kissed her warmly on the lips and felt the tip of her tongue caress mine. Putting my arms around her, I drew her slender warm body close to me and felt the soft curves pressing into my flesh. It was a tender, loving embrace but there was no lust in my loins and no desire to thrust my flesh into hers.

Pulling away from me, she threw the bedclothes back and kneeling between my legs teased my dicky with playful fingers until he began to swell a little. I felt him throb and harden as she gently caressed with the tips of her fingers.

Abandoning my stiffened dicky, she lay back and looked at me expectantly with an inviting smile on her lips. Getting between her legs I had the feeling of being trapped in a pouch of clinging, suffocating, feminine flesh and drew back. My limbs lost their strength and my dicky became a floppy, useless piece of meat. Sitting back on my heels, feeling dejected and confused, I bit into my lower lip until it bled, like someone whose guilty secret had been exposed.

Dara sat up, full of tenderness and concern. Seeing the feeble thing that hung between my legs, she delicately caressed it with soft fingers. But it was all to no avail; it remained puny and weak, so she tugged at it and then rolled it between her hands.

Seeing that nothing she could do would alter the situation, she put her arms around my neck, kissed me and said, 'Never mind, darling. You have probably overtired yourself today with all that walking.'

She put her arms around me for heart's comfort, like a mother trying to reassure a frightened child. 'Don't let it bother you, James. Everything will be alright after you have had a good night's sleep.'

But to me, in a pit of abject despondency, the future looked bleak and sterile.

My futile attempts at sexual intercourse in the morning were but a repeat performance of the night before. Dara, cheerful and patient, tried to arouse my passions with loving kisses and clasping embraces. It was tantalizing but I couldn't rise to the occasion.

During the weeks that followed we endeavoured often to achieve the conjugal intimacy that is one of the blessings of married life. It always ended in embarrassed frustration with Dara worried and perplexed because I was a miserable failure as a husband.

There came a night when Dara, who had been a sympathetic angel of patience throughout my impotence, threw herself back and cried in a low, dispirited voice, 'If a woman can't be a woman to her husband, what can she be?'

We had little to do until Thursday when we were to meet with Jonathan Ede again. This idleness didn't suit me and I became listless and prone to frivolous disputes with Dara over matters of no importance. Her forbearance and concern for my temper only made me more irritable.

After what seemed an age of waiting, Thursday morning came at last and my spirits lifted when we set off in good humour for the National Theatre. We got a hearty and cordial welcome from Jonathan and the other members of the company assembled on the stage.

With a smile ever ready and genuine, Dara introduced us to everyone with a warm handshake and a 'Pleased to meet you. My name is Dara Kennet and this is my husband, James.' Her ingenuous, vibrant femininity brought forth some warm appreciative glances from the male members of the company.

Their good humour soon put us at our ease and, after some jesting and banter, we fell into their way of addressing each other in exaggerated tones of affection with words like darling, ducky and angel. This lively theatrical life was just what I needed.

Under Jonathan's supervision, we began our first rehearsal of a comedy entitled *Raising the Wind,* reading our parts from copies of a script that had been hastily prepared for us. As none of us knew the stage directions we stumbled about, constantly getting in each other's way. To the amusement of everyone, the play rapidly became a comedy of errors. Our laughter quickly subsided when Jonathan sternly brought us to order and, in a fit of impatience, sent us home with strict instructions to learn our lines and be word perfect by the morning of the next day.

I made my debut as a professional play-actor at the National in the first week of May, playing the part of a typical English gentleman. Everything had been put together only hours before our first performance. As an impudent miss, Dara's costume was an extravaganza of mixed colours in the worst possible taste. Her dress was a fly-a-way, starched-out Balzorina gown of bright ultramarine, picked out with a multitude of various coloured flowers and a blond lace cap with cherry-coloured rosettes and red ribbon streamers a yard long flying out from it in all directions. In a play which did little to amuse the audience, her costume certainly got a laugh each time she made an appearance on the stage.

The comic scenes were not funny, raising only occasionally a polite chuckle rather than a good hearty laugh. It was sentimental slush that aroused no genuine sentiment and would have been booed off the stage before the second act if it had been performed in London. The drama critic of the rowdy 'New York Herald' gave it the hammering it justly deserved. Nevertheless it laboured on for two whole weeks at the National before we set off on a tour that would take us to most of the towns in the Eastern States during the next three months.

The tour brought home to me the amazing size of America. What emphasized the dramatic scale of this extraordinary country was the view from the windows of the train as it speedily carried us along the railroads. I became very conscious of a wide open sky and the awesome, endless space spreading across the grassy plains from one horizon to another. The white-painted clapboarding of the houses, stores and taverns of the small towns we passed through was a refreshing change after the dull brown architecture of New York.

I was highly delighted with the generous hospitality and warm appreciation for our performances in Pennsylvania and Ohio during the first few weeks of the tour. On our way to Boston we stopped off at New York for a day to pick up more costumes for the players. I took the opportunity to call at the Chemical Bank on Broadway to collect the monthly allotment that Father was sending me. Funds now replenished, Dara and I had a sumptuous meal before rejoining our friends for the tour of the states north of New York.

We were in Baltimore by the middle of July where we put on three different plays in as many nights at Ford's Theatre: *The Fool's Revenge, Masks and Faces,* and, on the third night, Mrs Stowe's *Uncle Tom's Cabin.* Our audience were easily pleased. All they wanted was a play that entertained them with simple emotions, had plenty of pathos and was easily understood. They were most impressed when Little Eva ascended to heaven before their very eyes during our final performance. From there we moved on to another Ford's Theatre in Washington, D.C.

Some five years later I was to read in an English newspaper the shocking news that President Lincoln had been fatally shot in this theatre while watching a performance.

Throughout our tour Dara had tackled every part that was given her with enthusiastic exuberance and was often hugged and praised by Jonathan Ede for her performance and stage craft. I wish it were possible for me to say the same about myself. According to Jonathan, I had no insight into the characters assigned to me and seemed incapable of expressing deep emotion. He made it plain that, in his opinion, I would never make a name in the theatre as I wasn't cut out to be an actor.

I had great respect for his judgement and sagacity. In my heart of hearts I knew he was right although my intellect at the time wouldn't accept the truth of his words. His lack of faith in my acting ability gave me no encouragement to continue my pursuit of a career in the theatre and I was relieved when we arrived back in New York at the end of the tour and could part company with him.

There was a further shock coming to me when I visited the Chemical Bank to collect my money. The clerk handed over a letter addressed to me saying, 'Your allotment has been cancelled. There will be no money for you to collect in the future.' The letter was from my father, unsigned and consisting of only two sentences: *Have just learnt from your mother's cousin that you have deceived me. You are a degenerate, good-for-nothing knave and I have no desire to see your face again.*

We decided to stay on in New York in the hope that some work with another theatrical touring company would come our way. I still had the money we had received from Jonathan Ede and a little left over from my last monthly allotment. Avoiding luxury spending, we could, with care, finance our day-to-day expenses for at least six weeks. Working in theatricals is a precarious living at any time especially in the late summer period, and towards the end of September saw us still without work with only ten dollars in the domestic kitty. Dara sold a diamond-encrusted brooch which bought us more time.

In these impoverished circumstances, it became imperative that we gave some thought for the future. I felt sure that my father, despite his disappointment in me, wouldn't let me starve, but that would mean returning to London. He was my only hope as there was no one in New York I could turn to for help at this juncture in my life. After some discussion we decided to renew our efforts to get work and, if this failed, to book our passage across the Atlantic. I think both of us knew that we were only postponing, for a little while, the day when we would have to leave America.

Within two weeks our minds were made up. With no prospect of any theatrical engagements and funds getting low, we had no option but to book our passage to Liverpool as soon as possible. The whole of New York was seething with excitement at that time in anticipation of the forthcoming visit of the Prince of Wales who had been touring Canada and the United States during the summer months.

Dara and I were part of the huge crowd waiting at Emigrants' Wharf when Edward, the Prince of Wales, landed to be received by Mr Fernando Wood, the Mayor of New York. Under the command of General

Sandford, over six-thousand soldiers were lined up in his Highness's honour. He was rather like his mother, the Queen, in looks with his fresh, fair complexion and light brown hair. As he passed near us he gave Dara a wide bright smile when she screamed at the top of her voice, 'God save the Prince of Wales.'

We embarked on the thirteenth of October for our voyage to Liverpool. Just before we boarded the vessel, Dara had bought a copy of the 'New York Tribune' and entertained me reading the newspaper's account of a ball at the Academy of Music held in honour of the Prince. Although the Academy on East Fourteenth Street had been built to hold no more than three thousand people, five thousand turned up for the great ball. The Prince arrived at ten o'clock and, before the dancing had begun, a large part of the floor collapsed and everyone, including the Prince, had to stand around waiting for two hours while a small army of carpenters repaired the floor. In the hectic activity of effecting the repairs, a carpenter was nailed in underneath the floorboards, with the result that there was further delay before the dancing could begin while the frightened man was released.

The voyage was boring and tedious as it was raining most days. We were confined to our cabin for five days in mid-Atlantic while the ship strove to make headway against storming gale force winds that brought the rain down in torrents. The dreadful weather caused wearisome delay and twenty-five days passed before we came into Liverpool harbour. The next day we boarded a train for London and arrived just before dusk at St Pancras station, where we took a cab to 'The Eight Bells' hotel near Covent Garden. It was a modest hotel where I had previously lodged for the night during my forays to London theatres from Oxford and I knew its charges would be reasonable. We had just about enough money to pay for a week's board, but I had high hopes of solving our financial problems by writing theatrical reviews for some of the London magazines.

None of my reviews were published but in the course of trying to get my work accepted I became acquainted with John Sweetapple, a successful theatrical critic who had ambitions to be an actor manager. He had written a number of plays, all of which had been turned down by a number of theatre managers. Nothing daunted by the rebuffs, Sweetapple was scheming to raise money to produce his own plays. I learnt a great deal from him. We became good friends and his cheer and good humour sustained me through a difficult period. Dara and I spent several evenings at his lodgings listening to his grandiose plans to become an actor manager who would one day astound London with his genius and originality. John Sweetapple did eventually realize his dreams, but not during the short time that I knew him.

After three weeks with no income I was in such desperate financial straits I began to sell off my personal articles and continued to do so until there was nothing left but the clothes I stood up in. 'The Eight Bells' were now pressing me for money. The day when they threatened me with confinement in the debtors' prison and I was literally down to my last penny, I plucked up my courage and decided to beard the lion in his den. My father always resided at his town house in St. James's Street during the winter months.

Our butler at Astrel House was somewhat taken aback on seeing me. From his demeanour I judged that he knew something about the reception I was likely to get from Father. Embarrassed, he ushered me into the library, saying, 'I'll enquire if Lord Pulrose is at home.'

Half an hour passed before my father made an appearance. He stumped his way past me looking like thunder and sat himself down at the reading desk eyeing me nastily for a while. It was cursed unpleasant and my nervous tension brought on a persistent dry cough.

Shuffling my feet and coughing, I was getting into a proper tizzy when he suddenly shouted, 'Well? What the devil brings you here, you degenerate pup?'

My eyes were beseeching him to forgive and let bygones be bygones but all I could get out in a hoarse whisper was, 'Forgive me, Father—I'm deuced sorry for what I've done.'

'Why? Have you given up your disgusting desires and become a man? Eh?'

'Yes, Father. When I was in America I slept with an actress nearly every night.'

He looked at me in astonishment for a moment with an expression of disbelief showing plainly on his face. 'Did I hear you right? Is that the truth?'

I was about to reply but he raised his hand saying, 'No, don't answer. I can't abide a liar.'

He bowed his head for a moment muttering, 'If only I could be sure. If only I could believe you. Damme! I dearly want you to be a true son to me. To get married and give me grandchildren. You do see it my way, don't you, my boy?'

I could only nod my head in agreement. My pederasty of the past weighed heavily on me and I was ready to agree to almost anything he said.

'Suppose I get you a commission in my old regiment, the Grenadier Guards. Two years' service in the army would do you the world of good and make a real man of you, y'know.'

As he said Grenadier Guards it suddenly came to me like a flash out of the blue—Nicholas Dawney of my schooldays had become a Grenadier. My heart turned over at the thought of being once again with the one person in this world that I loved more than any other.

'Father,' I said like a dutiful son, 'I've been a fool in the past but from now on I will follow your guidance and do whatever you think is for the best. Now, if you will give me some money, I would like to look up some old friends of my days at Oxford.'

Immediately I said 'old friends' he looked at me suspiciously. 'No, you don't get round me like that. You will be confined to the house until I take you to Aldershot to take up your commission in the army. I'm not having you getting up to any mischief in London with your debauched friends of the past. You won't be here for more than two or three days. The Commanding Officer of the Grenadier Guards is an old friend. He will be only too pleased to welcome a son of mine into his regiment. Be patient, we will soon have you settled and safe from temptation.'

Although I was desperately anxious to get back to Dara and settle my account at the hotel, I was between the devil and the deep blue sea. If the old boy learnt that I had married someone of humble origin, an actress at that, and I had been married for over six months without making her pregnant, there would be the very devil to pay, and I would be kicked out into the street without a penny to my name. On the other hand, I had to devise some way of reassuring Dara that I would be keeping in touch with her and would be sending some money within the next two or three days.

Life can be sheer hell sometimes. The old man never left my side all day and when I went to bed he locked my bedroom door from the outside. I was virtually a prisoner in my own home. By the following evening I could stand the worry about Dara no longer and told my father I owed 'The Eight Bells' hotel for three weeks' board and lodging and it was urgent that I get to Covent Garden and settle the account.

'Put your mind at ease, James,' he said, 'I'll attend to your little problem,' and left the room before I could think of another excuse for getting out of the house. He was back within a few minutes to tell me he had sent a footman to pay my hotel account.

The footman returned in a little over half an hour to hand the money back to my father. 'What's all this?' my father asked, looking at the bag of sovereigns. 'Didn't I tell you to pay my son's account at "The Eight Bells"?'

'There was nothing to pay,' he answered. 'A young woman had already settled what was owing this afternoon, just before she left the hotel.'

'Gad! What young woman?' my father asked, turning to me for an answer.

I was just as surprised as he was and at a loss for words. The footman was smiling at me and, because I was playing for time and confused, I grinned nervously back at him.

My father gave me a quizzical glance and then, with a big smile on his face, thumped the desk top with his fist. 'You young scoundrel. Why didn't you tell me you had been staying at the hotel with a woman? By jove, you have become a proper ladies' man. You've got the taste for it, what!'

He stood up guffawing coarsely and slapped me heartily on the back. 'You young rascal,' he said, excited and full of good humour. 'Upon my soul I didn't believe a word of that story about the American actress but I do now.'

He suddenly went all solemn. Picking up the money the footman had returned, he handed it to me. 'You have made me a very happy man, James. Egad, I'm devilish sorry that I misjudged you. Now off you go and enjoy yourself, for tomorrow we journey to Aldershot.'

I couldn't get out of the house fast enough. At 'The Eight Bells' none of the staff were able to give me any information as to the whereabouts of Dara so I wandered the streets around Covent Garden until after midnight in the vain hope of catching a glimpse of her. I got very little sleep that night as I tossed and turned in a fever of anxiety as to what could have happened to her. In the weeks that followed I returned time and time again to the vicinity of Covent Garden but none of the enquiries regarding my wife ever came to anything. It seemed she had disappeared for good.

PART FIVE

The Golden Virgin

Tired out after our journey from Liverpool, I slept soundly throughout our first night at 'The Eight Bells' hotel. James was still asleep when I got out of bed, curious to see what was causing the continual roar in the street below. It was my first sight of bustling, thriving, noisy London. The street was filled with vehicles of every kind, costermongers' carts, lumbering market wagons filled to overflowing with vegetables. Their screeching iron-rimmed wheels on the cobbled surface added to the confusion and tumult of the bells of the barrow boys, the raucous shouting of men and women selling gingerbread, hot meat pies and other cooked food, whelks, watercress and a variety of wares. The pavements were strewn with cabbage leaves and litter of every description.

After breakfast James set off to call on some magazine editors and I sallied forth to explore the Covent Garden market. Stepping into the street I unwittingly became the cause of a dispute when two women, carrying baskets, converged on me.

One of them, an Irish woman, smoking a short clay pipe, shoved her basket at me, 'Gingerbread, lady? The best in London.'

The other woman, wearing a stiff gown tucked up with a large quilted petticoat, pushed Irish to one side with strong, brawny arms and thrust her red, bloated face towards mine. ''Ere y'are, lady. Buy me spiced gingerbread, smo-o-king 'ot, fresh out'a the oven,' she demanded in a coarse cracked voice.

Irish, outraged at this intrusion, forced her basket into me and cursed the other woman with some Celtic oaths.

First one basket and then the other pushed me backwards towards the hotel entrance as they argued and screamed abuse at each other. I could see that it wouldn't be long before they would be coming to blows. Pot-boys and ragged dirty-faced children, attracted by the screams of anger, gathered around us, eager to see a fight. As I extracted two pennies from my purse, a pot-boy shouted encouragement to Irish: 'Put the kye-bosh on her, Mary.'

Dropping a penny in each of their baskets, I fled across the congested street, negotiating my way through a higgledy-piggledy confusion of vendors of fried fish, hot pies, muffins, caged linnets, almond toffee and costermongers' barrows loaded with fresh fruit and vegetables. The pandemonium and cries of 'Hi-i-i! Carrots, penny a bunch; pahnd o' grapes for thrupence; hot chestnuts; cherry ripe, round and sahnd, fivepence a pahnd; fish alive-O,' vibrated through my head and filled me with an excitement that was a welcome change after weeks of boredom on board ship.

Resisting the tempting smell of hot coffee wafting out of an eating house on the corner, I turned into Mart Street where, although the thoroughfare was narrow, my movements were less restricted because the traders' vehicles were confined to one side of the street. I hadn't got very far when a voice, rising above the other street cries, clammered for my attention.

'Oy! Oy! Oy! Hi there, lady. Turn abaht and look at these 'ere apples. Rosy red and juicy.'

It was a young man about my own age. He was dressed in the usual costermonger's clothing, a long cord waistcoat with shining brass buttons and trousers tightly fitting over the knees and billowing out over highly polished boots. Beneath a cloth cap pulled jauntily down to one side, his mischievous eyes invited me to examine a large apple that he held in a hand outstretched in my direction.

Eve tempted Adam with an apple. On this occasion it was Adam tempting a woman with the same fruit. For that was indeed his name as I was soon to find out. The apple was all he said it would be: tasty and juicy. Little did I know as my teeth crunched into Eve's fruit that Adam Sutton's friendly face would be my introduction to the foul obscenity of London's underworld.

There was always a hearty welcome for me when I purchased fruit at Adam's barrow. In the first half of the week he was not to be seen in Mart Street as those were the days he pushed his barrow into other parts of the city. Our acquaintanceship ripened very quickly into a flirtatious friendship that kept me amused for hours as I stood chattering with him and his customers. It didn't take me long to learn the prices of the fruit and vegetables on his barrow and I often helped out when he was very busy with a crowd of housewives demanding quick service.

There was nothing else for me to do as James was out nearly every day and attending theatrical performances most evenings. He struck up a friendship with John Sweetapple, a theatre critic, who was more successful than James at getting his work published in the magazines that were in circulation in those days. I spent two or three boring evenings with James at John's lodgings listening to him reading out loud extracts from some of the plays he had written. Try as I may, I couldn't arouse any interest in his plays and he obviously wasn't concerned about me as he addressed most of his conversation to James.

Apart from John Sweetapple and James, the only person I could talk to was my costermonger. Adam was one of those people who have the knack of getting you to open out and confide in them. It wasn't long before he knew all about my adventures in America and how I had met James and wed him in New York.

I asked him once if I talked too much. 'Nah!' he exclaimed, 'I like listening to your la-di-da lingo.'

Puzzled by this remark, I asked what he meant by my 'la-di-da lingo'.

'You talk proper—like a toff. You're not like me; you're edicated, ain't yer. You've got the words for ev'ryfink. I s'pose you got to 'ave, bein' married to a gent that is. I don't know why you bovver wiv me. I'm just a costermonger.'

The idea of me talking with a 'la-di-da' accent seemed so absurd and ridiculous that I laughed out loud. My amusement quickly subsided when I saw the angry expression on his face. He thought I was laughing at him. To make amends I put a hand on his arm and said, 'Don't be angry, Adam. I'm laughing at myself not you. You are my friend. My best friend. Believe me I wouldn't do anything to upset you.'

To get over his embarrassment he began to pile up the apples into a neat heap. 'Don't just stand there like a loony,' he said brusquely. 'Make yerself busy. Tidy up them oranges.'

Because of this difference in speech he obviously felt some sense of inferiority. Up till then I hadn't given the matter any thought but he was painfully sensitive about his lack of education and somehow, when the opportunity arose, I would have to convince him that I loved his cockney accent. In fact, it added colour and life to his words. Everything he said held me fascinated and I never got tired of listening to the descriptive phrases he used.

We had been at the hotel about three weeks when I woke up one morning to find that James had dressed and left the hotel before I had opened my eyes. I was curious as to his haste because invariably I was the first one out of bed, but thought nothing of it, assuming that he had an early appointment that morning. Although I didn't see him that day, I wasn't unduly worried and settled down to sleep in the evening thinking that he was probably drinking with friends until the early hours of the morning.

Much to my concern, when morning came I found myself alone in bed. I dressed in a hurry of anxiety and went downstairs to enquire if anyone had seen my husband, as he had failed to make an appearance since the previous day. At a loss as to what I should do next, I sought out Adam to ask his advice.

He made light of my fretting saying, 'Nothin' to worry abaht. Got boozed up last night I s'pose. Mark my words, he'll wake up wiv a sore 'ead and crawl back to yer feelin' more dead than alive.'

His words were reassuring, but I couldn't help feeling apprehensive. It was unlike James to be out all night.

From the expression on Adam's face I could see he thought I was making too much of it. 'Don't just stand there lookin' like a sick cow. 'Ere, make yerself busy. I could do wiv some 'elp this mornin'.'

I stayed with him until midday then hurried back to the hotel. Mr Dawkins, the owner of 'The Eight Bells', was waiting for me and hailed me as I was about to mount the stairs to our bedroom saying, 'Just one moment, Miss. I want a word with you.'

Nettled by him addressing me as 'Miss', I asked sternly, 'Did you say "Miss"?' Impatient to get to our chamber to see if James had returned, I took a step up the stairs and turned and fixed my eye on him. 'Aren't you aware that I'm Mrs James Kennet?'

'Be that as it may. Your husband, if that's what he is, owes me a tidy bit of money and I want it now.'

'Have you seen Mr Kennet?' I enquired hopefully.

'No. Not for two days. That is, not since I threatened him with the debtors' prison if he didn't pay me the seventeen pounds he owes me.'

I looked at him aghast, hardly believing my ears. Whatever could James be thinking about, allowing us to run into debt like this. He had assured me on the voyage coming over that there would be no more money problems once we got to London.

Mr Dawkins snorted, 'Gents like him usually do a bunk when their debts get bigger than their pocket. I am sure we won't see him again so you're the one who will have to pay.'

'How can I pay you?' I exclaimed. 'I haven't got any money.'

'You can sell those two rings on your hand,' he answered. 'That's if they are genuine.'

'But it's all the jewellery I have left,' I protested.

'He has taken you for a right mug, hasn't he? I'll bet this isn't the first time you have had to bail him out when he has been living above his means. I'm sorry, Miss, but you'll have to come with me. I'll show you where you can sell your rings.'

For the first time I began to doubt James' integrity. I didn't know what to think. Crestfallen at this sudden turn of events, I allowed Dawkins to take me by the arm and lead me along the road to a shop showing a window display of clocks and watches. He released my arm at the shop doorway saying he would wait outside.

'Vot have you got for me?' the man in the shop asked as soon as I entered. 'Or is it you vould like a vatch . . . maybe a clock? Eh?'

His dark, grizzled hair, topped by a little black skullcap, hung down in ringlets on each side of his heavy, sallow face. The dark eyes above his hooked nose fired with interest when I removed the two rings from my fingers and placed them before him but his words belied his thoughts.

Picking up the rings he gave them a quick glance. 'Glass!' he sneered. 'Pretty, but just glass. Not vorth more than a few shillings. Vell, vot do you vant for zem?'

My attention was distracted by a tapping on the window behind me. I looked around thinking it was Mr Dawkins getting impatient for his money only to see a roguish street boy, nose and goggling eyes pressed up against the window with his tongue lolling out. Turning around I was about to speak when the tapping became more urgent and louder.

The shopman, furious at this interruption to our business, rushed to the door and shouted, 'If you vant to buy a vatch, come in and buy a vatch—if you don't vant to buy a vatch take your snotty nose away from my vindow!'

The boy pulled his mouth wide with his fingers, stuck out his tongue, then ran down the street. I made up my mind that I wasn't going to be intimidated nor was I going to enter into tedious bargaining about the rings.

'I want seventeen pounds,' I announced. 'And if you won't give what I'm asking for them I'll take them elsewhere.'

He took an eyeglass out of his pocket and examined the rings minutely, giving me a sharp hard look. 'Not vorth more than fourteen pounds.'

I reached out for the rings. 'I owe that man out there seventeen pounds. I can't take a penny less for them.'

He stepped back out of my reach.

'Give them back to me,' I said angrily.

'You owe ze man ze money?' His features softened but he wasn't going to give in without a protest. Raising his hands palm upwards he shrugged his shoulders. 'Pretty faces viz pretty rings vill be ze ruin of me.'

After he had slowly counted out seventeen sovereigns he gave them to me with great reluctance and an anguished expression.

An impatient Mr Dawkins wanted the money as soon as I left the shop but I wouldn't give it to him. 'You will have to wait until we get back to the hotel,' I said, 'where you can write me out a receipt for it.'

I went up to my bedchamber after settling the account where I intended to wait until James returned.

Sitting on the bed idly looking around the room it suddenly came to me that none of James' personal effects could be seen. Usually his hair brushes, writing paper, etc., were strewn around in various places. I re-

membered about a week ago having a fleeting thought about how tidy
the room was and assumed that James, for once, had put all his things
into drawers or his clothes cabinet. In a daze, I looked everywhere. He
had left nothing, not even a small item of clothing. Everything that belonged to him had gone.

Stunned, I stood in the middle of the room unable for a while to
accept the thought that he had walked out of my life without even saying
goodbye. He wasn't strong in character, that I knew, but he had always
been kind and considerate. It was unbelievable that he could desert me
in this way without any warning.

Flinging myself on the bed I cried out loud like a stricken animal. With
tears flowing down my cheeks I sobbed quietly into the pillow. He had
cast me aside when his debts had got too much for him. Cast me aside as
a thing of no importance. How could he do this to me, I asked myself
time and time again and spoke the words out loud but could find no
reasonable answer in my mind.

There was nothing for it. I would have to leave the hotel before I got
further into debt. Collecting clothing and everything that was mine I
slowly packed them all into my leather bag and walked out of the hotel.
With dragging feet and a feeling of rejection and dreadful loneliness I
returned to Adam and his barrow.

There weren't many people about and Adam was trying to whip up
some business by beating an old tin box and calling out the prices of his
stock.

'A-ho there! What d'you think of this 'ere? Carrots penny a bunch.'

Without a pause in his words he signalled me to come alongside of
him. 'Hurrah for free trade. Pertater, turnips, onions. All fresh and good.
Oy! Oy! Now's yer time. 'Ere y'are guv'nor, fine broccoli-i? Dirt cheap.
Oranges 'n apples, thrupence a dozen.'

When Adam heard my tale of woe he asked me what I was going to do
now that I was on my own.

'I've got no money and nowhere to go,' I answered tearfully. 'What can
I do, Adam?'

He averted his eyes, embarrassed by my tears and misery. 'It's an 'ell
'ole where I live. Not fit for the likes of you,' he mumbled.

I was becoming more and more aware of the hopelessness of my situation and couldn't see any way out of it. In this world you've got to have
either a man or money and I had neither. 'Where do you live, Adam?' I
asked.

'I've got a room in an 'ouse that's old and musty. You wouldn't like it.
It's the worst 'ouse on Exeter Street. Broken windows stuffed wiv rags
and full of street hawkers, thieves, sluts and cryin' babies—the scum of

London.' He hesitated. 'There's only one bed. You'd 'ave to sleep wiv me. How about that, my La-di-da Lady? You wouldn't like that—would yer now, eh?' He was grinning all over his face but uncertain as to how I would reply.

I had got the drift of where all this was leading to before he had finished and was ready with my answer. 'You're a lovely man, Adam. If I have got to share a bed, I would rather it was you than anyone else. Do you think you can put up with me? I'll try to earn my keep by helping you in any way I can. Whatever happens, I promise not to be a burden on you.'

It was obvious he hadn't expected such an easy conquest and I wondered if he thought I was too eager to get into bed with him, so I said, 'I can sleep on the floor, Adam, if you'd prefer it.'

'What d'yer take me for? I can relish a woman and bull 'er as good as the next man so don't let any of me mates 'ear yer say anyfink abaht sleeping on the floor. They would fink I was a proper Jessie boy.'

After many months of married celibacy his cheerful virility quickened my pulse and raised my spirits. What matter if I lived in a ramshackle old house with the castoffs of society? It wouldn't be anything new to me as I had experienced abject poverty in my years of childhood and had come out of it unscathed.

An hour or two passed before Adam decided that, as there was so little left on the barrow, it was time to knock off and get something to eat. We packed what was left into a sack and returned the barrow to the hiring yard. The hire of a barrow cost threepence a day during the winter months and fourpence during the summer.

There was no need to go to an eating house as all round us was a wide selection of food on the street stalls. There were pies, muffins, eels, plum puddings, fried fish, baked potatoes, all steaming hot, as well as ham sandwiches, pickled whelks and eggs. Despite the squalor and filth of the streets it was a cheerful scene with the warming red glow of the charcoal braziers and swinging oil lamps hanging from the stalls. Adam and I had two mutton pies each and finished off our meal with plum puddings.

On our way to Adam's favourite ale-house, 'The Half Moon' tavern, we passed several splendid gin houses with their glittering chandeliers lighting up the elegantly carved mahogany bars which extended the whole length of the saloon. I had a peek in one and viewed with awe the huge green and gold barrels of gin stacked behind brass rails labelled 'Corpse Reviver', 'The Real Knock Me Down', 'Blue Tarter', 'Mother's Favourite' and other enticing names.

At 'The Half Moon' tavern I was introduced to Tom Biggs, a crony of Adam's who was also a costermonger. He looked a slippery character to me and I was on my guard from the first moment he gave me an admiring leer. He had on the usual dandified costermonger's garb with a bright multi-coloured silk neckerchief. They were all proud of these pieces of silk around their necks. 'King's Men' they called them and when they took to living with a girl they usually gave her a similar neckerchief. Adam settled our arrangement the next day when he proudly tied one around my neck.

All Tom's words were over-emphasized by nods, sly winks, shrugging shoulders and extreme facial expressions.

Adam had a drink waiting for him. Tom raised his glass in a salute, ''Ere's to you, Adam; may your cock and purse never fail yer.'

His girlfriend turned up shortly after we arrived. She was coarse in language and manners but a pleasant, amiable girl who treated me with a certain amount of reserve until she got to know me better.

In answer to calls from Adam and Tom, Florrie, the barmaid, replenished our drinks. She was a full-breasted, plump, well-built woman, about forty years of age, who ruled the roost in the tavern, keeping everyone in order, including 'Pig Face', the landlord. When she returned to the bar I couldn't help commenting on the tattoos emblazoned on her arms. From her wrists upwards the tattoos covered almost every inch of her skin. The most outstanding was an impression of St Paul's Cathedral encircled by a multitude of pink roses.

Tom Biggs snorted and, with a wink at Adam, said, 'Yer should see the rest of 'er. She's tattooed from neck to foot wiv everyfink yer can fink of; ships, lovers' knots, sights o' London, devils and angels. You name it, she's got it. Up 'er legs, on 'er belly, everywhere.'

'But why?' I asked.

Tom laughed. 'Well, it's like this, see. She was married for two years to a tattoo artist who practised 'is craft on 'er when 'e 'ad nuffink better to do. At the time she worshipped the ground 'e trod on and would let 'im do anyfink 'e wanted wiv 'er. You women are bleedin' fools when a man takes your fancy. She's proud of 'em cos, now 'e's dead, she carries on 'er body the best tattooing 'e ever did do while 'e was 'er 'usband. She's got somefink to remember 'im by. See?'

Adam bent forward and whispered something to Tom which I didn't catch.

'What are they whispering about?' I asked Betty, Tom's friend.

'They're not gonna tell yer so I will. It's wot she's got tattooed dahn 'er back.'

'What's that?' I said, full of curiosity.

'Tell 'er abaht the fox,' said Tom, sniggering.

Betty ignored him. 'Startin' up near 'er waist she's got some 'untsmen on 'orses, jumpin' over fences and gallopin' like mad.'

'Tally-O!' shouted Adam. "Oo's gonna foller the fox?'

Betty was having difficulty suppressing her giggles and said, 'You've never seen anyfink like it. When she bends dahn you see all these 'ounds runnin' all over 'er backside arter the fox which is disappearin' up 'er arse 'ole.'

I looked round at Florrie. With her light grey hair tucked under a white bonnet, she looked so respectable and dignified it was difficult to imagine all those tattoos under her clothing and to understand why she had allowed her fair skin to be disfigured in this manner.

Adam and his friends were pushing each other and laughing uproariously at the shocked expression on my face. 'How do you know all this?' I asked.

Adam lit up a tuppenny cigar. "Cos she'll show it to anyone for 'alf a sovereign—would yer like to see it?'

'No!' I said quickly. 'It's bad enough thinking about it without seeing it.'

Adam sniffed. 'We've vexed Mrs La-di-da,' he said to his friends. Then he turned to me and spat out, 'Don't put on any airs and graces wiv us. Take us as yer find us, or 'oppit.'

Surprised and shocked, I could think of nothing to say in reply to his abrupt outburst. Luckily Betty chose that moment to get up from her seat and say to Tom, 'Well, I'm orf. If yer want to come wiv me put yer shillin' on the table.'

Tom looked at Adam, laughed and with a knowing wink gave Betty a shilling and followed her out of the tavern.

'What was all that about?' I asked Adam.

'Nothin' much,' he answered. 'She's a shillin' dolly mop. If she likes yer, she'll give yer all yer want for a shillin'.'

'Is she a prostitute then?' I asked.

'Nah. She works in the fish market. Yer get nuffink for nuffink in this world. The shillin's not important. She don't see no reason why she should give it for free. Even though she enjoys it as much as the cove 'oo's on top of 'er.'

'If you ask me,' I said, 'she's nothing but a common tart, selling herself cheap.'

'Ah. Yer don't understand. Yer not like us. She's just a good sport. I remember the first time Tom and me met 'er. They say two into one won't go but it did that night. Tom and me 'ad 'er sandwiched between us, piggin' it in the same 'ole as yer might say.'

It was pitch black when Adam and I stumbled up the stairs to his room later that evening and I paid scant attention to the decaying, fetid smells that seemed to infect the whole house. Adam's room was spotlessly clean but barely furnished, with its cold floorboards, bed, wash stand, clothes cupboard, small table and two chairs. In the fluttering light of a tallow candle I undressed and he did likewise, removing all his clothing except his shirt, before jumping into bed.

When I pulled my shift over my head and stood naked before him he turned his head away. 'Put yer bloody shift on,' he shouted. ''Ave yer got no shame, showing all yer got like that? Wot d'yer fink this is, a broffel?'

This was my first experience of lower class prudery. Later, as time went by, I was to learn that Adam was no exception to the idea prevalent amongst the poor that it wasn't decent to expose your private parts to anyone however intimate the relationship had become. In all the time I was with Adam I never saw him naked; he always undressed with his back to me and held the front of his shirt over his private parts until he got into bed.

Wasting no time on kisses or caresses, he pulled me roughly under him. He was what you might call a 'knee-elbow lover'. Taking most of his weight on his forearms he crouched over me and viciously thrust deep into my giny saying, ''Old yer breaf when I pass yer 'eart.'

In spite of the rough manner of his entry into my soft underparts, it was good to feel the warm full flesh of a man inside me again. The deep probings of his aggressive cock began to arouse my passions but the warm, sensual feeling wasn't to last for very long, for in less than two minutes his frantic stabbing brought him to a head. Gasping for breath, he flopped down on me.

Bitterly disappointed, I said with feeling, 'Is that the best you can do for a girl?'

Without any warning I was stunned by a stinging blow across the mouth from the back of his hand. 'Shut yer mouf, you stupid cunt,' he growled, 'or I'll shut it for yer.'

I could hear the slumbering anger beneath the surface of Adam's words the following morning when he bid me rise and dress. 'Come on, woman, there's work to do.'

He was determined to bring me down a peg or two to keep his own self esteem. The difference in our education and speech irritated and belittled him. His constant harping on what he called my 'la-di-da' speech and genteel manners exposed his sense of inferiority with those who had the advantages that he associated with the self-assured gentry. What he wanted from me was admiring respect.

It was obvious that if our intimate relationship was to continue he
would have to be top dog and I his subservient woman. It would be
difficult for me to play such a role but it would be easier for me than
have us both tearing each other to pieces in constant bickering. A long
day of sullen resentment was not a happy prospect so I decided to put
the matter to rights immediately.

Standing before him with eyes downcast in an attitude of meekness
and submission bare-footed and wearing only my shift, I murmured in an
apologetic voice, 'Adam, I'm sorry for what I said last night. Please forgive me.'

The angry resentment he felt was still boiling up inside him and had to
come out. He scowled at me. 'Yer're a tight-arsed, snooty bitch and I
won't stand for it so yer'd better knuckle dahn and mind yer tongue.'

He waved his fist in front of my face. 'Yer fink yer're better than me—
don't yer?'

'No, Adam, I don't,' I protested.

Stuck for words, he mumbled hesitantly, 'Mind yer place—or I'll wal-
lop the 'ide off yer.'

By the time we arrived at Covent Garden, Adam was his usual lively,
agreeable self. It was hard work helping him push the barrow through
dismal streets and into gloomy courtyards to get the sales for the fruit
and vegetables. Despite the drizzling rain that soaked us to the skin, he
remained talkative and entertaining, doing his best to bring good cheer
and laughter to the pale, pinched-up faces of the women who came out
from crumbling houses to buy our vegetables. Their thin, tawdry dresses
gave them little protection against the cold wind and rain.

I was dog tired at the end of the day and ready for bed but Adam
insisted on us having another evening at 'The Half Moon' tavern. The
cosy atmosphere and warm welcome I received from Florrie soon revived
my spirits.

Sitting next to Tom Biggs was a little dwarf. He was so hideous and
grotesque that I couldn't take my eyes off him. I tried to concentrate on
the conversation between Adam and Tom, but became increasingly uneasy as the fixed staring eyes that bulged from the monstrous head of the
dwarf followed all my movements. He never took his eyes off me from
the moment I sat down in a chair opposite him. The diabolical grin on his
fat lips unnerved me every time I glanced at him.

Adam seeing the dwarf's interest in me, gave him a push and said,
'Take yer eyes off 'er, yer randy little bastard. Anyway she'd get nuffink
from your short stick.'

The dwarf turned with his heavy head lolling to one side. 'My short
stick 'as pleased a lot of women.' Sticking out a thick, wet tongue at

Adam, 'Yer know what they say, "Long and thin, goes right in but it's short and thick wot does the trick."'

I took my eyes off the dwarf just for an instant and in that fleeting moment he had disappeared from view. Looking around the tavern to see where he had gone, I became aware of something crawling up my leg. My searching fingers found a hand half way up my thigh. Letting out an outraged yell, I flung myself backwards toppling over onto the floor. Scrambling to my feet amidst a roar of laughter, I caught sight of the dwarf's head rising above the table, and thumped it hard with a clenched fist.

Florrie intervened and with a comforting arm around my shoulders ushered me behind the bar and poured out a glass of brandy.

'Here you are, luv, drink this. That bloody dwarf, you never know what he is going to do next.'

To my disgust Adam and Tom were splitting their sides with laughter. When they saw me looking at the dwarf with an excess of loathing they hooted even louder. To everybody's amusement the dwarf climbed onto the table and, with tongue lolling out, 'cunt thumbed' me with a thumb folded into his fist. In triumph at my discomfort his fat little legs danced a mad Irish jig to the accompaniment of Adam and Tom's hand clapping.

The landlord, with a scowling face, gestured for me to get back to my seat and I was about to do so when Florrie muttered, 'Don't take any notice of him. Stay where you are.'

Pig Face, as Florrie so aptly named him, was a big bully of a man with a florid complexion. His scanty crop of hair was plastered over the top of his head in a vain effort to hide a bald patch.

With some harsh words he was ordering Sniffler, the little waif who helped out at the back of the bar, to bring more glasses. Sniffler had obviously got her name because she was constantly sniffing a wet nose. For something to say, I asked Florrie if she and Sniffler slept on the premises.

'Yes, we share a room upstairs. That way I can protect her from Pig Face. Poor little sod, she's never had a chance. Born in the Poor House and kicked out to fend for herself when she was twelve, she knew nothing of the world outside and was scared stiff when I found her, curled up in the doorway. I brought her in and gave her some hot soup. We needed some help so I persuaded Pig Face to let her stay and she's been with us now about twelve months.'

She shot a quick look at her boss and her voice dropped to a whisper. 'You wouldn't think it looking at that belly of his but he's a right randy sod. He's always at her. She never complains because she's frightened he will chuck her out into the street. I've caught him more than once having his way with her in a cupboard. Yesterday he had her bent over on the stairs and was ramming it into her like a street dog with a bitch.' She sighed. 'I do my best, but you can't have your eyes everywhere, can you?'

'What about you?' I asked. 'Doesn't he try it on with you?'

Florrie snorted, 'Just let him try; he will get what he got last time.'

'What was that?' I asked with a laugh.

'Well, it was like this. I was born and bred in Chelmsford.'

'So that's why you don't talk cockney,' I exclaimed.

'I couldn't, luv—even if I tried. The doctor taught me how to speak proper and I've done so ever since.'

'What doctor?' I asked.

'Well, I was going to tell you if only you would stop interrupting. When I was twelve I got work as a serving maid with a Dr Huddle. Although he had a wife he crept into my bed the first night I was there saying, "Huddle wants a cuddle." You couldn't help laughing at the things he said. He was always coming out with comic remarks like that and, mind you, always with a straight face.'

'Well go on,' I said, interrupting her again. 'What happened?'

'To tell you the truth I was frightened out of my wits. Being a virgin and in the flower of my youth, as you might say, what with his wife asleep downstairs and him up with me, I didn't know what to do. I put up a struggle but he got it in me just the same. It hurt a bit at first but not all that much.'

She broke off for a moment to serve some drinks then came back to me. 'Where was I? Oh, yes. He was a handsome forty at the time and very clean about his person—if you know what I mean. I was big for my age, a grown up girl before I was fourteen and that's when I started to get as much pleasure from it as he did.'

As she seemed to have run out of words, I asked, 'How long did it go on for?'

'Oh! Let me see. I was twenty-three when he collapsed all of a heap on the kitchen floor one day. His heart gave out I think. About eleven years I would say. The day after they buried him, his widow had a stand up row with me and kicked me out, bag and baggage. You see she had known all along what was happening but never let on until after her husband had died. He had always given me a shilling every time he did it and as I never spent any of it I had quite a bit put by for me when I needed it.'

'What did you do when she kicked you out? Come to London?'

'Yes, that's right. I had never been anywhere but Chelmsford and I had always wanted to see London. That's when I met Fred. Oh, he was a lovely man, was Fred. A wonder in bed and a wonder with his tattoo needle. That's how I got all the tattoo pictures on me. I'll show you them some time. You will be amazed. I'm a living work of art. It wouldn't be decent,' she said with a giggle, 'but sometime I would like to walk around stark naked so that everybody could admire Fred's pictures.'

She came to an abrupt stop when Pig Face brushed past me, nipping my bum as he went by. 'That's just like him, the dirty old sod,' said Florrie. 'This was Fred's regular drinking place and after he died I came to work here. Pig Face's wife was still alive then, but that didn't stop him trying to get his hand up my skirt. He didn't get very far because I pushed my thumbs into his eyeballs and kneed him hard in the nutmegs. He never tried it on again after that.'

Awakening before Adam the following morning, I found myself cuddled to him with a hand on his crotch. I don't know how long I had been in that position but he was firm and sticking up proudly. It jerked each time my fingers stroked. Each twitch of his cock brought a tremor to my giny and sent a thrilling spasm of desire through my burning flesh.

His eyes were still closed in sleep as I eased under him and guided him into me. In this drowsiness he lay heavy on me but that's the way I wanted it. After all those months without ever feeling the full weight of a man on me it was good to feel the hard muscular belly pressing into mine. Twining my legs around his, I levered my hips upwards, forcing my giny hard up against him. Swooning with joyful bliss my swiggling buttocks raised my fevered passions to the dizzy heights of fulfillment.

Adam was fully awake by this time and in his usual crouched position driving himself deep into me. I lay back with languid limbs, in blissful submission, as he savaged my throbbing giny and rose again to join him in a thunderous whirling storm that left us clasped tight against each other.

Clinging to him in warm contentment, I opened my tear-smeared eyes to find him smiling at me with tender amusement and, for the first time since we had met, received a fond kiss on the lips. A kiss that opened the flood gates of my affections, but he pulled away when I reached out to caress his lips with loving fingers and rolled out of bed to pull on his trousers impatiently, as if ashamed of showing the soft underside of his nature.

It didn't happen all that often but whenever I awoke before Adam my persuasive caresses soon had him ripe and ready for loving. With his head clouded in sleep I could take full advantage of his drowsiness to have it my way. My clinging legs held him close to me until my giny tensed and I lay back, all passion spent.

It was only on such mornings that we got together as lovers should, allowing the deep longing of the flesh for union with someone of the opposite sex to reach fulfilment. It seems contradictory but, after I had risen in joy and happiness to achieve the sensual bliss that follows desire satisfied, I welcomed the onslaught of his aggressive lust. Satiated with sensual warmth I submitted willingly to the rapist that is in all men and opened my thighs wider to further his passions. Clinging to him after he had emptied his loins into me I would await the tender kiss of gratitude that was my reward for awakening him with loving caresses.

It was about this time that I discovered who was living in the cupboard on our landing. I can only assume that in better days, when the house was occupied by a family with servants, it had been used to store bedding. It protruded into our room to a depth of about three feet.

Adam was having an evening out with Tom Biggs and had left me to my own devices. As I sat mending a small tear in my skirt, my concentration was disturbed by scraping and scratching sounds coming from the space taken up by the cupboard. Often during the night I heard rats scuffling under the floorboards but this was altogether different. Coming out onto the landing I cautiously opened one of the doors of the cupboard to find a ragged boy about eight-years-old, smeared in oil and grime, scraping away at a piece of copper by the light of a tallow candle. He was squatting on a straw-filled mattress which covered most of the floor of the cupboard. His clothing was tattered and torn and between his open legs was a basket of odds and ends; bones, copper nails, pieces of coal and a filthy variety of other curious objects. I was about to ask him what he was doing there when a girl of about ten or eleven rudely pushed past me to sit down beside her brother.

'Wot d'you want?' she demanded of me.

'Nothing. I heard a scraping noise and wondered where it was coming from. How long have you been living in this cupboard?'

'Wot's it to you?' she said and pulled the door to.

I went back to my sewing, intrigued at the thought that Adam and I had neighbours who lived practically in our room. More in a sense of fun than anything else, I knocked three times on the wall that was the back of their cupboard. In less than a minute there was a knock on our door.

'Come in,' I shouted.

The door swung open and there she stood, bristling with indignation.

'Wot the 'ell d'yer want now?' she asked, prepared to do battle with me.

She was completely disarmed when I took two apples from our fruit sack and offered them to her. Viewing the apples with a stark, hungry look she licked her lips and slowly moved towards them. When she was within reaching distance she grabbed the apples and stepped backwards and took a bite out of one of them. Munching away she looked at me doubtfully. 'Wot's yer name?' she asked through a mouth full of apple.

'Dara—what's yours?'

'Polly Barnes.'

'And your brother?' I asked.

'Peter. You frightened 'im when you came on 'im suddenly like that. You're a bit of a nosey parker, ain't yer?'

I laughed. 'Bring him in here and I will give him an apple.'

She banged on the wall and shouted, 'Peter, come in 'ere.'

When he appeared in the doorway I offered him an apple and asked what he was doing with the bits and pieces he had in his basket.

'Sortin' 'em aht,' he mumbled as he chewed on the apple.

'We're "mud larks",' said Polly in the way of an explanation.

'What the hell is a "mud lark"?' I asked.

'Cor. Where've you been? Mean ter say yer never 'eard of mud larks?'

I shook my head. 'Alright, tell me what you do when you are mudlarking.'

'Well! Everyday we search in the mud by the riverside for coppah, nails, coal, old iron, bones—anyfink that we can get a penny or two for. Las' week Peter fahnd a shillin' an' I pulled aht a baby's shawl. We got thrupence for it—it was a good 'un—that's arter I'd washed it.'

As the weeks went by we became good friends. On the nights that Adam was out I would often sit in their cupboard helping to sort out and clean the pieces of copper and iron. Everyday they were down by the river banks, up to their knees in mud and floating scum, searching the dregs of the tide.

They had previously lived with their mother and her man in the room now occupied by Adam and me. When their mother died the man just got up and walked out on them. They had no money for rent so they sought sanctuary in the landing cupboard and since then had made a precarious living as mud larks. I took them under my wing, giving them what I could in the way of fruit and vegetables and occasionally buying them meat pies. They always looked lean and hungry even with the extra food I gave them.

Polly was always trying to sell various little items to the people in the house. She knew them all and was brutally frank in her descriptions of the characters who slept and fed in this dingy warren of a place. First she warned me about the man in the attic above us.

''E's a thievin' bastard,' she said. 'Nothin's safe when 'e's arahnd. 'E'd take the pennies off a dead man's eyes, 'e would.'

In the room below us lived a 'tosher' with a wife and six children. A tosher's work was extremely dangerous. They were often bitten on the hands and face by rats as they scavenged with seven foot long poles for anything of value in the sewers that flowed into the Thames. Some of them suffocated in the poisonous vapours that arose from the foul sewage. The risk of being crushed by the roof of a sewer falling on them was always there and so was the danger of being sucked down in the perilous quagmires of mud and sewerage where the floor had collapsed. There were terrible stories of toshers' skeletons being found picked clean of skin and flesh.

Upstairs there was a married couple not yet fifteen, who Polly said had just moved in. At that time there was a well-known dubious church in the East End which married youngsters for sevenpence and no questions asked, provided both partners were over fourteen-years-old.

According to Polly, a drunken Irishman rented the basement cellar and charged beggars, prostitutes, thieving vagabonds and the like, twopence for a night's rest on the stone floor. Most of the other rooms were occupied by large families sleeping as many as ten in a room. Of them all, the worst was a dirty old cadger in filthy rags, who slept on the landing or wherever he could find a place to lie down. His melancholy face was pitted with smallpox marks. Even the corners of his eyebrows seemed eaten away by the awful disease. He was forever getting into trouble for groping one of the dozen or so little girls that swarmed all over the buildings. He would lie and wait in dark corners on the stairs and jump on them, getting his hands on their private parts before they had time to scream. Then he scuttled down the stairs and into the busy street before anybody had time to catch him.

It was about this time I began to notice that Adam seemed very flushed with money, spending it freely on clothes and amusements. He became very bumptious and overbearing when he donned his new 'togs', strutting and swaggering like a proud peacock.

Puzzled as to where all this money was coming from, I would ask him how he came by it only to be told to mind my own business when my questions became too pressing for his peace of mind. Of course, life became a lot easier for me. We only worked weekends when we were in Mart Street market. The rest of the week we were free to do as we wished. As we strolled at our leisure through the busy streets, frequently stopping to chat with his costermonger cronies, he would show off by giving me some money to spend on whatever took my fancy.

They were balmy days and nights. We became regular visitors to the theatres that catered for the lower orders and I was often taken to such sports as cock-fighting, the savaging of hordes of rats by terriers in private rooms at the rear of some tavern and bare-fisted fights between burly women who were compelled to grasp a coin in their hands as they were likely to scratch each other's faces with their finger nails. The first woman to drop a coin being accounted the loser.

Our favourite theatre was the Queens in Tottenham Street, London's most disreputable playhouse and consequently nicknamed the 'Dust Hole'. At the Queens we were entertained by melodrama, comic songs, acrobats, jugglers and dancing girls singing lewd songs.

Friday nights were reserved for 'The Half Moon' tavern where the dwarf was constantly catching me off my guard while I was talking to someone. On the night of the new year when we were celebrating the end of 1860 and the beginning of 1861, he was nowhere in sight as we entered the tavern and I settled down happy that he was absent from our revelries.

You could never predict what would happen next when he was around and I would sit, knees tight together in an agony of apprehension, waiting for a sly assault on my private parts by the lecherous little monster. I couldn't understand why Adam was so genial with him. Every time the dwarf looked at me I could plainly see the hatred and lust that lurked behind that fixed grin on his face.

I was leaning back in my chair, legs astride, laughing at something Adam had said when I felt a finger sliding into my giny. For a moment I couldn't believe my senses and was too stunned to move. Somehow the dwarf had come into the tavern and had got beneath our table without me seeing him. The revulsion and shock I felt at that moment cannot be described. Speechless with raging emotions, I ran behind the bar to stand beside Florrie.

Adam and his friends burst into laughter when they saw the cause of my sudden retreat as the dwarf emerged from under the table prodding the air with his forefinger. They roared with raucous laughter when the dwarf put the moist finger to his nose, sniffed and pulled a wry face. My humiliation was complete and there arose in me an ice cold hatred for this repulsive creature who had become a loathsome nightmare which often haunted my thoughts.

Florrie's soothing words did little to still my agitation. Trapped behind the bar I watched the dwarf climb onto the table with a helping hand from Tom Biggs. Looking directly at me with an obscene grin he put a hand between his legs and cunt-thumbed me once again.

'Now yer up there, yer little bugger, sing us a song,' Adam cried out.

In a voice as thick as treacle, the dwarf began to sing:

'All you that in your beds do lie,
Turn to your wives and occupy;
And when you have done your best
Turn arse to arse, and take your rest.'

This lewd little ditty was greeted with loud laughter and applause, giving him the encouragement to sing another song but my attention, being drawn elsewhere, I didn't hear the words. There was a respectably dressed woman, about forty, sitting near the door with a small glass of gin before her. I had seen her many times before, sitting alone staring into space, but what caught my interest this time was her exposed breasts and something wrapped in a white baby shawl which she cuddled close to her chest.

My curiosity got the better of me. Moving away from the bar as far as the door I got a closer look. Inside the shawl was a rag doll with a white bonnet on its head. There were two bright, wide-open, blue eyes painted on patches of kid leather sewn into the doll's face, and lower down one could see soft leather red lips in an open smile.

The woman looked up at me and smiled. 'Do you want to see my baby?' she asked.

After my latest encounter with the dwarf I was wary, suspecting another trick to humiliate me but nodded dumbly, keeping an eye on the dwarf who was now dancing an Irish jig on the table top.

Opening the shawl so that I could get a better view of a broderie anglaise gown she said, 'It's my first,' and then with a face glowing with motherly pride, 'Isn't he lovely?'

Taking a firm hold on one of her breasts she pushed the brown nipple between the doll's red lips and softly hummed a lullaby.

Looking around the tavern to see if anyone was observing what was going on, I became aware of Florrie beckoning me back to the bar.

'Who is she?' I asked Florrie. 'I've seen her before but didn't know she was deranged.'

'She's been like that for about two weeks now. I think her mother's death turned her head. You see, apart from when she was with her husband, Maggie has lived alone with her mother all her life. Twenty years ago her husband fell to his death when he was replacing some roof tiles. Three weeks after, Maggie gave birth to a baby who only lived for a few hours.'

'How awful,' I exclaimed.

'The way I see it,' Florrie said, shaking her head, 'Maggie can't stand being on her own in that big house where she lives so she has made another baby to keep her company through the long lonely days and nights. The first time she opened her blouse and put the breast to the doll's mouth there were a few coarse remarks from the men here but I soon put a stop to that. After all, she is not doing any harm so leave her to get on with it, that's what I say.'

I think it was about the end of February or the beginning of March when they hung Mrs Lucy Flowers outside Newgate Prison. We left 'The Half Moon' tavern just after midnight to join the streams of people converging on the prison. When we got there Adam pushed me into the jostling crowd already assembled around the gallows. As more and more people came to witness the dawn hanging, I was so squeezed by the swaying dense multitude that it was a wonder some of my ribs did not get broken. From the way almost everybody was behaving you wouldn't think we were waiting to see someone meet with a sudden death. Brutish ruffians, boozed up to the eyeballs, were shouting obscenities as they fought with bottles of beer; tipsy whores with arms linked sang the most disgusting bawdy songs; young bloods, the sons of the aristocracy, dangerously drunk, lashed out with their sticks at the slightest provocation, and slippery villains picked pockets as they slipped through the crowd.

When Lucy Flowers appeared on the platform of the gallows she was greeted by a deafening roar from the crowd. She was a stoutish woman of middle years who had been condemned to death for poisoning a relative to get her money. It was a wicked thing to do but I couldn't help feeling sorry for her, shrinking back before the onslaught of fearsome oaths and filthy language directed at her as the hangman slipped the noose around her neck. It was a gruesome spectacle. I couldn't bear to look and had to close my eyes just before she dropped through the open boards. Adam said that because she was a heavy, well-built woman 'she fell beautiful.'

The night after the hanging we were in 'The Half Moon' tavern. I was talking to Florrie when Adam came to tell me that he and Tom Biggs had some business to see to and they would be back at the tavern within the hour. He had done this often enough before, returning full of cheer and good humour. I had no reason to be concerned but I became agitated with worry when an hour passed and they were still absent.

It didn't help to stand in the doorway of the tavern peering anxiously into the darkness of the street so, after a time, I came back to our table to have another drink. I had hardly got seated when Tom Biggs rushed in all of a sweat and breathless with excitement. He helped himself to my drink, took a deep breath, looked across the room vacantly, and in a low voice said, out of the side of his mouth, 'They got 'im!'

'Adam?' I queried.

'Yus. The police collared 'im wiv the swag. It was lucky they didn't see me, 'cos I 'ad stopped to tie up me boot lace when they nabbed 'im.'

'You were out thieving?' I asked in shocked surprise.

'Gaw blimey! Didn't yer know?' he exclaimed. 'I fought you were in on it. Gawd, luv a duck, where did yer fink all the money was comin' from?' Shaking his head in wonder, he exclaimed with admiration, ''E put up an 'ell of a fight, kickin' an' buttin' 'em. They 'ad ter knock 'im aht wiv their truncheons before they could get the grapplin' irons on 'is wrists.'

I sat deflated in stunned silence, unable to take it all in. 'Can I go and see him?'

'Nah, yer'll 'ave to wait 'til after the trial,' he answered gruffly. ''E'll be at least a year on the treadmill if yer ask me. Poor bugger, it'll bleedin' break 'im—you'll see.'

I tried to see Adam after he had been sentenced to two years' hard labour on the treadmill but was brusquely turned away by an officer at the prison gates. Two weeks later, a sovereign discreetly passed into the 'turnkey's' hand opened doors for a brief visit. With a heavy bunch of keys clanking by his side he led me through long passages to a room divided by an iron grille.

Adam looked at me through the bars. 'Yer shouldn't 'ave come,' he said in a low, lifeless voice. 'I told 'em I didn't want no visitors but they forced me to come an' meet yer.'

He was a pale shadow of his former self, a hollow thing with all the stuffing knocked out of him. I could have wept but held the tears back and tried to put on a bright smile.

With head hung down he muttered in a whisper of bitterness, 'I'm not stayin' 'ere. You'll see. I'll break aht of 'ere some'ow.'

There was a long pause with neither of us knowing what to say next. Moving away from the iron bars, he looked at me with an expressionless face. 'Get aht. I don't want yer to see me like this and, for Gawd's sake, don't come again.'

With a heart heavy with sorrow I watched him shuffle to the guard who took him through a stout oak door at the back of the room, and out of my life for ever.

Now that I was left to my own resources the problem of earning a living was uppermost in my mind. Selling some of my clothes and other personal items brought in sufficient money to stock the barrow with an assortment of fruit and vegetables. Pushing the loaded vehicle from Covent Garden to Mart Street just about exhausted me and I had little energy left to shout for trade. All around me were costermongers much more experienced than I. We were in fierce competition to attract people to our stalls. As the day wore on I learnt that owing to my inexperience I had bought at too high a price and, if I was to clear what remained on the barrow, I would have to sell at a loss. By nightfall there was less money in my pocket than I had started with.

The money from selling my personal possessions had to feed three mouths as my two little mud larks were going through a bad patch, unable to find sufficient odds and ends on the riverside to feed them. They would have starved to death without my help. Altogether it was getting to be a desperate situation. When I got down to the last few items that would bring in some money I decided to consult Florrie in the hope that she might come up with an idea that would solve my financial problems.

As I was about to enter 'The Half Moon' tavern a voice from the shadows alongside the door said, 'Dara, I got a message for yer. It's Adam, 'e wants ter see yer. 'E's 'idin' at my place.'

It was the dwarf. At first I thought he was up to one of his usual tricks, then remembering Adam's words at the prison, 'I'm not stayin' 'ere. I'll break aht of 'ere some'ow', I began to wonder; was it possible that he had made an escape from the jail after all?

The dwarf tugged at my skirt. 'Come on. We don't want ter wait arahnd 'ere. Somebody might foller us.'

I still hesitated, unable to make up my mind if the dwarf was speaking the truth, but if Adam was in need of help I ought to get to him as soon as possible. Adam had told me on one occasion when we had been discussing the lecherous little maniac that the dwarf lived behind some empty warehouses. It would be just the sort of place for Adam to make for if he had escaped.

There was urgency and impatience in the dwarf's voice as he stepped away from me. 'Are yer comin' or aren't yer? P'raps Adam'll believe me now. I told 'im wot a fool 'e was, expecting 'elp from a toffee-nosed sod like you. S'only when yer dahn 'n aht yer find aht 'oo yer real mates are.'

I hesitated no longer. 'Shut your mouth,' I said angrily. 'Take me to Adam.'

To avoid being seen, he led me through darkened, stinking back alleys, stopping from time to time to listen in case someone was following. Convinced that he had been speaking the truth after all and that Adam was anxiously waiting for me, I was in a fever of impatience to get to him as quickly as possible and urged the dwarf to quicken his steps.

The wooden stairway we ascended took us to a jetty jutting out above the swirling waters of the river. Moving cautiously along a gangway to a small building at the very end of the wharf, we came to a door which the dwarf unlocked and pushed open, then made way for me to pass him. I couldn't see a thing as it was pitch black inside.

'Hurry up,' the dwarf whispered. 'I want to get the door shut before I light a candle.'

Treading warily, I moved slowly forward with hands outstretched in case I bumped into something and asked, 'Adam, where are you?'

I had hardly got the words out of my mouth when I was sent sprawling by the weight of the dwarf jumping on my back. We fell face downwards with his arms around my shoulders.

'Don't move,' he said in a hoarse, menacing voice. 'I got a knife at yer froat and I'll cut yer fuckin' 'ead orf if yer move as much as an inch.'

The sharp tip of the knife was pressing into my gullet as he lay astride me. I knew by the sound of his voice he meant every word of his threat and was scared spitless, waiting for what might come next. Terrified that this demented monster who had tricked me into this dark, lonely place might take it into his head to finish me off, there and then, I lay, my whole body paralysed with fear.

He forced me to crawl to a low, iron bed and onto a coarse mattress. He turned me onto my back and said, 'I'm puttin' the knife between me teef where I can get at it quick so lie still or else yer'll get yer bleedin' froat cut.'

Shuddering in fear with the blood pounding through my head, I felt a rope being tied around my wrist, and then jerked tight as he attached it to a corner of the bed; then he did the same with the other arm. He pulled the skirt away from my trembling legs, then tied my ankles to the bottom corners of the bed. I lay spread-eagled, limbs apart and unable to move more than an inch or two.

Scrambling on top of me, he pressed the razor sharp tip of the knife into the tender skin of my throat and loosened the buttons of my blouse. There were screams of terror rising from the whirlwind of my mind which only I could hear, that ended in deep sobs in my throat and left me in a cold sweat. Although I opened my lips at each scream it was only to gulp in more air, breathless with a shuddering which shook my whole body again and again.

Loosening his neckerchief, he forced it between my teeth and tied it in a strong knot at the back of my head. The darkness of the room seemed to cause him no hindrance in his movements.

I could only make muffled sounds of protest as he tore open my shift and pressed his wet, thick lips around my nipples. He went at them as if he was going to eat the tender flesh of my breasts, nibbling with his teeth and making disgusting nasal snuffles.

Getting off the bed he sunk his teeth into the soft rounded flesh of my belly. I gasped and let out a muffled cry of pain.

'That's nuthin' ter wot yer gonna get,' he sniggered as he undressed.

'Yer'll wish yer'd never been born by the time I've finished wiv yer. No-body knows yer 'ere so when I've 'ad all I want the fuckin' fishes can 'ave yer.'

Climbing on top of me, he attacked my breasts again. His thing was hardening against my belly as his lips and teeth savaged at my nipples. Crouching down between my thighs he got an inch or two of it into my giny then, getting a firm grip on my breasts, pulled himself up until he had got it all inside me. The strain on my breasts was unbearably painful and brought tears to my eyes. No words can express the agony I felt as his fingers dug into the tender skin each time he drew himself up to thrust himself into me. The stench of his sweat filled my nostrils and the spittle from his mouth dribbled onto my chest when his heavy breathing became harsh with lust. I was choking with nausea at the foul indignities he was inflicting on my defenceless body when the pig-like grunts from his slobbering lips quickened and he galumphed to a finish.

Throughout the hours of darkness my body was frequently defiled by his bestial, obscene attacks. I lay awake all night prostrated by grief and a burning humiliation that left a deep scar in my memories for many years.

Some slivers of daylight penetrating the oak boarded walls of the room shortly after dawn awoke the dwarf from his slumbers. Without a word to me he donned his clothes and departed, slamming the door behind him.

Soon after he had left, a storming rage of angry frustration set me struggling with the bonds that tied me to the bed. In a vain attempt to break the ropes around my ankles I gripped the iron bar of the bed and cut one of my fingers on a protruding splinter of metal. Casting my eyes upwards at the slight wound on my finger gave me the notion that if I could get the rope around my right wrist to that sharp point of metal I might, given time, be able to fray the strands of rope fibre and break free.

The possibility of being released from my bonds filled me with excite-ment and hope. Moving my body to the right hand side of the bed put a painful strain on my left ankle but slackened the rope around my wrist and made it possible for me to get part of it onto the sharp splinter. Holding it by the tips of my fingers, I moved it backwards and forwards in the hope of tearing one of the strands. A good hour passed before I felt something give. My fingers were losing their strength and I had to rest for a while before I was able to continue with my labours.

Some hours later I had sawn through most of the rope and was strain-ing with all my might to break free. Mad with anger and fear, I threw the whole weight of my body about the bed in a desperate struggle and suddenly rolled over onto my left side when the torn rope snapped under the strain. Exhausted and exhilarated, I wasted no time in loosening the knots that bound my other limbs.

When I got off the bed my knees buckled under me and I lost my balance several times before I could pull my skirt up to my waist and stand upright. Walking around the room, swinging my hands around, brought the blood back into my arms and legs again. I was overjoyed to be on my feet but my spirits were soon dampened when I tried to open the stout oak door. It was firmly locked and wouldn't budge an inch.

My hopes of freedom dashed to the ground, I gave vent to my anger by kicking at the door until my toes hurt. I went berserk, throwing a small table against a wall and hammering a wooden chair on the floorboards until it fell to pieces. I picked up a leg that had come off the table when it crashed against the wall and hit the door repeatedly with it until all the energy went out of me and I had to sink to the floor exhausted.

Panting for breath, I looked at the table leg, eyes glazed with tears of despair and thought of the dwarf coming back to get me. Picking up the table leg I swiped at the door, resolved to put up a fight to the death rather than let him ravish me again.

Sitting with my back to the wall I fell asleep and awoke with a start just before nightfall, sweating at the thought that he might have got in while I slept. Standing behind the door I waited for his return. The room was in complete darkness when I heard his footsteps on the stairway. With my heart thumping in my chest and my legs trembling, I raised the heavy leg high above my head as the key went into the lock, and held my breath in fearful suspense.

He pushed open the door and cleared his throat as he was about to close it. It was the sound of a dry cough that followed which directed my aim. Summing up all my strength I brought my wooden bludgeon swishing down with such a force that it must have cracked his skull open when it hit his head. Emotions of fear, hatred and vengeance flooded my mind, drowning all reason and sanity. In a fit of madness I repeatedly hammered the dwarf until, in a hot sweat of exhaustion, I pitched forward onto the battered body, gasping for air.

After a little while I struggled slowly to my feet. It felt like moving in a dream where everything seemed vague and shadowy, arousing no interest or curiosity. Pulling the door to, I locked it and dropped the key into the waters sloshing around under the river wharf. I have only a hazy memory of walking with quiet, timid steps along dark back-alleys, emerging into the gas lit Strand and ascending the stairs to my room with heavy feet.

Dirty and dishevelled and feeling dreadfully weary, I undressed leaving the clothes to lie where they had fallen. With soap and water the foul filth of the dwarf was scrubbed from my skin. Dropping onto the bed I pulled the cover up over my head and floated uneasily on the surface of a fitful sleep.

Awakening at daylight, shaking with a fever which consumed my flesh in waves of heat, I quenched my thirst with two glasses of water and returned to bed to fall into a deep sleep that held me fast until late the following afternoon. My first thoughts were of food for pains of hunger gnawed my innards. Rising from bed much refreshed, I quickly dressed and went into the streets to look for a seller of hot meat pies who traded nearby. As I approached his stall I searched my skirt pocket for coins to discover that there was only just sufficient money to purchase two pies.

The first pie tasted a treat and I wolfed it down before you could say Jack Robinson. As I hurried back to the house, street vendors were lighting their oil lamps against the dark shadows of nightfall. Looking at the remaining pie which I had intended giving to my two mud larks, the temptation was too much and with greedy hunger I ate half the pie before getting to my room. The tearful face of Peter looked up at me as I opened the cupboard door. The sight of his pitiful skinny little body and shrunken cheeks made me flush with shame that I had only half a pie to offer him. He was like a ravenous animal as he stuffed the remains of the pie into his mouth. It disappeared down his throat in no time at all.

"Ave yer got anyfink else?' he asked hopefully. 'We 'aven't 'ad nuffink to eat for nearly free days.'

'Where is Polly?'

He didn't answer, so I asked him again where his sister had got to.

'She's gorn ter get some money so we can eat.'

'Where?' I asked.

'A broffel 'ouse in Windmill Street.'

Stunned, I looked at him in astonishment. 'I don't believe you. That's a terrible thing to say about your sister. You shouldn't tell lies like that.'

'It's not a lie—it's true, I tell yer. I 'eard 'er askin' a girl where it was. Polly's gorn there now. She won't be back till late and she's bringin' me some food.'

He was obviously speaking the truth but it didn't make sense. What sort of work would a girl of eleven be doing in a brothel, I asked myself? Whatever the work, it was no place for a girl of her age and I made up my mind to fetch her straight away before any harm was done.

I knew Windmill Street was near the Queen's Theatre so it didn't take me long to find it, but none of the buildings looked like a whore-house. I'd never been in a place of that sort, which didn't help much, and I couldn't see me knocking on a door and asking 'Is this a brothel?' It was then I remembered a house in Tottenham Court Road where police were stationed. They would know the whereabouts of the brothel.

The policeman immediately showed concern when he heard I was seeking a girl of eleven who was thought to be in a brothel. He left me for a moment and returned with a police inspector, a thick-set, pugnacious, good looking man, who wanted to be assured that the girl was not yet twelve.

'Oh yes,' I answered. 'It was but three weeks ago that Polly told me it was her eleventh birthday. What difference does it make whether she is twelve or eleven?'

The inspector drew himself up. 'All the difference in the world, my dear. It's against the law for a man to have carnal knowledge of a girl under the age of twelve.'

'Do you mean to say it's alright for a man to sleep with a girl at that young age?'

'You shouldn't be surprised, young lady. I can detect some American in your speech. Am I right in thinking you have spent some time in that country?'

'Yes,' I answered, 'but what's that got to do with it?'

'Well . . . in some states of America the age of consent for girls is as low as seven years.'

'Seven years?' I echoed. 'It's too horrible to contemplate. What I want to know is can we do something about Polly?'

'If she's under twelve we can run Ned Dawkins into jail tonight, have no doubts about that. He has been too cunning for me up to now. I have visited his house three times but to no good purpose. He's got all his girls trained to answer that they are over twelve years old. That way he is on the right side of the law and I can't touch him.'

'Who is Ned Dawkins?' I asked.

'Ned is the whore master of the house you are looking for in Windmill Street. His pimps are everywhere, handing out little cards to gentlemen. "All the girls are under fifteen—fresh and clean—disease free" it says on the cards. He is an impudent villain who laughs behind my back every time I question his girls. I would like to get him behind bars and I'll do just that tonight, if your Polly tells me she is eleven. You will have to come with me to point out which is Polly.'

Turning to a police sergeant, 'I'll need you, too, to keep an eye on Ned while I search the rooms.'

The door of the brothel wasn't locked so the inspector pushed it open and almost bumped into Ned Dawkins as we entered. He gave a sharp command to his sergeant, 'Hold on to Ned' then, grabbing me by the arm, rushed me upstairs and into the first room on the landing.

An elderly gentleman, wheezing and blowing like a boiling kettle, had just finished his congress with one of the girls. The poor little thing was so small she was out of sight, completely covered by the old man's fat, naked body. The inspector, moving very quickly, got alongside the bed and rolled the man onto his back. Taken by surprise, a fair-haired young girl looked up at us with innocent blue eyes. There were no signs of developing womanhood on her youthful, baby skin.

'What's your name?' the inspector enquired gently.

'Ann Mundy, sir,' she replied nervously.

'How old are you?'

'Twelve, sir.'

'You don't look more than ten. Are you speaking the truth?'

'Yes, sir.'

Throughout all this the stout gentleman by her side just lay there with eyes closed. The inspector wasted no further time with her and made for the next room.

The uniform of an army officer was neatly folded over a chair and on the bed lay a well-built, muscular man about thirty. The hands of two naked girls, kneeling beside him, held his thick upright cock. It was only when they turned their faces towards us that I realized one of the girls was Polly. No bigger than walnuts, her protruding virginal breasts stood out on her skinny, ribbed chest.

'Polly,' I cried out. 'Get dressed at once. You are going back to Exeter Street straight away. This place is not for the likes of a young girl. I don't know what's got into you.'

'So this is Polly,' the inspector exclaimed in triumph. 'Now we are getting somewhere. What's your age, Polly?'

'Twelve,' she answered, right smartly.

'But, Polly,' I protested fervently, 'you told me it was your eleventh birthday about three weeks ago.'

'Nah, yer got it wrong. Yer want yer ears washed aht. I said twelve.'

'Twelve or eleven, I don't give a damn. Get your clothes on. I'm taking you home.'

'I 'aven't eaten for days. 'Ave yer got six shillin's cos that's wot this 'ere gentleman 'as given me.'

The older girl, kneeling on the other side of the man and still holding on to his cock, looked at me with an insolent grin on her face. 'Fer Gawd's sake give Polly six shillin's so she can give the gent 'is money back an' then get the 'ell aht of 'ere.'

I stood there exasperated, looking at the two girls, who, ignoring my presence in the room, had returned to their task of caressing the man.

Descending the stairs, fuming with anger, I vowed never to allow myself to get into a situation again where I was without money. But for a miserable six shillings, I could have saved Polly from becoming a prostitute. There is no justice in this world, especially for the hungry poor.

The following morning I made my way through a not particularly salubrious neighbourhood to the Queen's Theatre, determined to make a living somehow. My experience in American theatricals, I thought, should stand me in good stead in applying for work on the English stage. Viewing the bill posters exhibited on the facade of the theatre gave my hope of employment a further boost. They announced in large, bold letters a new version of *The Marble Heart*, a melodrama by Charles Selby, which would simulate classical statuary by means of living models. The theatre was to be re-opened by its new owners, Venus Productions, the following Saturday.

I was about to knock on one of the main front doors when a tall uniformed theatre commissionaire appeared by my side with a large key in his hand.

'And what can we do for you, young lady?' he enquired.

I explained briefly that I was an actress looking for work in the theatre.

'If that's the case you'll need to see Mr George Guyatt, the new owner and producer of this play,' he said, waving vaguely at the posters. ''E's probably still abed. Sleeps in one of the dressin' rooms,' he added, by way of an explanation.

I had to wait a good half hour before seeing Mr Guyatt who was busy frying a kipper for his breakfast. He was a large, fat man with a beetle-browed face and a completely bald head. Chewing slowly at a mouthful of kipper, he surveyed me from head to tail.

Swallowing his fish he compressed his lips and then questioned me in a loud, deep voice. 'Are you modest, bashful or given to prudery?'

Giving the matter some thought before answering, I replied with a grin, 'No, not particularly.'

'Then I may have some work for you. It's good pay. Eight pounds a week and all you will have to do is stand still through the first and third acts.'

Eight pounds was a great deal more than I had expected. I considered myself indeed fortunate to be offered such a sum when skilled craftsmen were earning less than two pounds a week for working twelve hours a day.

Swallowing another mouthful of kipper, Mr Guyatt went on to give a summary of the play. 'It's about a sculptor who loves unworthy women and neglects his mother and gentle sweetheart. Much of the melodrama takes place in Raphael Duchatlet's studio in Athens. The studio has a number of statues of Greek women, nude from waist upwards. How do you feel about having your tits whitewashed to look like marble? For that's the effect we will be aiming for: live women looking like marble statues.'

Once again I took my time before answering. The idea of exposing my breasts to the public took some getting used to. On the other hand, I was desperately hungry and without a penny to my name. As the saying goes, 'Beggars can't be choosers', and so I agreed to be one of the statues for the play.

In my impoverished circumstances I needed a friend who would loan me some money to tide me over until I received my first week's wage of eight pounds. The only friend that came to mind who might give me a loan was Florrie, the barmaid at 'The Half Moon' tavern.

Good, kind Florrie was generosity itself when I asked for a loan to see me through till pay day. Without a moment's hesitation she placed five sovereigns on the bar and asked me if that would be enough. Overcome with emotion and faint with hunger, I collapsed on a chair and burst into tears. Florrie's answer for anybody in trouble, a glass of brandy, was placed in my hands with her usual words for these occasions: 'There, there, luv, drink that up. It will do you good.'

I wanted so much to open my heart and tell her about what the dwarf had done to me and how I had left his battered, dead body locked away in a deserted wharf shed above the river—but managed to restrain myself. That was a secret I dare not reveal to anybody.

We had only three days for rehearsals before our first performance on Saturday. There was little for me to do but learn to stand very still which wasn't as easy as it sounds, as I soon discovered. Most of the work was done before we 'living statues' got onto the stage. With two different shades of whitewash we covered all our flesh from the waist to the hair line on our heads. I arrived before anybody else to apply whitewash to cover up the bruises and bite marks that the dwarf had inflicted on my breasts. The second coating of whitewash was of brown stain colouring which was brushed on lightly in streaks to give an effect of old marble. When it was dry, glycerine was dabbed on to make the marble colouring look smooth and shiny.

I must admit that when we put on the thin, wet pieces of cloth across our eyes and the papier mâché helmets which had received the same treatment of whitewash we really did look like Greek statues. The final touch was the white material which hung in folds from our waists.

The theatre was packed to full capacity for the opening night. When the stage curtains were drawn the audience gasped in amazement at this realistic display of semi-nude living statues and showed their appreciation with loud, prolonged applause. I could see very little of the audience through the tiny slits of my eye coverings but the thunderous applause lifted my spirits and I listened with great interest to the dialogue of the other play actors as the plot of melodrama unfolded.

In conversation with the other girls that evening I queried how the play had passed the censorious Lord Chamberlain. To my knowledge no English theatre had ever staged half-nude women. One of the older girls retorted with a sniff, 'It won't last for long, maybe a few weeks, before it will be closed down. It has escaped the eye of the Examiner of Plays because it has never been submitted to him.'

'If that is so,' I exclaimed in alarm, thinking of the five pounds that I owed Florrie, 'the theatre could close tomorrow.'

'Calm down,' a woman replied. 'A sleazy, backstreet theatre like this holds little interest for the Examiner of Plays. It will be weeks before he gets round to venturing into a notorious neighbourhood like Tottenham Street.'

The physical spectacle of women nude to the hips while a melodrama was being enacted on the stage created a sensation that brought in the crowd, including certain members of the nobility who were attracted to any place that offered something exceptional. The old 'Dust Hole' theatre was therefore enjoying a prosperity that, in my opinion, couldn't last for more than a few weeks. Every night the nearby streets were lined with rows of coroneted carriages and other expensive conveyances. We had been playing to full houses for over a fortnight. Surely it couldn't be long now, I thought, before news of our scandalous play reached the ears of the Examiner of Plays.

As it happened there was no cause to worry. Destiny had something else in mind for me. The commissionaire at the theatre entrance approached me one afternoon as I was about to go into the changing room. Could I spare him a few moments of my time, he asked politely, adding that he had a message of some importance for me. Intrigued, I accompanied him to a coffee house in Goodge Street where I was introduced to a Dr John Kersley. After shaking me by the hand, he passed over a fist full of sovereigns to the commissionaire who thanked him profusely, then made his departure.

Ordering coffee and cakes from an obsequious waiter, Dr Kersley then turned his attention to me. With a sonorous, authoritarian voice he declared, 'On the advice of a friend, I visited the Queen's Theatre last night with the sole purpose of seeing if you are the type of girl I am looking for to be a special attraction at my Palace of Health and Beauty in Pall Mall.'

He paused while the waiter placed on our table a pot of coffee and a plate of cakes. His tall, thin figure and elegant attire gave him the appearance of a man of some distinction. I must say I was impressed and a little overawed by the piercing dark eyes under a rather large forehead.

Viewing the cakes with some distaste, 'It's a poor assortment,' he announced. 'Would you prefer something else?'

On the plate were some 'Jumbles', thin crisp slices made from a mixture of treacle, butter and flour, and three-cornered puffs filled with sweet preserve.

'Not for me. "Coventrys" are my favourite cake,' I said, biting into the puff pastry and letting the delicious warm jam fill my mouth.

Handing me a steaming cup of coffee, he said, 'Now to business. I will give you thirty pounds a week for what you are doing for eight pounds.'

Astounded, my mouth full of pastry and jam, I gazed at him in wonder, astonished that anyone was prepared to give me thirty pounds a week, just for exposing naked breasts. There must be a catch in it somewhere, I thought. 'Just for showing my breasts?' I exclaimed.

'Well no. Not exactly. You will appear before my clientele with your skin covered in gold paint and completely naked but for a small piece of silk pasted over your vagina. For, make no mistake about it, you will be painted everywhere except on your back which will be covered by a rich, purple cloak, edged with white ermine.'

I sipped at my coffee, taking time to clear my confused thoughts. The idea of appearing before an audience without any clothes on didn't trouble me a great deal. After all, I wouldn't be completely naked, with a piece of painted silk covering my private parts. 'What will the Lord Chamberlain say to me appearing without clothing?' I asked doubtfully.

'He and his lackey, the Examiner of Plays, have no jurisdiction over medical establishments. There is nothing to fear from that quarter. We are not to be compared to a common playhouse,' he snorted with indignation. 'You will meet only the corps d'élite at my house in Pall Mall.'

It was clear from his angry expression that I had committed a faux pas and that I had better watch my P's and Q's in the future. 'The Palace of Health and Beauty sounds a grand place,' I said deferentially. 'When can I see it?'

Somewhat mollified by my change of tune, he replied, 'There is no time like the present. I will take you there now.'

'Oh! But I have to prepare for this evening's performance at the theatre.'

'Don't talk such nonsense, girl. They have no claim on you. You are working for me from now on. I will pay you for this week's work. Come along, there is no time to waste.'

In a hired Brougham drawn by two fine bay horses, the doctor confided that the display of live statues at the Queen's Theatre had attracted many of his clientele. The result of this had been an alarming reduction in the number of people who usually attended his lectures on health and beauty. Sir Charles Cheyney, a close friend, had seen me on the stage and had returned to Hebburn House full of enthusiasm for my physical charms. In a long discussion with the doctor that had lasted until the early light of dawn, they had come up with the idea of a Golden Virgin, and had worked out all the details of how it could be presented to the upper crust of society.

When the driver of the Brougham drove his carriage through the pillared entrance of Hebburn House I got my first glimpse through the foliage of the trees and shrubs of the impressive front of the Adam-designed mansion that was the Palace of Health and Beauty. On each side of the driveways that wandered across the spacious lawns of the front garden a number of elegant carriages were drawn up. Guarding the door were two very tall muscular porters wearing superb colourful liveries with large gold-laced cocked hats.

There were several ladies and gentlemen, attired in the height of fashion, conversing in the reception hall. Every room inside was set out in the most lavish style with magnificent furnishings. The walls were hung with long draped, ornate gilt mirrors and oil paintings of languid nudes displaying their beautiful bodies in most provocative poses.

A former banqueting hall was now used by the doctor for his lectures. About fifty carved mahogany chairs with rich red velvet seating faced a small stage at the rear of the room where there were two exquisite marble statues of the Greek goddesses, Hymen and Psyche.

I was taken to a sumptuously furnished, large bedchamber on the second floor where two women, seated before a glowing coal fire, immediately rose to their feet as the doctor entered. One of them, a handsome woman about forty, was introduced as the matron and housekeeper. After a few words with Dr Kersley she took her leave of us with a polite apology for her hasty departure. I was to learn at a later date that she had the honour of sharing the doctor's bed and had his authority to dismiss any member of the staff who didn't meet with her approval.

The other woman, Betty, was in her early twenties and a different class of person altogether. An overblown blonde, plebeian in looks and thoughts and, as I was soon to discover, prone to excitable, shrill laughter when a man was present. She was to be my personal maid when not working downstairs, so the doctor informed me.

The next morning and during the days that followed experiments were made with various shades of gold paint on my skin to see which would shine most brightly when dry. My first ordeal was of having a triangular piece of silk pasted over my private parts and, later, the pain of it being removed. It was not to the doctor's liking as the covering showed a marked line beneath the paint. He refused to have any further experiments until all the hairs at my armpits and crotch had been removed.

It took Betty and me nearly a whole day with small, metal tweezers to painfully pull out every hair on the parts affected. This harsh treatment left the skin inflamed and sore and another two days elapsed before I could bear to have the silk pasted on me again. The doctor was still not satisfied and, taking up the material, he cut out a small oval, pasted this miniscule of silk over my slot and insisted on a fold running down through the middle. The gold paint was then applied and he stood back, well pleased with his efforts to achieve the natural appearance of the nude female body and announced that invitations could now go out to the crème de la crème of high society for the first tableau of the Golden Virgin and her male attendants.

'What male attendants?' I asked.

'Two magnificent coal-black negroes wearing only brief loin cloths,' was the answer as he departed hurriedly from the room.

In the early mornings before the ladies and gentlemen arrived, I was allowed to wander around as I pleased in the company of the ebullient Betty. Hebburn House was nothing less than a celestial paradise of sensuality, solely devoted to pleasing the sexual whims and vanities of the nobility. Health and beauty were its supposed aims but little attention was given to either. Private rooms for 'treatment' abounded everywhere. What went on behind those closed doors would have brought a blush to the face of Satan himself.

All the staff had been chosen for being personally agreeable, blooming in health, sweet tempered and with a commitment to indulge the clientele in whatever they desired. They were attired in white, diaphanous chiffon robes drawn in at the waist by a gilt, chainlink girdle. Beneath their robes there was only a small loin cloth for the men and lace-edged pantaloons for the girls. The pantaloons were really two separate garments, one for each leg, and held at the waist by a silk tape.

For ladies suffering from ennui but fearing pregnancy there were dildoe rooms where negroes, or white males, administered to their need for excitement and satisfaction.

Young women with a rare talent for giving pleasure by massage served the noble gentry in chambers set aside for that purpose. The medical needs of the aristocracy were not entirely forgotten. Baths of warm sand mixed with aromatics and healing herbs gave relief to those with in-flamed and swollen joints. The Hermippus technique of gaining new life and vigour by inhaling the breath of young maidens was very popular with the more elderly gentlemen whose hands were allowed to stray between the open pantaloons during treatment.

Punctuated with bursts of shrill laughter, Betty went into lengthy de-tails that left nothing to the imagination as she described these activities with obvious enjoyment. Although I liked the girl, despite her faults, the other members of the staff had a very poor opinion of Betty for being always ready to oblige any man who asked for it without thought of reward for services rendered. They considered she was as common as a barber's chair and just as easy to get into. What I liked about Betty was that she never had any reverence for titles. Dukes, lords, or randy porters were all the same to her; she made no discriminations. To her they were just men who had what she described as the 'necessary dilator' between their legs that gave her so much pleasure.

With gold paint applied, auburn hair brushed until it shone like the gold on my body, I stood waiting to be called for my first appearance as the Golden Virgin. After Betty had tied the ribbons of the purple cloak around my neck in a neat bow, she led me to a full-length mirror. The transformation was such that, apart from the hair, I was unrecognizable as my former self. The mirror reflected a gold statue of lifelike propor-tions. Following out the doctor's instructions, I arched my back and straightened my shoulders. This stance brought a pert, upward tilt to my gold breasts, bringing a statuesque beauty and dignity to my naked body. The hazel eyes in the mirror reflected admiration and pride for the gold goddess image.

The oily black negroes were about to lift me to their shoulders when the doctor hurried into the room with a many-faceted, highly polished piece of glass that sparkled like a large, cut diamond. With the aid of some very sticky substance he placed it firmly in my navel.

Sitting high on the shoulders of the negroes, I looked down at the doctor as he slowly, with measured steps, led us into the lecture hall to the sound of a fanfare of trumpets. There must have been nearly a hun-dred people in the hall, all agog and impatiently waiting for my entrance. About fifty or more were seated in the mahogany chairs, the rest of the people standing at the rear and against the side walls. The sound of the trumpets ceased as I descended to stand on a raised platform covered in rich red velvet.

At the first sight of my gold nakedness the audience were awe-struck, mouths agape and eyes nearly popping out of their heads. The men were gasping for breath and devouring every inch of my body with their lustful eyes. The ladies were admiring the muscular proportions of the negroes who stood at a lower level on either side of me. They were all spellbound for a moment or two, then quite spontaneously, they started to clap and cry out their applause.

As soon as the excitement died down, Dr Kersley commenced his lecture. I thought it was very interesting but very few of the people seemed to pay much attention. The theme of his talk was fertility and virility. Using his cane to point out on my body the positions of various organs in the female, he launched into an attack on the faith some persons had in the aphrodisiac powers of Spanish Fly. He said more natural methods of arousal would bring about true happiness and conception.

He then spoke of the 'Celestial Bed' that, until I arrived on the scene as the Golden Virgin, had been the main attraction of the establishment.

'This bed of fertility,' he said with pride, 'is the only bed of its kind in the whole, wide world. It is my invention to stimulate any gentleman and his lady desirous of progeny. Twelve feet long and nine feet wide, it is supported by forty pillars of brilliant glass of the most exquisite workmanship, in richly variegated colours and surrounded by eight large mirrors whose reflections fire the limbs with greater energy.

'We all know how virile and excitable a stallion becomes when taken to a mare. To bring vigour and warm desire to the gentleman, the mattress is stuffed with hair from stallions' tails that have a buoyance which is most helpful to the male in his efforts to propagate. To invigorate both parties the mattress has numerous inlets which are filled with ethereal spices and a pot-pourri of aromatized essences which give off, with each bounce, a most pleasing fragrance to stir the emotions of love.'

Throughout the discourse his face remained at all times solemn and his voice extremely earnest. 'Primitive tribes in tropical climates have a form of contraception where the woman, after intercourse with the male, jumps violently up and down. My bed is designed to achieve the opposite result. It has a mechanism that, after coitus, tilts the lady's hips upwards to facilitate impregnation. The female desiring pregnancy must then lie in this position for at least half an hour to allow the spermatozoa to drain into the ovum.'

Carried away by his own eloquence, he spread his arms out wide as if he was about to bestow a blessing on the audience. 'The superior ecstasy which the parties enjoy in the celestial bed can bring about the utmost satisfaction, for the barren are more likely to become fruitful when they are powerfully agitated in the delights of love. Any gentleman wishing to spend an evening in the celestial bed with his lady wife, for a complement of a fifty pound bank note, may be permitted to partake of the heavenly joy it affords.'

Night after night, for weeks, I had to listen to these lectures while the men explored every inch of my body with lust-filled eyes and the women speculated on the virility of the negroes flexing their muscles beside me. Nevertheless, it was an easy way to earn thirty pounds a week. There was little need or opportunity for me to spend my money as I was only allowed out for two mornings each week. The doctor didn't want me to mingle with his clientele.

There was much curiosity as to my identity and Dr Kersley, knowing that a mystery is always an object of great attraction, added further interest to the enigma of the Golden Virgin by hinting that I was an illegitimate child of a European prince. Everyone actually believed that I was a virgin and some of the more wealthy gentlemen had offered the doctor considerable sums of money for the privilege of being the first man to bed me. He had to refuse these requests for the honour of depriving me of my maidenhood, for once it became known that I had lost my virginity I would lose my attraction as a desirable female.

In the exciting intoxication of my life as the Golden Virgin, I had scarce given a thought to my value as the star attraction of Hebburn House. It wasn't until the end of June that I learnt from Betty that people were paying two guineas for admission to the lecture hall to see my naked, gold-painted body. It didn't take me long to work out that Dr Kersley was collecting over fourteen hundred pounds a week for displaying his Golden Virgin.

That very evening, five minutes before I was due to appear in the lecture hall, I demanded a wage of one hundred pounds a week for my services. I was prepared for the angry consternation of Dr Kersley when I made a claim for more money, but not for the abuse that came from the tongue of his matron and housekeeper, Mrs Murdock.

In the convivial company of the nobility Mrs Murdock was all grace and charm, aping their manners and speech but if any of the staff upset her she upbraided them with a stream of scurrilous obscenity. Lurking behind that sweet smile and snooty voice was a vitriolic, foul-mouthed harridan.

'Shut your filthy gob, you cock-teasing, dirty bitch or we'll throw you back into the gutter where you belong,' she yelled in an intimidating voice.

It was obvious that she had been nursing a jealous hatred of me for some time, and it was bursting to be released. In a blazing temper she made a swipe at me with an open hand and I reeled back as she screeched at the top of her voice, 'You've got a bloody cheek, you greasy-arsed slut. A hundred pounds just for showing your tits and buttocks? You brazen whore, who do you think you are?'

My hackles rose and, looking at her with lips curled in contempt, I spat out, 'You are a two-faced hypocrite, coarse and disgusting and clearly not a lady. I only wish those people waiting in the lecture hall could hear you now. The stench from your filthy mouth turns my stomach.'

She rushed at me, tooth and nail, ready to tear me to pieces. Before we could get to blows the doctor intervened, holding us apart at arm's length, and ordered Betty to take Mrs Murdock to her room.

With angry eyes wet with tears of vexation, she hurled further abuse at my head before Betty could get her through the doorway.

Glaring at me, the doctor gasped fiercely, 'Get down to the lecture hall at once.'

I stood my ground and answered calmly, 'Not before I get your solemn promise that you will pay me a hundred pounds a week from now on.'

He cast his eyes about the room as if seeking inspiration, took out his watch and looked at it anxiously and sighed in resignation at the stubborn expression on my lips. 'Alright, you ungrateful hussy. You have my word that's what your wages will be in the future.'

My ears were deaf to the lecture that evening. I was too busy calculating how much money I had banked since coming to Hebburn House and what it would soon amount to. Seven weeks at thirty pounds plus two months at my new wage came to a sum exceeding a thousand pounds, which meant that within a short period I had risen from abject poverty to become a woman of independent means. I was cock-a-hoop at the thought of having enough money in the bank to keep me in comfort for at least three years. When you are flat broke you only have the choice of digging your own grave or getting back up on your feet, determined never to be penniless again. Money is a commodity you can depend on, which is more than you can say about men.

Mrs Murdock never ever spoke to me again but from that time on I knew she would be scheming to find some way of getting rid of me. It took her three weeks to find a girl who could stand in for me as the Golden Virgin if ever, as she put it to the doctor, I was ill or unable for some reason to take my place on the podium in the lecture hall. I could see how her cunning mind was working. With a substitute Golden Virgin waiting in the background I would never again be able to hold the doctor to ransom for more money.

Mrs Murdock's prodigy, Virginia Norman, was well-named but ill-equipped for the part intended because she was inexperienced, shy and, actually, was a sixteen-year-old, untouched virgin. I knew instinctively that in her innocence she would be unable to stand as I did, stark naked before the hungry lust of dozens of male eyes, and yet pose as an unruffled virgin, cool and confident in her superiority.

I took to her straight away. You couldn't help liking Virginia; she was so sweet natured and eager to help Betty when she was applying the gold paint to my body.

After my appearance on the podium they worked together removing most of the gold paint with a solvent especially prepared by the doctor. And then, with me lying in a warm soapy bath, they would gently pick away at any remnants of the paint still adhering to my skin.

Virginia was about my height with the same colouring in hair but her under-developed body needed to be filled out if Mrs Murdock intended to fool the clientele that they were looking at the same female who had appeared before them since the beginning. Every day the poor girl was stuffed with fattening foods and the best cuts of meat in an effort to get her to put on more flesh. I knew my days as the Golden Virgin were numbered and estimated that it would take at least a month before she came up to my proportions.

One evening near the end of July, I had just finished my bath and was about to dress when the doctor marched into my room, ordering Betty and Virginia to go downstairs, and sat in a chair with an annoyed expression on his face waiting for me to finish dressing.

After a while, he coughed nervously and asked, 'Do you remember, Dara, when we first met I spoke to you of Sir Charles Cheyney, the gentleman who saw you at the Queen's Theatre and recommended you as the girl to be the Golden Virgin?'

'Yes,' I answered, wondering what was coming next.

'He has become quite obsessed with the idea of seeing you in the nude, without the gold paint, and has been pestering me for some weeks now with his requests. It has been very difficult for me because it was his idea in the first place to present you painted in gold and also he happens to be a friend of long standing.'

'If that is all he wants,' I said, 'and you want to oblige him, I have no objections.'

'Believe me, Dara, I've done my best to put him off but now he is threatening to tell everyone where we found you if I don't give way.'

'Is he here now?' I asked.

'Yes. He's waiting downstairs for your answer.'

'See to it that Betty and Virginia are kept busy elsewhere,' I said, 'then bring him up here. The sooner we get this business over with the better.'

I was trying to tidy up my room when the doctor returned to introduce me to Sir Charles Cheyney. Bowing from the waist, he then took my hand in a refined, delicate manner and brought it to his lips. 'I am most charmed and very grateful that you have granted me this favour.'

This gentlemanly approach was in keeping with his dress and deportment. His savoir-faire and courtesy were far from what I had expected. I had assumed a man who wanted a private view of a girl in the nude would be an old reprobate, physically gross and mentally repellant. With such a man I would have had no qualms about displaying myself naked provided he didn't touch me, but Sir Charles didn't fit into this picture by any means.

He was about my age, tall and slender, with very handsome features. I liked the sound of his voice, too, which was low and melodious. Because he was so attractive I was overcome with modesty and embarrassment. The thought of being just a nude object to him filled me with self disgust. Under different circumstances I would have set out to gain his admiration and respect.

He must have sensed the confusion of my feelings for, as soon as Dr Kersley left us alone together, he said, 'Dara, I know so little about you that my principal aim in seeking this assignation was in the hope that we may become better acquainted. There is no need for you to undress. I have seen your beautiful body many times in the lecture hall for I am one of your most devoted admirers. Please be seated so that we can converse in comfort.'

Relaxed in a chair, I now examined him more closely. He was undoubtedly the most beautiful man I had ever seen, with short dark hair, tightly curled, greyish-blue eyes beneath thick masculine eyebrows which gazed at me quizzically. There were small lines of humour around his mouth and eyes which softened the effect of his strong cleft chin and brought a warm expression of geniality to what would otherwise have been a stern face.

'Is Dara your real name?' he asked diffidently with an amused expression on his face.

'Yes. I am Dara Kennet from the Isle of Man but recently returned from a visit to America.'

'Kennet,' he repeated. 'An uncommon name, if I may say so. I know of only one Kennet, a man of my own age with whom I was well acquainted when we were at Heaton together; a rather effeminate boy who shared a school desk with me for a number of years.'

He mused on the matter for a moment, then exclaimed, 'Why, that is quite extraordinary! James Kennet was also in America last year. Maybe you met him?'

'Yes, maybe,' I answered in some confusion. 'Where is he now . . . I would very much like to meet him?'

He gave me a long searching look. 'You know this man, don't you. Is it possible you are a relation of his?'

Getting no answer to his questions he asked, 'Have I stumbled on to some secret in your past? Why the reticence? Surely you can trust me; I wish you no harm.'

He was right, of course. There was no need to hide the truth from him. It was possible that the man who had been his schoolboy friend was the same James Kennet to whom I was wed. The only way to find out if this was so would be to trust him.

'Sir Charles,' I said, but got no further for he interrupted me to exclaim with a smile, 'Forget the title; just address me as Charles. There is no need for formalities between friends.'

'Very well,' I replied. 'The truth of the matter, Charles, is that the James Kennet you speak of could be the man I married in New York and who deserted me shortly after we arrived back in England. But I cannot be sure. Where and how can I meet him? Is he in London?'

'Yes, to be sure. But from what I know of him he is hardly likely to be the type of man YOU would choose for a husband. I saw him but only yesterday, strolling down the Strand with his lover, Nicholas Dawney. No, not your man, I'm sure.'

While he was speaking I remembered something that would be a means of identifying this James Kennet as my husband: a birthmark on his neck that looked like a small red ladybird.

'Tell me, Charles, has your James got a birthmark?'

'Why, yes,' he answered quickly. 'I saw it often enough when we sat beside each other at school. It was like a little red beetle just under his left ear. I know it was on the left side of his neck because he always sat to the right of me.'

That clinched it. There was no longer any doubt in my mind that he was speaking of my James. In my agitation I stood up and declared that I would go to him at once.

'Not before you satisfy my curiosity on one or two questions that puzzle me,' Charles replied calmly. 'In my opinion James is incapable of husbanding any woman, however attractive she may be. How did you come to marry him?'

I told him the truth of how we met, our first night together in bed and the celibate months of marriage that followed the wedding.

When I had finished, he said, 'How dreadful it must have been for you, my dear, and yet how fortunate for, as it turns out, you are married to one of the wealthiest men in England. A man who owns thousands upon thousands of acres of land, an elegant town house, a huge mansion in Berkshire and an equally large house in Kent. His father died about two months ago. He was out hunting and his horse threw him head first into a tree. James, being his only child, succeeded to the title and inherited a great fortune.'

'What shall I do, Charles? Please advise me.'

'It is much too late for you to go calling on James tonight. Besides, think of the embarrassment for all parties concerned if we found him in bed with his lover? Will you put yourself in my hands and allow me to protect and support you in what could be a very tricky confrontation with your husband? It will have to be in the morning for later in the day I board a ship bound for Australia where I am to be secretary and aide to my uncle who is taking up a very responsible position out there.'

'What will I say to Dr Kersley?' I asked, anxious as to what I should do next and very much disturbed by this news of titles, great wealth and male lovers.

'Dr Kersley? Ah, I can see trouble there. It would be better for your future position in society if he knew nothing about this. Will it take long for you to pack your belongings? We could make our escape now, before he returns to your room.'

I threw some clothing into my leather bag and followed Charles down some back stairs to an exit at the rear of the building. Once out in the open we ran helter-skelter across the grassy lawns to his waiting carriage. 'Hurry, Baldwin,' he shouted to the coachman. 'Make all haste to Cheyney House.' In the plush, dark interior of the carriage I lay back to recover my breath.

Charles put a protective arm around me and I snuggled up close to him feeling warm and secure in his embrace. He kissed me warmly on the lips and I responded with all the affection of my nature. Cool fingers loosened the buttons of my blouse and delicately caressed the nipples of my breasts. To my hot delight he made free with my body. His hands were everywhere. When his fingers began to gently probe between the tender lips of my giny I arched my back in an intensity of feeling.

My clothing was in great disarray when the coachman brought the horses to a halt outside Charles' home in Catherine Place. All was quiet in this by-street sheltering near Buckingham Palace. Luckily there was nobody about to see me descend from the coach and enter the house. Taking up the small lighted candle placed in a china bowl on the hallway side table, Charles led me upstairs to his bedroom.

Clothing was scattered all over the room when our bared bodies came together in a breathtaking embrace. His cock filled out and pressed against my burning flesh. It was so sturdy and thick when I grasped it in my hand. Getting down on my knees, I held the throbbing cock firmly as I delicately licked its swollen head with the tip of my tongue. I nearly choked when, in a spasm of quickened lust, his hips thrust forward and it penetrated the top of my throat.

Throwing me on the bed he came on me like a raging bull, churning my innards with savage lust. Strong hands gripped the cheeks of my bottom and pulled me into him as he strove with rapist thrusts to get deep inside me. I brought my knees up high and submitted willingly to this ravishment. Swirling in a storm of passion that shook my innermost senses, my feelings rose and clashed in an explosive climax as his hands pulled my buttocks up to him for my giny to receive the gushing sap from his dilated, pulsating member. We lay, released from all earthly desires, our senses dissolved in a blissful nirvana of extinction that the French speak of as 'the little death'.

Bright sunlight was filtering through the window curtains when I awakened from a night of Elysian dreams. The polished oak of the wall panelling and the wide floorboards shone in the morning light making a perfect setting for the satinwood cabinets and gilt chairs. Stretching out, I looked up at the canopy of the ornate four-poster bed and sighed in the luxury of happy contentment. Charles chose that moment to come out of his sleep and pull me close to him.

'Good morning, Lady Pulrose,' he murmured in my ear.

'Is that really my name?' I asked.

He nodded. 'Yes. Your James is now the seventh Lord Pulrose.'

'Is it all true, what you told me last night?'

'What in particular?' he replied with a smile.

'About James being very wealthy and his lover, Nicholas Dawney.'

'Of course it's true, every word of it.'

'I'm not looking forward to meeting them. What shall I do? And, oh, Charles, where shall I go afterwards? It'll be impossible for me to live in the same house with them. I just couldn't do it.'

'You can live here. I shall be in Australia for at least two years. In my absence the family solicitor will be paying the servants and other household expenses. But the house needs a trusted occupant to keep an eye on the servants who tend to get lazy and negligent if there isn't anyone to give them their orders daily. Will you do that for me while I'm away?'

'Charles, you are a most kind and generous man but I haven't the means to keep this place in the style your servants would expect.'

'Nonsense,' he retorted. 'You are forgetting that your husband is very wealthy. We will see him this morning and demand an annual financial allotment that will enable you to live in accordance with your social standing as a member of the nobility.'

Wasting no further time on words, Charles threw back the bedclothes, got between my legs and showered kisses on my breasts. Flushed with excitement, he rolled onto his back and brought me above him to suck at the nipples of my breasts. When he came up to give me a kiss on the lips I got into a kneeling position and guided him into my moist giny. Moving with a gentle rhythm up and down on him as you would with a cantering horse, aroused my sensual desires to a fever pitch. With a desperate, urgent need to reach the heights of my passion I flung myself down on him and, with my hands gripping his shoulders, I ravished him as fiercely as he had possessed me the previous night.

Crying out in the intensity of my ecstasy, I gave myself up to him when he got a firm hold on the cheeks of my buttocks and forced me hard up against his loins each time he thrust into me. I lay limp across him, all passion spent as he had his way with me, rotating my hips with strong hands until he could hold back his seething lust no longer. My belly, pushed up tight against his, convulsed as he emptied his spurting, manly essence into me.

When Charles recovered his breath he patted me on the bottom and asked me to move over as he was going to ring for breakfast. After giving two strong pulls on the bell rope he got back into bed. Shortly after that his butler arrived holding a large wooden tray of cooked food—kippers, sausages, bacon, eggs—and chunks of bread. Placing the tray on a side table he asked his master if he would prefer tea or coffee. On receiving the answer that it would be a coffee morning he gave a slight bow and departed to go downstairs. I was watching him closely the whole time he was in the room and not once did he glance in my direction. Indeed he didn't look at Charles either and yet he returned with another plate and cutlery within less than a minute.

While we were eating I commented on Billings, the butler, not looking at either of us as we lay in bed.

'A well-trained butler should never look at you when he is speaking or when you are addressing him,' he answered. 'This applies to all the servants. If any of them should have the impertinence to do so in my absence, dismiss them immediately. I will not tolerate servants who do not know their place. Just remember, Dara, that they are employed to do your bidding at any time of the day or night. Believe me, you will lose their respect if you do anything for yourself. Don't even brush your own hair. There is a personal maid to do that and if, by chance, you wish the fire to be stirred to life with a poker, then you must ring for a servant to perform this service for you.'

'Won't they talk about you and me being in bed together?'

'Only amongst themselves. Never to anyone else,' he answered. 'Our conduct in or out of bed is none of their business. Don't concern yourself with what they think or talk about. They are our inferiors, in every respect, little better than dumb animals and to be treated as such.'

* * *

When the front door was opened to us at Astral House, Charles instructed the butler to inform Lord Pulrose that Sir Charles Cheyney awaited him.

Taking me by the arm Charles pushed the butler to one side just as he was about to knock on a door and entered the room unannounced. James and his friend were lounging in armchairs near a large marble fireplace. Hearing the butler's outraged protests at our rudeness, James looked round and went pale when he caught sight of me.

Quickly recovering from the shock of my sudden appearance in his morning room, he got to his feet and stood before me. 'Dara! Is it really you?' he said in a voice just above a whisper, then flung his arms around me.

I thought he would never stop hugging me. When he did, I saw that he was wet-eyed and overcome with this unexpected reunion. While James was wiping the tears from his eyes I took a quick glance at his friend, Nicholas Dawney. There was a sardonic expression on his face and, in his eyes, a look of derisive contempt for James and me as we struggled to contain our emotions.

'It is such a relief to see you, Dara, standing there, alive and well,' exclaimed James as he stood back and viewed me fondly. 'I got back to the hotel only hours after you had left and have been on the lookout for you ever since. Where did you get to? Nothing ever came of my enquiries as to your whereabouts.'

'I don't want to talk about it James.'

He embraced me again. 'I understand, Dara. It can wait. Oh, it's so good to see you again. I'll get the servants to prepare a room for you. This is your home from now on.'

'No, James, I cannot stay here,' I said quietly, looking meaningfully at Nicholas Dawney, who was staring at me with a supercilious grin.

James had momentarily forgotten Nicholas Dawney's presence in the room and had the decency to blush in embarrassment when he got the meaning of my words.

'There are other houses where you can stay,' he said hesitantly. 'You can have Kennet Towers in Berkshire and we have another great house in Kent. I will make out an allotment so that you will have sufficient money for all your needs. After all, Dara, you are my wife and I want to look after you and make amends for . . . Please let me try to make up for all that you have suffered in the past.'

I felt ashamed at the vile thoughts I had harboured about him since we had parted at 'The Eight Bells' hotel. Although obviously infatuated with

Nicholas Dawney, he was still very fond of me and concerned for my welfare. His desire to make amends was very touching but I was determined to be free and uninvolved in his liaison with Nicholas.

'Charles is sailing for Australia on the first tide tomorrow and has kindly offered me the hospitality of his home in Catherine Place while he is abroad,' I said.

Getting on to his feet, Charles decided this was the moment to discuss the question of my allotment.

'Well, James, friend of my schooldays, have you forgotten me?' he asked.

'Of course I haven't,' replied James quickly. 'Forgive me, I was so overcome that I had thoughts only for Dara. Accept my heartfelt thanks for bringing her back to me. I owe you a great debt of gratitude which I will never forget. Please allow me to pay all your household expenses while Dara is a guest at your home. It is the least I can do under the circumstances, my dear fellow.'

'Why, that's very decent of you,' said Charles with a smile. 'I'll instruct my solicitors to send you a monthly account. Now, what allotment are you going to bestow on your Lady Pulrose?'

James thought for a moment. 'Would ten thousand a year be adequate?' he asked tentatively.

Charles fixed his eyes on James' nose in a steady stare. He told me afterwards that this was his habit when he wished to make anyone feel uncomfortable.

'Twenty thousand?' James stuttered questioningly.

Charles didn't answer. The silence was painful as he continued to stare at the tip of James' nose.

'Tell me, what do you think would be an adequate allotment to settle on Dara?' James asked, appealing to Charles and squirming with embarrassment.

'One must take into consideration that a lady in high society has many expenses if she is going to mix with the nobility on equal terms,' answered Charles gravely. 'You are a man of great wealth, James. You wouldn't want your friends to think that your wife was living on slender means.'

'Would thirty thousand be sufficient do you think?' asked James doubtfully.

Charles pursed his lips. 'Yes, that is possibly the right figure.' Then, turning to me, he asked, 'Will you settle for thirty thousand, Lady Pulrose?'

These large sums of money they were bandying about as if they were discussing pennies just left me dizzy and speechless. I could only nod my head in amazement at Charles' perspicacity.

'Good,' exclaimed James with relief that satisfactory arrangements had been made for my future welfare. 'Will you stay and have coffee with us?'

Charles, with polite apologies, explained that there was insufficient time as many arrangements had to be made before he departed for Australia.

James embraced me at the front door and extracted a promise that I would call again as soon as I had settled into my new home.

I was very upset when Charles departed for Tilbury Docks in the afternoon. Although I had known him but a short time, I was heartbroken at the thought that we wouldn't see each other again for a very long time and wept bitter tears when he kissed me goodbye on the doorstep. In less than twenty-four hours he had brought great changes to my lifestyle. His friendship and affection was something I would treasure in the conviction that destiny would somehow bring us together again.

Later that afternoon Billings, the butler, assembled all the servants, including Baldwin, the coachman, in the hall for my inspection.

'This, my Lady,' he said, pointing to a pleasant, plump woman, 'is the cook, Mrs Wakeford,' and so went on down the line introducing maids and other servants. There were nine of them in all and everyone showed great respect in my presence. I could think of nothing to say so I dismissed them with a nod of the head and they went off downstairs to attend to their various duties.

PART SIX

Midnight Lover

During the days that followed I revelled in the luxury of being waited on hand and foot and spent over eight hundred pounds on fashionable, expensive costumes and millinery. An even larger sum was spent on jewellery. I was delirious with excitement each time a package of clothing was delivered at the door and my personal maid, Tilly, helped me dress in my new attire. She fussed around me smoothing out the creases as I stood admiring myself in front of the bedroom mirror.

Some of the costumes were really beautiful and did much to enhance my appearance. My favourite was a rose pink walking out dress with a bodice that hugged my figure and open sleeves that revealed the puffed chemisette underneath. The skirt had a very wide base with broad white ribbon bands below the knee.

I was wearing this costume on the day I spied John Sweetapple in the vicinity of Westminster Abbey and invited him back to Cheyney House for coffee and a chat.

His was the first familiar face I had seen since Charles sailed for Australia. Now that the excitement of buying new clothes and jewellery had died down, there was little to occupy my time. Money and a title don't necessarily bring friends. Life had become tedious and boring and I longed for company and conversation for I am very gregarious by nature.

It was plain that John Sweetapple, a thin man with pale, watery eyes, didn't recognize me for there was a puzzled look on his grey, wrinkled face when I greeted him like an old friend. I had to remind him of the times when James and I first arrived in London and spent several evenings at his rooms listening to him reading his plays.

His face cleared as the memory came back to him, but, to my disappointment, he showed little desire to continue our acquaintanceship and was about to move on when I exclaimed, 'There have been great changes in our lives since last we saw you. Following his father's death, James has succeeded to the title of Lord Pulrose.'

It seems everyone loves a lord for this news brought about a tremendous change in Sweetapple's attitude to me. Stunned, he looked at me with great interest, admired my dress, shook my hand with enthusiasm and said in a deferential low voice, 'And you, of course, are Lady Pulrose . . . Er . . . How is . . . er . . . James these days?'

I explained briefly that we were living apart but remained good friends.

By this time he was leading me by the arm in the direction he had been walking when I first approached him. Releasing my arm from his hold, I beckoned to Baldwin to bring the carriage alongside and asked Sweetapple if he was refusing my invitation to have coffee with me. The poor man was all confusion and apologies, tripped on the step of the carriage as he was getting in and nearly fell into my lap.

At Cheyney House, with fancy cakes spread out in front of him and a cup of coffee in his hand, he calmed down to tell me what he had been doing since we last met. I learned that he had given up writing his boring plays and had become an actor manager with his own theatrical company touring provincial theatres. His play-actors were pressing him to arrange another tour. Theatres in Manchester, Liverpool and Dublin were available to him; all that was lacking was the finance to set it all in motion.

I knew this talk was leading up to a request for money and was prepared with an answer. The intoxicating excitement of a group of theatricals on tour was still fresh in my memory. It was just what was needed to lift my spirits.

He eventually came to the point. 'Lady Pulrose . . . er . . . I wonder, er . . . if you have given thought to . . . er . . . being a patron of the arts?'

'Certainly not,' I snapped, 'and I have no intention of doing so. How much money do you want?'

Flustered by direct speech, he hummed and ahed. 'Er . . . a hundred pounds.' Seeing the smile on my face gave him more confidence. 'Er . . . that would be the rental for . . . er . . . the theatres.'

'John Sweetapple,' I said accusingly, 'you are not being entirely truthful with me, are you? I will finance your tour up to the sum of three hundred pounds on condition that, at one of the theatres, you put on *Romeo and Juliet* and I play the part of Juliet.'

When he stopped gulping in surprise at this windfall of money that was coming his way, we discussed details of the tour and, because he had doubts about a Shakespearian play, it was agreed we would have two or three rehearsals before our first performance of *Romeo and Juliet* in Dublin.

This suited me perfectly. I would have the company of the other actors for two weeks without any responsibilities and, on the third week, realize an ambition I had nursed for a long time of playing Juliet.

There were one or two other conditions I insisted on before we parted that day. 'No one,' I told him, 'must know that I am a titled lady or that the financial backing for the tour is coming from me.'

'By what name shall I . . . er . . . introduce you to the rest of the company?' he asked.

'We must think of a name. What do you suggest?' But nothing he came up with met with my agreement. In despair, I asked him for his mother's maiden name and promised to accept it as my stage name, whatever it was.

'Er . . . Nellie Clifden,' he answered, looking at me warily to see how I would respond.

'It is not the name I would have chosen but it will have to do. I refuse to discuss the matter any further but do remember in the future to address me by that name and not as Lady Pulrose.'

That was how I was known throughout the tour. Nellie Clifden, an actress who had recently returned to England after a lengthy tour of the theatres in America. I enjoyed myself immensely and impressed everyone at rehearsals, including John Sweetapple, in my role as Juliet. By the time we got to Dublin for my debut at the Theatre Royal, I was word perfect. Judging by the applause and the three curtain calls made at the insistence of an enthusiastic audience on our first night's performance of the play I was undoubtedly a great success.

The following morning, taking a stroll around the harbour, I came across a Manx fishing boat moored to the dockside. The crew were busy preparing to sail back to the Isle of Man but not too busy to chat to someone from their island. It was good to hear the Manx tongue again and I took the opportunity to ask news of my family in Baldwin Valley. They had little to tell me except that my brother, Simon, had emigrated to New Zealand with the intention of working his own farm. I was reluctant to leave them and waited at the dockside until they had left the harbour and set sail for the open sea.

Simon was the eldest in our family. We were very close, there being only one year's difference in our ages. I had no regrets about leaving the island but would have liked to have kept in touch with him. Simon was the only one who truly cared about me. Returning to the hotel my mood became sad at the thought that now he was living on the other side of the world it was unlikely we would ever see each other again.

Removing the greasepaint from my face after the curtain had fallen that night, I heard a discreet knock on my dressing room door. Upon my call to enter, there appeared, to my surprise, a handsome young man in the full-dress uniform of an officer in the British Army.

'Lieutenant Stanley at your service,' he announced, giving me a half salute.

I viewed him up and down for a moment. It is not uncommon for young gents to enter the dressing room of an actress with an invitation to dinner in the fond hope of a sensual reward afterwards.

'What can I do for you, Lieutenant?' I enquired casually.

Receiving no reply I turned to face him.

'The Devil take me' he said. 'Now that I am here I don't know what to say.' Picking at an imaginary speck of dirt on his sleeve, he got his message out in a great rush of words. 'The fact is the Prince of Wales attended the theatre last night. He was in a state of excitement and interest each time you appeared on the stage. By jove, he couldn't contain himself. He has done nothing but talk about you ever since. Most distressing.'

'I'm very flattered,' I said, 'but, if that's all you have got to say, you can go now . . . and . . . oh, yes . . . tell the Prince I thank him for his interest and regard.'

'You don't understand,' he protested fervently. 'His Royal Highness is in a frenzy of desire for you and doesn't know what to do with himself. I have a cab waiting in the street to take you to Curragh Camp.'

Outraged at his impertinence, I cried out, 'How dare you make such a proposition to me. If you think that because I am an actress I am freely available to any gentleman who desires me, you are very much mistaken.' Opening the door wide I gave him a withering look of contempt and said in an ice cold voice, 'GET OUT!'

After he had gone I changed my clothing and was about to don my cloak when the Lieutenant popped his head around the half-opened door. 'Please, Miss Nellie, may I say I'm deuced sorry?'

He looked so miserable and down in the mouth that I took pity on him and invited him to be seated. 'Tell me why you have undertaken the task of procuring girls for the Prince of Wales?' I asked sternly.

'By jove, that's a cursed unpleasant way of putting it,' he protested with an expression of indignation. 'Please be patient with me, Miss Nellie. I'm not very good with words but I want to try to explain my mission.'

'Alright,' I replied, 'I'm listening.'

'The Prince has been my friend since boyhood. All his life he has been under the constant surveillance of someone or other, never getting an opportunity to meet girls of his own age. I'm one of the few friends he can confide in.

'To complete his military education he has been sent to Curragh Army Training Camp under the supervision of his "Governor", Colonel Bruce, who has been entrusted by Queen Victoria with guarding her son from all temptations of the flesh. With the result, here he is, nearly twenty years of age and still a virgin.

'You are not just an actress to him. You have aroused deep emotions of sincere affection in His Royal Highness. Please take pity on him, Miss Nellie.'

His appeal on behalf of his friend touched my heart. The more I thought about it, the more attractive the invitation became. To be the first woman to be intimate with the Prince of Wales was as tempting as a delicious apple hanging from a tree waiting to be plucked by whoever saw it first. I remembered him as he was on Emigrant's Wharf in New York, with his fresh complexion, light brown hair, and the most pleasing smile he gave me when I shouted, 'God save the Prince of Wales.'

On impulse, I arose to my feet and said, 'Very well, Lieutenant, take me to Curragh Camp.'

In the cab on the way to the camp I became concerned about the ever-watchful Colonel Bruce and learnt that, as he was addicted to card games, some fellow officers had been induced to keep him playing whist in another part of the camp until it was time for him to retire to his bed. The Lieutenant stressed how important it was that if Royal wild oats were to be sown they must be sown discreetly.

Quietly and stealthily we walked along dark corridors until we came to my companion's quarters. After lighting a small oil lamp he left me to inform the Prince of my arrival. I removed my cloak and was about to kick off my shoes when the Prince quietly entered the room.

I had been instructed by Lieutenant Stanley how to address this illustrious person but what was one to do with a young man who was so dithery that all he could say was, 'Oh, Nellie! Oh, Nellie!'

It was obvious that he was extremely embarrassed and suffering from the turbulent lust that gathers force in a young man's blood and drives him mad with storming emotions. I could see the agony in his eyes as I stripped off and exposed my naked body to his gaze. His youthful naïvete appealed to the woman in me and I said in almost motherly tones, 'Come, dear boy; it will be alright,' and began to help him undress.

When I got his clothes off I threw back the bed coverings and turned to him. He trembled at my touch; beads of sweat began to form on his forehead, his eyes were beseeching me for help. 'Oh, Nellie! Oh, Nellie!' he whispered when I brought him to the bed and manoeuvred myself underneath him. He had worked himself into such a state that he couldn't get it in me. Folding my hands around his cock I guided it into my giny. It was just as well I did for he emptied himself with the first thrust upwards. Hot and breathless, he rolled off and onto his back.

After a while his breathing became more even and he hesitantly touched my breasts. 'Oh, Nellie!' he whispered once more and moved closer to me.

'My name is not Nellie,' I burst out somewhat irritably. 'It is just a name I've borrowed for the week while I'm playing Juliet. I couldn't very well appear on the stage as Lady Pulrose. It wouldn't do.'

Startled, he sat up and gazed at me in doubt and confusion. 'Lady Pulrose—James Kennet's wife? How could that be? He isn't married to anyone as far as I know.'

I spent some time telling him how James and I had met in America. He was so delighted when convinced that he was actually in bed with a titled lady that I couldn't help thinking he was a little bit snobbish and that he hadn't been altogether happy in his intimacy with what he thought was a woman of plebeian origin.

'Does your husband know about this escapade of yours in the theatre at Dublin?' he asked.

'No,' I answered, 'and I hope you won't tell him or anyone else.'

'Your secret will be safe with me,' he replied with some dignity. 'What puzzles me,' he said after a thoughtful pause, 'is how you can be a wife to Pulrose. From all accounts he is a most effeminate creature with little interest in women.'

'Yes, this is true,' I said with a sigh. 'I discovered that after we married. I'm his wife in name only and am now residing at Cheyney House in Catherine Place while Sir Charles Cheyney is in Australia.'

Our little talk had given the Prince some assurance and helped him to regain his confidence. Clasping a hand around one of my breasts, he kissed me most warmly. He knew what to do, this time, to assuage the lusty desires that my feminine wiles had aroused in his loins and he set to with a vigour and enthusiasm that was most admirable. He made no bones about enjoying the delights of my female flesh and his virility boded well for the procreation of further royals in the years to come.

My lover was sound asleep when I kissed him goodnight. His loyal friend, Frederick Stanley, was waiting to escort me to the cab for the journey back to my Dublin hotel. The first faint rays of daylight were emerging from the silhouette of the eastern horizon when I entered the vehicle. The Lieutenant held the open door for a moment to whisper, 'Will you honour us with another visit tonight?'

'Yes,' I replied, 'if it is the wish of your friend.'

I had two more assignations at Curragh Camp before the Prince left Ireland on the twentieth of September to return to London. He had been attached to the Second Battalion of the Grenadier Guards under the command of Colonel Percy. Although he had gained great satisfaction from the ten weeks of the comparative freedom of military life, he was now looking forward to seeing Vicky, his elder sister, the Crown Princess of Prussia.

As he had two or three days at Buckingham Palace before visiting

Berlin, we made detailed arrangements for a nocturnal meeting at my home in Catherine Place, the first of many visits by the Prince to Cheyney House, so conveniently close to the Palace that he could make the journey on foot in less than five minutes.

When I got back home there was a sealed letter from the Prince awaiting me.

'My Dearest,

You are constantly in my thoughts. I think about you with deep affection, a feeling I am sure that will abide with me always. Because of your rank and situation amongst the nobility I am delighted that we will be able to meet often at social functions and private dinner parties. I look forward to being with you tonight. Your sincere admirer, Bertie.'

Reading this letter brought it home to me just how much this affair with the Prince was going to affect my life style in the future. My servants could be a problem if I was unable to count on their loyalty and discretion.

I broke the news to Billings, my butler, by informing him without any hesitating preliminary talk that the Prince of Wales and I had become good friends and that we could expect His Royal Highness to be a frequent visitor to the house from now on as I wanted my home to be a comfortable refuge for him when seeking relaxation.

Try as he may, Billings was incapable of hiding his pleasure and excitement. From the expression on his face I knew we would get his full cooperation to keep this affair a secret and he would see to it that there would be no seepage of gossip from the house to the world outside.

Our plans for the autumn went steadily forward. After his visit to Berlin, the Prince would return to Cambridge on the thirteenth of October to continue his studies at Trinity College and I would find lodgings at one of the numerous inns or taverns in the town. The Prince had his own private accommodation at Madingley Hall, a spacious country mansion about four miles outside the town.

I was enraptured by Cambridge with its venerable colleges and quiet cloistered courts. The great antiquity of the pleasant and extensive buildings surmounted by pinnacles and minarets absorbed my interest. My social life was enriched by association with the Prince's friends in the Amateur Dramatic Club. Because of his royal influence, I became the resident actress at the Club's premises behind 'The Hoop' hotel in Jesus Lane and a good friend of Francis Burnand, the founder of this theatrical group for undergraduates. Soon after his arrival at the university the Prince was an appreciative spectator of the farces and extravaganzas to which the Club's programmes were confined, and his favour secured for it a fuller academic recognition than it had enjoyed before.

We had much pleasant intercourse both in conversation and in physical intimacy in my dressing room near the stage whenever he was able to escape from the watchful eye of his Governor at Madingley Hall. His close companions and fellow students at Trinity College, the Duke of St Albans, Charles Beresford and Nathaniel Rothschild, often joined us for supper in my rooms at 'The Hoop' hotel.

One evening he arrived in great agitation, looking a little off colour and a bit pale around the gills. It seems that one of the cabbies in Dublin had talked of a liaison with an actress. The scandal had become the gossip of London high society and had reached the ears of his parents. Deeply shocked by the news of this fall from grace, the Queen had sent her husband to Cambridge to administer a very severe reprimand to their wayward son. Prince Albert inspired nervous reverent awe in Bertie, who, under stern admonishment, broke down and admitted he had 'yielded to temptation'. He assured his father that the affair with Nellie Clifden was now over, which to some extent was true, as, strictly speaking, I'm not known by that name. His father was much relieved to hear this and told him: 'As the future sovereign of the British Empire you must not, under any circumstances, stray from the path of righteousness. The consequences for this country, and for the world, would be too dreadful to contemplate.'

Discussions immediately got underway at Windsor Castle as to what to do about the future of the Prince of Wales. His father began to arrange for a five month tour of the Near East for his son, and the Queen drew up a list of seven young European princesses for consideration as Bertie's future wife on the principle that if one must yield to temptations of the flesh, it should be done in accordance with God's will in wedded bliss. But all these plans were overtaken by something even more catastrophic.

Prince Albert caught a chill from the cold, wet weather that prevailed during his stay at Cambridge and within two weeks died of typhoid fever at Windsor. Much to Bertie's distress his mother, in her grief, blamed him for the death of her husband, because Prince Albert was on his way to discipline his son when he contracted typhus. In the first stupefaction after the death of her husband she vowed fidelity to all his views and said she would: 'Apply them particularly to Bertie whose future has been planned so carefully by my beloved Albert.'

The Queen went ahead with arrangements for her son's tour, determined to carry out her late husband's wishes. So I was deprived of Bertie's company for five months while he toured Lebanon, Palestine, Egypt, Greece and a number of other countries in that area. When he got back on the thirteenth of June he regaled me with his accounts of shooting wild boar in Albania and shooting crocodiles on the banks of the River Nile. During his tour abroad the Queen had proceeded with negotiations for her son's marriage to the beautiful Princess Alexandra of Denmark.

Shortly after his return to London at his request I took him, one dark night, to see some of the slums where I had lived at one time. Horrified by the degradation of the poor and moved almost to tears, he began to hand out gold sovereigns to the starving ragamuffins who quickly surrounded us. He had to be restrained as I feared we would have a riot on our hands. I got him back into our waiting cab as quickly as possible and away from a demanding crowd that was threatening to get ugly and dangerous.

From the time of his sister, Alice's, wedding to Louis at Osborn House on the first of July until the eve of his own wedding to Princess Alexandra, we were on a constant merry-go-round of private dinner parties and visits to palatial mansions throughout the land. Where the Prince went, I was sure to be nearby. Shrewd hostesses of high society soon got the message that if they desired the company of His Royal Highness at any of their intimate dinner parties or any other social events, an invitation to attend would also have to be sent to Lady Pulrose.

We occupied adjoining bedrooms, usually with a connecting door, when we were entertained by the nobility at one of their country house parties, where flirtation, dancing and practical jokes were the order of the day. Bertie had little time for straitlaced prudes which was just as well for shortly after we all retired for the night, there would be much nocturnal toing and froing along the passageways of these great houses as people left their chambers to join up with their lovers in some other bedroom. There was no scandal for we were all members of an exclusive club of the wealthy élite who conducted their affairs of the flesh discreetly and quietly. Almost everything was condoned provided it was done behind locked doors.

Bertie loved the chaff and levity of this free and easy company with their good humoured wit and gaiety. Nevertheless, within this convivial atmosphere he still expected from his associates a certain deference, tolerance for his own idiosyncrasies, and respect for his royal rank. He did not stand obtrusively on his dignity but any undue familiarity was discouraged with an icy stillness that could be very embarrassing for the offender. We went from one great mansion to another enjoying the pleasure and comfort and the sumptuous, warm hospitality extended by our hosts.

Like his mother, he had a gargantuan appetite for food. Nothing less than haddock, poached eggs, bacon, chicken and woodcock would do for him for breakfast. This greed for rich food and thirst for claret which he preferred to champagne and brandy was nearly his undoing when he mounted me with strangled gasps and breathless croaks after consuming to the full a twelve course dinner. When he finished with me he was blowing like a grampus with eyes popping out of an apoplectic, flushed red face.

'My God, he is dying!' I thought and, in panic, poured a full glass of brandy down his throat. Which didn't help matters one little bit for he was horribly sick afterwards.

We kept good company at my house in Catherine Place where, in the full glory of the grand hostess, I wined and dined them, doing my best to charm and beguile the Prince's closest friends with a familiarity that I had long taken for granted. Of all his companions, I took to Nathaniel Rothschild most, known to his intimates as 'Natty'. He was a brusque man with strong personality and didn't suffer fools gladly although he could be very kind and generous with those who sought his advice and help.

I was fascinated when, in answer to my questions, he told me a story about his grandfather, Nathan, the first of the Rothschilds to arrive in England. Apparently the Bank of England refused to discount a bill drawn upon Nathan by his brother, Amschel of Frankfurt. His messenger was informed that the bank only cashed their own bills and not those of private persons.

'I am no ordinary, private person,' Natty's grandfather exclaimed, highly indignant. 'They will rue the day they refused my bill.'

Walking over to the bank, he took a five pound note out of his satchel and asked for gold in exchange. When the clerk gave him five sovereigns, Nathan then brought out a second five pound note with the same request. He kept this up for seven hours and ended the day with twenty-one-thousand pounds all in gold sovereigns but as he had nine clerks doing the same thing the bank had lost in one day two-hundred-and-ten-thousand pounds from its gold reserves.

Nathan and his nine men were at the bank again the next day. 'These gentlemen refuse to take my bills, so I will not keep theirs,' he exclaimed to the restless customers who could not find any tellers free to help them. He solemnly warned the Bank of England that he had eleven million pounds in notes which he intended to change into gold sovereigns with the aid of his employees, even though it would take up to two months of his time and that of the bank tellers to cash the lot. The bank directors were in a panic and quickly agreed to send Nathan an abject written apology and a promise never to refuse a Rothschild's bill in the future.

The financial acumen of the Rothschilds was well known throughout

Europe and, indeed, the rest of the world. Following Natty's advice, I increased my fortune considerably by careful investment. I knew the Prince lived far above his means and gossip had it that Natty and his two brothers, Alfred and Leo, often paid the debts incurred by His Royal Highness. As to the truth of this accusation, I cannot say.

Bertie was forced to be with his family at Windsor Castle for the celebrations of Christmas and we were unable to meet each other again until the third week in January of the new year because of other commitments he had at that time. We had a long-standing engagement to attend a house party at Kintburly, aptly called 'The Palace of the Shires', one of the greatest of the stately homes of England, the ancestral seat of Lord Wawcott who was noted for his lavish hospitality.

On the train we shared a compartment with Freddie Stanley who had acted as the Prince's messenger when we first met at Curragh Camp in Ireland. He was still in the army and had a batman called Geordie who kept us well supplied with drinks throughout the journey.

I had a long lie in bed the first morning as Bertie was out shooting hares, rabbits or anything else that moved in the long grass of the moorland. A chamber maid informed me as I descended the stairs that His Royal Highness had injured his leg and was limping badly. Supported by Freddie and his batman, the Prince, with his right leg raised, painfully negotiated the ascent to his chambers. Apparently he had stumbled into a rabbit hole and sprained his ankle rather badly. When he got his boot and stocking off, I could see how swollen his ankle had become and applied a cold wet compress to the swelling while we waited for the doctor.

Suffering a great deal of pain, he was confined to his bed for the rest of the day. We ate our meals in his bedchamber and I tried to do all I could to alleviate his discomfort. About nine o'clock the doctor gave him a strong sedative that he assured me would dull the pain and allow His Highness a good night's sleep. I had drunk half a bottle of wine with our evening meal and was feeling heavy with drowsiness when I retired to my own bedroom.

In the fantasy of my dreams I felt skillful hands caressing my body, gently exploring the soft lips of my giny, conjuring a divine rhapsody of tenderness that held me in a heavenly rapture of desire. As if in a trance, my thighs were gently persuaded to open wide to receive angelic kisses that slowly crept up to the apex. Warm lips that, in my dream-like, half-awakened state, seemed real and yet ethereal, thrilled my sensitive private parts with exquisite sensual kisses which sent me into an uncontrollable convulsion of passion. My hands reached down and my fingers slipped through a head of short curly hair that I dimly realized wasn't the same as Bertie's. The firm flesh of his cock pressed between the lips of my giny and I lay back breathless with urgent desire, not caring whether it was a devil, an angel, or earthly man between my legs so long as he assuaged the burning desire that consumed me in fires of passion.

The passageway to my womb clasped the ardent male member of my unseen lover and I felt my buttocks being raised as he came down on me. Swooning under the onslaught of his savaging thrusts, my hips writhed in an ecstasy of raging passions which swept me up and ever upwards in a spasm of emotion that silently screamed for release and fulfilment. When I came to my limbs were quivering and my eyes were wet with tears of blissful joy.

His vigour and virility were astounding. On and on he went, thrusting that lovely big cock deep inside me, only pausing briefly for a moment or two when the sap burst from his shuddering member. Twice more I rose in a fervent, sensuous, breathless intensity to reach the pinnacle of my hot desires.

I lay in a warm blush of ravishment after he left my bedroom as silently as he had entered it. Slowly the finger of curiosity began to stir my thoughts. Who could it be, this lover who came out of the darkness and just as quietly disappeared into the shadows of the night? But I was too exhausted to continue the questioning and, with a deep sigh of content-ment, snuggled my head into the pillow and fell asleep.

At various times during the next day I cast a speculative eye on some of the male guests. I was looking for a tall, lithe, muscular youngish man with short curly hair. Whilst there were one or two possibilities, none of them entirely fitted the image I had in mind of my midnight lover. Bertie, confined to bed with a painful ankle, was petulant and irritable all day long. I tried reading to him and playing cards, but it seemed nothing was going to lift his spirits and my own detached smug good humour only made him more irascible. I had high expectations of another nocturnal visit from my unknown lover and longed for bedtime.

The long case clock downstairs was striking the hour of midnight when I thought there was a sound of some movement at the door but couldn't be sure and clenched my fists to control my excitement. Taut and tense, my heart pounding in my chest, I felt the bedcoverings being raised and jumped involuntarily when he placed his lips on my open mouth. He got into me immediately, wasting no time on preliminaries, and humped me with savage desperately urgent thrusts until the sap spurted from him. He lay hard inside me for a moment or two while he recovered his breath and then, with fingers entwined through my hair, gave me a long sus-tained passionate kiss, the kiss of a man determined to dominate and possess the female beneath him. With his lips clasped to mine and his cock jerking inside me, my blood warmed to the passion that was rising in me. This perfect union of our two bodies soon brought me to a loving orgasm of great intensity.

In the tumult of my emotions he said something that sounded like, 'Eeh! Hinny, yer a grand fuck and a reet canny lass.'

We had one more night together before our return to London. At the local station Freddie Stanley and his batman, Geordie, carried Bertie into the royal carriage reserved for our party.

When we arrived in the great metropolis there was lots of bustling activity as they got Bertie off the train and out of the railway station. When it came for my turn to descend to the platform I tripped over someone's small leather bag and would have fallen head first onto the asphalt platform but for the timely intervention of Geordie's out-stretched arm.

'Eeh! Hinny, mind yer step,' he exclaimed as his strong hands supported me.

I gazed at him stupefied, unable for a moment or two to associate him with my mysterious lover of the past three nights. A nervous giggle gur-gled in my throat at this startling revelation, while he, for his part, stood confident and proud with dancing eyes and a broad grin spreading across his strong handsome features.

With that accent spoken by the people of the north east of England, he said in a voice a little above a whisper, for Freddie Stanley was speaking to a station porter nearby, 'I wanted yer t'knaa who it was.' Then, before turning round to pick up his officer's baggage, he gave me a conspirato-rial wink of the eye and whispered, 'Gudbye, Lady Pulrose, and God bless yer.'

By the beginning of March all London was agog and buzzing with inter-est in the Prince of Wales' forthcoming wedding, and many decorated triumphal arches were being erected for Princess Alexandra's short drive through the capital on her way to Windsor Castle. This excitement was hardly surprising considering that Bertie was one of the world's most eligible bachelors and that despite keen competition from six other prin-cesses, Alexandra was the chosen bride to be.

She seemed to meet with everyone's approval. The Queen was very favourably impressed with the Danish princess's quiet, ladylike manners and her lovely refined profile. The Prime Minister, Lord Palmerston, thought she was 'charming and beautiful but, what was more important, Alexandra was a Protestant.' Disraeli, who had an invitation to the wed-ding, which was to take place in St George's Chapel at Windsor on the tenth of March, praised her because 'she had no need to smile to look gracious' and thought she was 'very handsome, with fine delicate features and a lovely mouth.'

'What chance did I have with Bertie?' I thought, 'with all that admiration for the future Princess of Wales.' It became evident as the date of the wedding approached and the Prince's visits to Catherine Place were less frequent than formerly that his desire for his bride to be obviously preoccupied his thoughts. Nevertheless, he spoke often of our last night together just before the wedding.

A sumptuous supper was prepared for that evening when he was due to call at ten o'clock. Wanting everything to be perfect I went to great lengths to be at my best for I wanted it to be a night of love that would last in his memory for a long time.

Hearing the sound of horses' hooves outside at ten o'clock, I rang for my butler to tell him to be ready to serve the meal within a few moments. When Billings answered my summons he informed me a footman from the royal household had delivered a sealed envelope addressed to me. Breaking the seal, I took out a hastily scribbled letter from the Prince.

'My Dearest,

I received a letter from the Queen this morning requesting my presence at Windsor for a meeting in the afternoon with the Prime Minister to discuss the final details of the arrangements for the wedding.

It is impossible to express in mere words how distraught I am that we will be unable to be together tonight because Mama insists on my staying with her until Princess Alexandra and I are man and wife.

You will often be with me in my thoughts, for I remain ever yours. Affectionately, Bertie.'

To Nathaniel Rothschild   22nd September 1863

'My Dear Natty,

It is with some concern for the welfare of Lady Pulrose that I address this letter to you. I am informed that no one has seen or heard of her for some considerable time and the servants at her home in Catherine Place can give me no information as to where she may be.

As you well know, she was always an excellent friend and an amusing companion and now that my dear wife is confined to Marlborough House as she is expecting our first child sometime in January I am finding life rather *dull and boring. So do be a good fellow and make some enquiries on my behalf as to the whereabouts of our mutual friend, Dara.*

Bertie.'

To the Prince of Wales   *30th September 1863*

'My dear Friend,
   After making many enquiries regarding Lady Pulrose, I am somewhat aggrieved that I have so little to report as to her situation.
   Using my influence with financial associates led me to an interview with her bank manager. As you know, banks are reluctant to disclose any information about their clients but he did inform me that about mid-summer he received from Her Ladyship a letter with a New Zealand postmark, instructing him to transfer several thousand pounds to a bank in Auckland. If I should receive any further knowledge on this matter you can be sure it will be passed on to you immediately.
   I remain your trusted friend, as always,

Natty.'